PRAISE FOR *IT'S ALWAYS*

'*It's Always the Husband* is a totally ad
A masterclass in misdirection with cl[
reveals right up until the final ⸺
Claire Douglas

'*Desperate Housewives* meets *Big Little Lies* – a propulsive page-turner, brimming with intrigue. Utterly addictive!'
Andrea Mara

'I devoured *It's Always the Husband* in a day. Fantastic pace and twists!'
Fiona Barton

'The queen of the psychological thriller is back. With twist after twist, C.L. Taylor expertly unravels the secrets and lies that will forever bind a group of middle-class school mums. A barnstormer of a book. Highly recommended.'
M.W. Craven

'C.L. Taylor had me gripped from the very first page and didn't let go until I'd turned the last. Another addictive, twisty thriller that I devoured in a weekend.'
Nadine Matheson

'Dark, unsettling, and full of intrigue – a compelling story packed with complex characters, tangled relationships and long-buried secrets.'
Rachel Abbott

'*It's Always the Husband* is an absolute bloody masterclass in suspense. It's so terribly accurate that I was dragged straight back to all those years standing at the school gates. A cunningly constructed plot, a web of secrets and lies, and Taylor's usual superlative writing. Outstanding!'
Helen Fields

'*It's Always the Husband* is a razor-sharp thriller full of secrets, suspicion, and twists. I couldn't tear my eyes away from the pages. Dark, addictive, and impossible to put down.'
Caroline Mitchell

'A masterclass in tension and suspense. Twisty, addictive, and impossible to put down. For me, it's always C.L. Taylor who delivers the most satisfying read!'
Lesley Kara

'From everyday school run to a tale of murder, blackmail and a frantic quest to find a killer; a compulsive small-town thriller with a stunning final twist.'
Jackie Kabler

'With more twists than a noose, this propulsive, whip-smart read is your new obsession.'
C.J. Cooke

'C.L. Taylor has done a brilliant job. It's *Motherland* meets *24 Hours in Police Custody* . . . a perfect blend. I loved it.'
Chris Bridges

PRAISE FOR C.L. TAYLOR

'Wow. Addictive. What an ending!'
Claire Douglas

'*The Guilty Couple* is a red-hot, nonstop rollercoaster of a book. Every time I thought I knew what was happening, C.L. Taylor pulled the rug, and I read the last few chapter so fast I felt dizzy.'
Lisa Jewell

'From the moment I picked this book up, I resented every minute I couldn't spend between its pages. *The Guilty Couple* is a one-breath rollercoaster ride, with twists, turns, ups and downs . . . then just when you think it's over, there's another loop ahead! A proper, classy thriller.'
Janice Hallett

'I loved *The Guilty Couple* so much I was up until 2 am finishing it. Twisty and compelling, tense and fast-paced and thoroughly unputdownable.'
Angela Marsons

'Twisty and gripping – another brilliant book from C.L. Taylor.'
Jane Fallon

'With high stakes and a killer premise, *The Guilty Couple* takes the reader on a thrill ride of a journey. A perfectly paced and propulsive read, told with C.L. Taylor's trademark instinct for edge-of-your-seat reveals.'
Lucy Clarke

'Pacy, surprising and with some brilliant twists – C.L. Taylor's best yet. Brilliant.'
Catherine Cooper

'Compelling. Compulsive. Crafted. Cleverly calculated.'
Jane Corry

'C.L. Taylor has done it again. A fast paced, thrilling read that I couldn't put down – with a twist I didn't see coming. I loved it!'
Heidi Perks

'Wow, *The Guilty Couple* doesn't let up for a moment – you're in for a ride!'
Sarah Pinborough

'Wow, *The Guilty Couple* was everything I needed it to be and more. I raced through it, hardly coming up for air. It's twisty, taut, unbearably tense and a masterclass in nerve-shredding storytelling. Brava, C.L. Taylor, you've done it again!'
Emma Stonex

'A brilliantly written, fast-paced and very clever thriller – I couldn't put it down!'
Susi Holliday

'Absolutely ripped through this belter of a story. A pacy plot full of her trademark twists, and characters that don't leave your head until long after you finish the final pages. C.L. Taylor has smashed it out the park with this one.'
Lisa Hall

'When you sit down with this book, you won't be getting back up until it's finished. Fast-paced, fun, packed with twists, this is a gem of a read.'
Jo Spain

'Whip-smart, perfectly paced and absolutely unputdownable, *The Guilty Couple* is a masterclass in edge-of-your-seat writing. I loved it.'
Rosie Walsh

'Dark, devious and devilishly twisting, *The Guilty Couple* is another breathless, one-sit-read from the brilliant C.L. Taylor.'
Chris Whitaker

'A clever, suspenseful story about secrets, blurred boundaries and a whole lot of betrayal. C.L. Taylor is a master at writing twisty thrillers, and this one is no exception.'
Samantha Downing

'Wow! Packed with ever-increasing suspense, vivid characters and twists that'll give you whiplash, it's one hell of a read. Utterly brilliant!'
Steph Broadribb

'It hooks you from the start. The cast of characters are so well drawn and so believably flawed. It's original, chilling and utterly page turning . . . One of those books that's impossible to put down.'
Debbie Howells

'A one-sitting read. Breathless pacing from the opening chapter to its twisty turny conclusion. Taylor is a writer at the top of her game and never disappoints.'
John Marrs

'Cancel your appointments, kick off your shoes and get comfortable. There's a new C.L. Taylor book in town – and it's a corker.'
Cass Green

'A killer premise, a propulsive plot and a gasp-inducing reveal – C.L. Taylor has done it again!'
Catherine Ryan Howard

'A plot that whips about like an eel held by the tail, peopled with morally dubious characters and propelled relentlessly forward towards the final twist. Another accomplished slice of psychological noir from a writer who knows the genre inside out.'
Vaseem Khan

'This has all the twists and turns and WTFs you could possibly want from a thriller.'
Red

'One of her best thrillers to date'
My Weekly

'A twisty tale'
Crime Monthly

C.L. Taylor is a *Sunday Times* bestselling author. Her psychological thrillers have sold over two million copies in the UK alone, been translated into over thirty languages, and optioned for television. Her 2019 novel, *Sleep*, her 2022 novel *The Guilty Couple* and her 2024 novel, *Every Move You Make* were all Richard and Judy picks. C.L. Taylor lives in Bristol with her partner and son.

By the same author:

The Accident
The Lie
The Missing
The Escape
The Fear
Sleep
Strangers
Her Last Holiday
The Guilty Couple
Every Move You Make

For Young Adults
The Treatment
The Island

C.L. TAYLOR

It's Always The Husband

avon.

Published by AVON
A division of HarperCollins*Publishers* Ltd
1 London Bridge Street
London SE1 9GF

www.harpercollins.co.uk

HarperCollins*Publishers*
Macken House, 39/40 Mayor Street Upper,
Dublin 1, D01 C9W8
Ireland

A Hardback Original 2025
1
First published in Great Britain by HarperCollins*Publishers* 2025

Copyright © C.L. Taylor 2025

C.L. Taylor asserts the moral right to be identified as the author of this work.

A catalogue copy of this book is available from the British Library.

ISBN: 978-0-00-860156-0 (HB)
ISBN: 978-0-00-860157-7 (TPB)

This novel is entirely a work of fiction. The names, characters and incidents portrayed in it are the work of the author's imagination. Any resemblance to actual persons, living or dead, events or localities is entirely coincidental.

Typeset in Sabon LT Std 11.75/14.5pt by Palimpsest Book Production Limited,
Falkirk, Stirlingshire

Printed and bound in the UK using 100% Renewable Electricity
at CPI Group (UK) Ltd

All rights reserved. No part of this text may be reproduced, transmitted, downloaded, decompiled, reverse engineered, or stored in or introduced into any information storage and retrieval system, in any form or by any means, whether electronic or mechanical, without the express written permission of the publishers.

Without limiting the author's and publisher's exclusive rights, any unauthorised use of this publication to train generative artificial intelligence (AI) technologies is expressly prohibited. HarperCollins also exercise their rights under Article 4(3) of the Digital Single Market Directive 2019/790 and expressly reserve this publication from the text and data mining exception.

MIX
Paper | Supporting responsible forestry
FSC
www.fsc.org
FSC™ C007454

This book contains FSC™ certified paper and other controlled sources to ensure responsible forest management.

For more information visit: www.harpercollins.co.uk/green

To everyone who has survived the school run, particularly Kathryn Chiswell Jones, Sarah Maddox and Jenny Smith.

Chapter 1

Jude

WEDNESDAY

To Jude, the school run is like Pamplona's running of the bulls; to survive you need tenacity, speed and balls of steel. The faster she navigates the groups of parents that crowd the street outside St Helena's Primary School, the sooner she drops Betsy off in the playground, and the less likely she is to be charged by the terrifying school mum clique. She's seen them watching her from the gates, the slow eye-sweeps, the analysis, the judgement. Whilst Betsy may have made friends in the five weeks since she started Year 5, Jude's kept her head down. She'd rather unblock a toilet than make small talk at the school gates. It's not that she's antisocial, she just hasn't got time for that particular kind of shit.

'Milly! Milly!' Betsy abandons her hand and speeds across the playground in the direction of a small, curly-haired girl with wide-set eyes.

Jude follows, shrugging off her daughter's backpack.

'I've been invited to Eloise's party,' Milly says proudly. She clutches Betsy's arm. 'You've been invited too!'

As Betsy jumps up and down, Jude glances around in search of a tall, broad man with closely cropped hair and a brooding expression. Will Ledger, Milly's father and St Helena's answer to Tom Hardy, is the one parent she *has* got to know since Betsy started school. Her friendship with the history of art lecturer, and the only single dad (as far as she knows), began tentatively. Forced to make small talk as their daughters ran around the local play park, Will was taciturn while Jude filled the awkward silences with inane facts, random observations, and meandering stories. She was pretty certain that, if their daughters hadn't become best friends, Will would have avoided her. Instead, he tolerated their initial interaction, nodding and shaking his head in all the right places. Well, *almost* all the right places. When she'd described, in dramatic detail, the funeral she'd held for Betsy's deceased hamster he'd started laughing.

Delighted to have found a chink in his socially awkward armour she told him another funny story. He laughed again, then batted back a silly story of his own. How that led to them sleeping together three weeks later she wasn't entirely sure. Booze and proximity – chatting on her sofa as their daughters snoozed upstairs on a sleepover – certainly helped. Half an hour later – sweaty, flushed and awkward – Will kissed her chastely on her cheek and muttered something about needing to get home. His body language spoke volumes – *let us never speak of this again* – and, equally mortified, Jude inwardly agreed.

'Is your dad not here?' she asks Milly.

'He's gone home. He forgot to bring my violin.'

IT'S ALWAYS THE HUSBAND

'Your dad did, or you did?'

'He did!' The indignation on Milly's face makes Jude smile. Oh to be nine years old again and have someone else to blame for everything that goes wrong in your life.

'Well, I hope he turns up soon.' She bends to kiss Betsy on the cheek, then hands her her bag. 'I need to get going. I've got a Zoom in . . .' She checks her watch and swears under her breath. If she jogs home she might just make it on time but, considering she hasn't run at speed since Betsy made a break for freedom at a train station when she was two, she's going to have to settle for a fast walk.

'Love you!' She squeezes her daughter's shoulder, then sets off at a trot, weaving between parents, children, scooters and prams as she squeezes her way through the gates. She rounds the corner onto the pavement, mentally rehearsing the presentation she put together last night, then stops abruptly as someone taps on her shoulder.

'Sorry, Jude, didn't mean to startle you.' A tall, slim blonde, head to toe in gym kit, looks her up and down. 'It is Jude isn't it? I'm Victoria. Victoria Routledge, Sophia's mum.'

Jude holds out a hand, only for it to be crushed against her body as Victoria gathers her into a hug that feels like being gored by a bull. She peers over Victoria's shoulder and spots the rest of the clique watching from the pavement, sniffing the air, sensing blood.

'I'm surprised you know my name,' she says as Victoria finally releases her.

It's almost terrifying, the way the other woman's smile appears, like there's a light switch on her back.

'I know everyone's name,' Victoria says breezily. 'I see it as part of my role, being head of the PTA. Talking of which. Are you coming to the meeting tonight?'

'Depends if you can catch me.'

'I'm sorry?' Victoria blinks at her. Back in Fairford, Jude's friends would have laughed.

'I said . . . Oh screw it . . . yes, fine, I'll be there if I can.'

'Wonderful! I'll see you tonight then. It's at 6 p.m., school hall.'

Before Jude can respond Victoria spins away, having spotted her next victim in the crowd of scurrying mothers. Jude watches her go, too stunned to care that she's now got just five minutes to get home in time for her meeting. Sod jogging, she needs to learn how to fly.

It is the sound of a scooter crashing to the ground – the clanging bell of metal on concrete – that makes her whirl around. At first, she thinks the two writhing, shifting shapes at the end of the street are children, then realises her mistake. These aren't Year 6 children, scrapping before the school bell rings – they're men. One, standing, is in his twenties; the other, lying on the pavement, is in his early forties. It's like a scene from a film – parents and children frozen, the only movement the pounding of the younger man's fist into the curled body of the older man. Jude catches a glimpse of closely cropped hair, a tweed waistcoat, and a violin case in the road and starts to run.

She's only vaguely aware of the other parents gawping at her as she sprints through them, shouting, 'Stop! Stop!'

Startled by the commotion, the shouting, or possibly the insane expression on her face, the younger man jumps back from Will, grabs his e-scooter, and takes off. Two of the dads drift closer, regaining their bravery now the attacker has fled, but it's Jude Will looks at as she crouches over him.

'I'm fine.' There's a tightness to his voice that she hasn't heard before. He's pale with shock, a bruise blooming on one of his cheekbones and his bottom lip is split. Shame radiates off him like heat as the other parents watch like he's a science experiment, about to explode.

Jude glares at them. 'You can stop staring and fuck off now!'

There's a sharp intake of breath and one of the dads mutters, 'Charming,' as he swerves around them, dragging his offspring in his wake.

'The violin.' Will groans as he tries to sit up, one hand groping for the case. 'I've got to—'

'Don't worry about that right now.' Jude moves to pick him up but he shakes his head and, groaning, gets to his feet. Sensing the drama is over, the other parents – who aren't comforting their traumatised children – drift in the direction of home, or the school.

'I could take it to Milly.' A woman in a multicoloured scarf, and her hair in plaits, steps into the road. 'Harper and Henry are in the same class.'

An objection forms in Jude's mind – oh look, another middle-class do-gooder who only steps in when the danger has passed – but there's something in the other woman's expression that makes her pause. She looks tired and kind and there's no curiosity in her eyes, just concern. Will must see it too because he says, 'Thank you. I'd appreciate that . . . I'm sorry, I don't know your name. With ninety kids in the year it's a lot to—'

'Sorrell.' She bends to pick up the violin case, then glances back towards the pavement, where her three children – two school-aged and a toddler in a buggy – are growing restless. 'That was very brave,' she gives Jude an earnest nod, 'what you just did.'

Jude shrugs awkwardly. 'It wasn't anything.' She waits until Sorrell has gathered her children and headed towards the gates, then turns to Will.

'I haven't got my car but I could walk you back home. Or I could help you to mine and then drive you to hospital.'

'I'll be fine.' His tone's softened now. The shock's worn off and he looks exhausted.

'You might have a head injury.'

'The only thing that's hurt is my pride. He came out of nowhere. I didn't have chance to fight b—'

'Don't do that. The guy was a psycho.'

Other than the split lip and swollen cheek she can't see any serious injuries, although he'll probably be a riot of bruises by the end of the day. 'Are you letting me walk you home or not? That's not a question by the way. I'm letting you think you have a choice.'

'Fine. Back to mine, no hospital.' He takes tentative steps until they reach the end of the street.

'You all right?' Jude asks as he draws to a halt and looks up and down the main road.

'Yeah, just . . .' He tails off and keeps walking, but she knows why he paused. He wanted to make sure his attacker wasn't lying in wait.

They continue on to the traffic lights, and the school gate clique who've gathered on a patch of grass nearby, Victoria in the middle, holding court. They fall silent as Jude and Will pass them.

'He deserved that.' Victoria's voice rings out clear and sharp as Jude and Will cross the road. Then, in a pitchy tone that almost hints at fear: 'You can deny it, but we all know what you did.'

Chapter 2

Victoria

WEDNESDAY

Victoria was as shocked as the other parents when the fight broke out by the school gates. Her primary concern was for the children – school-aged and younger – who were witnessing violence, probably for the first time, in an environment that should have been safe. Her secondary concern was for the man on the ground, curled up in a ball. But when she realised who was being attacked her fear vanished. She was witnessing karma kick someone's arse, literally, in Will Ledger's case and, from the expression on her friends' faces, she was sure she wasn't the only one who felt that way.

She'd never trusted him, not from the moment she laid eyes on him when their children started Reception, five years earlier. Jude was a fool to run and comfort him. She needed warning about the company she kept.

Now, as Victoria parks up in the driveway of her detached four-bedroomed Georgian house, her heart leaps. Grade II listed, it's the home of her dreams. She adored it the moment she saw it listed on Rightmove ten years earlier, then fell in love with it the moment she walked through the door. It was run-down, rotten and unloved but with its large room sizes, and even larger grounds, she could see its potential. Unusually, Andy could too and they'd walked through it, pointing, commentating, tapping and touching. It was a home they'd fill with children and laughter, a project to work on together, the ideal place to start their married life.

Her mood sours as she spots Andy's car outside her beloved house, and when she turns the front door handle it swings open. She bloody *told* him to call before he comes round. It's not his home anymore; he can't just waltz in when he wants.

'Andy!' The word has a sharp snap to it as she takes off her shoes. There's no reply but she can hear the floorboards creaking overhead. He's in her bloody bedroom, probably going through her drawers, looking for something – anything – that will get the judge on his side.

'Andy!' She speeds up the stairs and flings open the door to her room. 'What—' she stares in horror at the mound of clothing on the bed and floor '—the hell do you think you're doing?'

Her husband, his back to her, ignores her, and continues to sort through the pile. It's exactly the kind of infuriating behaviour that led to the breakdown of their marriage – Andy does what he wants, when he wants, and to hell with her feelings. Compartmentalising his feelings, acting with authority and decisively leading a team might be great qualities for a detective inspector, but it made him the worst kind of husband. Victoria rounds the bed so she's directly facing him and lunges at the pile of clothes, gathering them towards her. Andy snorts with irritation, then straightens up.

'I was looking through those.'

'For what? You're not to take *anything* from my house without agreement.'

'Your house?' He laughs drily. 'That's for the court to decide.'

It's a battle that's been raging ever since their first couples counselling session. Andy – arms crossed, sullen-faced – answered the counsellor's question: 'Am I right in thinking that you don't really want to be here?' with a curt nod. 'Victoria doesn't want to save this marriage. She's trying to save the house.'

The accusation had stung. How dare he imply that the house was more important to her than their children. Their happiness, their stability, their self-esteem and self-worth; *that* was what mattered more to her than anything else. The house was a bonus. The only trouble was, even with help from her parents, she was still a hundred thousand pounds short of the sum she'd need to buy him out and, with Andy also scrabbling around to find the money to buy her out, it was quickly becoming a case of 'whoever finds the money first gets the house'.

'Tell me what you're looking for,' she says now.

'My dress shirt and my black bow tie.' The glare he gives her from across the bed is pure irritation. 'There's a function tonight and—' He breaks off and looks at his watch. 'What are you doing back at this time anyway? Shouldn't you be out torturing someone?'

She gives him a long look. 'I could say the same to you.'

'Fuck off, Vic.'

Inwardly she smirks. If he wants to trade blows he

shouldn't do it with someone who knows how to hit where it hurts.

'My client cancelled,' she says, feigning indifference when the truth is she feels a bit sick. The client didn't just cancel their session, they cancelled full stop, telling her they'd decided to sign up for Peloton instead. Two sessions a week, four times a month. That's £480 she's going to be short. The only way she's going to be able to fill the shortfall in her income is if she jumps onto social media and drums up some trade. Instead, she's having to deal with her soon-to-be ex-husband and the mess he's made of her life.

'Your bow tie's in your sock drawer,' she says curtly, 'and you threw your dress shirt away because it was stained with red wine.'

Andy's lips part in objection and Victoria raises her eyebrows, waiting for him to accuse her of lying, but his mouth snaps shut and, without so much as a thank you, he yanks open his sock drawer, roots around and yanks out his bow tie.

'Bye then!' she calls after him as he stalks out of the bedroom. 'Thanks for your help, Victoria! I'll tidy up the mess I made, Victoria!'

He doesn't reply and, as the stairs creak under his weight, she runs after him. How dare he just waltz into her home and waltz out. She's not his maid or his PA.

'If you did your job properly two years ago,' she calls after him as he reaches the bottom of the stairs, 'there wouldn't be traumatised children crying at school.'

Andy continues to head for the front door then, as Victoria readies herself to shout something else, he pauses and turns back.

'What the fuck are you on about?' The words 'you mad bitch' are implied, but not said.

IT'S ALWAYS THE HUSBAND

She grips the banister and looks down at him. He seems so small and insignificant, so scruffy and unkempt. She can't believe she ever looked up to him, as a policeman, a husband, or a man.

'Someone beat up Will Ledger outside the school gates this morning. If you were a better detective he'd be in prison now, but no, you didn't have enough evidence to convince the CPS to charge him with—'

'You sound frustrated,' Andy cuts her off. 'Why don't you do a jumping jack and calm the fuck down?'

He flicks his middle finger at her then, before she can respond, slips out the front door.

Chapter 3

Sorrell

WEDNESDAY

With the twins deposited at school, and Scout dropped off at nursery, Sorrell heads home. She smells burning the moment she opens the unlocked front door.

'Finnley!' She sprints into the kitchen where black smoke is billowing from a saucepan. Eyes stinging, she turns off the gas, grabs the saucepan's handle with a tea towel, opens the garden door and dumps it on the patio.

'Finnley!' She takes the stairs two at a time, stomach hollowed with fear. Where is he? He wouldn't have left a saucepan on the hob and just gone out.

I don't want to be here anymore. The phrase haunts her.

She searches the top floor of the house. She's terrified, relieved, then terrified again as she throws open the doors to their bedroom, the children's bedrooms, the nursery and the bathroom. She runs back downstairs, only vaguely aware of the draught from the still-open front door as she darts from room to room. Finnley's not in the living room, the dining room, the downstairs toilet, the kitchen or the utility room. His car is still in the driveway. He wouldn't head out on foot and leave the front door unlocked.

He can only be in the garden or her studio. He's never liked their garden; he hates the fact it's overlooked by their neighbours, and the only time he ever enters her studio is to bring her a cup of tea, but she has to check everywhere before she calls the police. With no sign of her husband in the garden she tries the door to the studio and her breath catches in her throat. Her six-foot husband is sitting on the floor beside the kiln, curled into himself, his head in his hands.

'Finnley?' She crouches beside him and touches a hand to his shoulder, tears of relief filling her eyes. 'What's happened? What's going on?'

He shakes his head, and she hears despair and desperation in his strangled sigh.

'Tell me, please!'

Still her husband says nothing, and the well of fear in Sorrell's gut bubbles with frustration. For the last month that he's been off work with stress, she's been holding their family together. She's taken on all the childcare, the cooking and the cleaning. She's taken on more one-on-one classes in her pottery studio to pay all the bills, and she's been looking after – and worrying about – Finnley. Most days she feels like she can't breathe, but someone's got to adult. And there's no one else but her.

'We can get through this.' She moves her hand over her husband's head, mentally sending him some of her strength as she gently strokes his hair. 'We've got savings, and my parents will always step in if we need them. I know it's hard, but we've got each other, the kids, our home. Promise me you won't do anything stupid. I can't do this without you.'

Her husband doesn't reply but she can feel him shaking beneath her hand.

'You need to talk to someone,' she says. 'A therapist or a life coach.' *Someone more qualified than me,* she thinks but doesn't say. 'You were under so much stress, doing overtime when the surgery was so short-staffed. You were bound to break at some point. God knows anyone would have. Just because you're off work doesn't change the fact that you're an excellent dentist. You're hardworking, you're compassionate and you're honest. This is a blip, that's all. We'll get through it.'

Finnley mumbles something that makes her pause.

'What was that?' she asks but he shakes his head.

'I'm fine. Just give me a minute.'

'Okay. I'll put the kettle on. I'll be in the kitchen if you need me.' She backs away from him and heads out of the studio. What he'd mumbled had sounded a lot like: 'I'm not honest at all.'

Chapter 4

Jude

WEDNESDAY

As Will puts a key in his front door Jude hangs back, readying herself for a tricky conversation – one where she insists he rings the police, and he tells her no.

She can feel her phone buzzing in her pocket; her client, no doubt, asking why she's not in their meeting, but she doesn't answer it. She'll ring them back later and explain. What's more important right now is ensuring that Will's okay. During the ten-minute walk back from school, he had explained what had happened: he'd shouted at the e-scooter rider to get off the pavement because there were children around, then the next thing he knew he was being punched in the head. It made sense, God knows Jude had shouted at enough e-scooter riders herself, but it didn't explain Victoria's parting shot – *He deserved that. You can deny it, but we all know what you did*. The accusation hung in the air between them until Jude could bear it no longer.

'What was Victoria on about? *We know what you did.*'

Will had glanced at her. 'Are you friends with that group?'

She'd shaken her head.

'Good. Keep it that way.'

'Why?'

He'd shrugged. End of conversation, and no amount of prodding could get him to reveal more.

'Have you got any painkillers?' she asks now as he steps into his hallway. You're going to need them.'

'Yeah.' He turns and looks at her questioningly, a small smile playing on his lips. 'Are you coming in or are you just going to stand there and make the place look untidy?'

She laughs in surprise. 'Who even says that anymore? How old are you? Seventy-five?' then follows him into the kitchen where he plucks a pack of ibuprofen from a ridiculously well-organised medicines cupboard. The kitchen isn't dissimilar to hers in size and shape but, where her kitchen has dirty coffee cups next to the sink, piles of washing stacked up on the table and 'Star of the Week' certificates, sponsorship forms and pieces of artwork affixed to the fridge, Will's kitchen is so clean and uncluttered it looks like a show home.

He clocks her raised eyebrows. 'When I get bored I clean.'

'Want to get bored round my house?'

He laughs and pops two ibuprofen into his mouth, swallows some water, then puts the empty glass in the dishwasher.

'Do you alphabetise your tins as well? Make sure they're all facing the same direction, like David Beck—' She presses a hand to her mouth – simultaneously delighted and horrified – as Will throws open a cupboard door. It's the neatest food cupboard she's ever seen – with tins, cans, bottles and packets perfectly organised in labelled plastic trays and containers. 'You're Stacey Solomon's wet dream.'

He snorts in amusement as he closes the cupboard door. 'Is she a fan of insomniacs? I have been known to scrub the bathroom at 2 a.m.'

'Want to sleep at my house?'

Will laughs then clutches his side. Instinctively Jude moves to check on him, but he raises a hand. 'I'm fine. I'm fine.'

As he straightens, his eyes meet hers and the mood in the kitchen changes. It becomes loaded with possibility, like the moment before a kiss. Jude returns his gaze, breathing shallowly. Maybe he doesn't regret sleeping with her. Maybe she misread the way that he left. He's attractive and there's an off-beat quirky side to him that she finds intriguing. Plus, it was the best sex she's had for years.

'Tea?' Will reaches for a shiny chrome kettle and, just like that, the tension in the room dissipates, like a wave breaking on the shore.

'Yeah' she says, wondering what the hell just happened. 'Can I use your loo?'

'Sure. Upstairs, second door on the right.'

She climbs the stairs then, having forgotten which room Will said was the toilet, tries the handle of the first room she comes to. It's a riot of pink and purple, glitter, soft toys, unicorns and fluffy pillows. It's very young-looking for a nine-year-old; there are still alphabet stickers on the wall. There are also clothes scattered on the bed, chair and floor. It's somewhat reassuring that, while Will is anally obsessive about tidiness and cleanliness in the rest of the house, he doesn't insist that his daughter does the same.

Drawn by a hamster, nibbling at the bars of its cages, on the dressing table, Jude moves into the room. Unlike Betsy, who barely acknowledged the loss of her hamster, Jude cried on and off for three days after Dobby died. For two years Jude would say hello to him whenever she walked into the kitchen and Dobby would return the greeting by frantically gnawing at the bars. She fed him cashews, cucumber and spinach, watching in wonder as he either nibbled his food delicately, or stuffed it in his pouches then returned to the bars for more.

'Hi!' She gently touches one of the hamster's tiny paws, gripping its metal jail. It pauses its gnawing to look at her, its black beady eyes regarding her warily. 'What are you call—' She breaks off, distracted by two bejewelled frames to the right of the cage. Both photographs are of women, one a redhead gazing lovingly at the baby in her arms, the other a willowy blonde, ethereal and joyful in a field of sunflowers. The redhead has to be Milly's mother – as well as the same wild, curly hair, they share the same smile and dark-rimmed green eyes. The other woman looks nothing like Milly, or Will for that matter. He hasn't told her much about his personal life. Whenever she's broached the subject, he's changed the subject or caught her off-guard with a joke.

Jude traces a finger over the glass. 'Who's this?' she asks the hamster.

'Robyn.'

Will's in the doorway, a basket of clean, folded washing in his hands, an unreadable expression on his face.

Jude's hand falls away from the photograph. 'I didn't mean to pry. It was the hamster; it lured me in.'

A smile pricks at the corner of Will's mouth. 'With a pumpkin seed? Soft bedding? Sexual promises?'

'That's how rumours start.' She gestures towards the other photo. 'That has to be Milly's mum. She looks so much like her.'

'Correct.'

'And Robyn is . . . her auntie?'

'Stepmum, as was.'

'Oh.' She's found out more about Will and Milly's lives in the last couple of seconds than she has in the last five weeks. 'Does she see them – her mum and ex-stepmum – very often?'

Will doesn't respond immediately and, as the silence stretches into awkwardness, an apology arranges itself in Jude's brain. She's being too nosy, it's none of her business, it's probably time that she—

'She doesn't see them at all,' Will says flatly. 'She can't. They're dead.'

Chapter 5

Sorrell

THURSDAY

Hi Sorrell! Just wondering if you'd like to come over for drinks and nibbles tonight. The usual crowd will be here. Be lovely to see you. V x

Sorrell rereads the WhatsApp message from Victoria, certain that there's been some kind of mistake. She hasn't been invited to join the other mums for a night out in well over two years. She doesn't know why – she hadn't fallen out with anyone – and she wasn't even aware that she was missing out until she logged onto Facebook for the first time in forever, and saw photos of the others together – at a cocktail bar, in Victoria's enormous garden, on a weekend day trip with the kids. The realisation that she'd been excluded was a sharp spike through the heart.

She messaged Audrey, the school mum she was close to,

asking why she hadn't been invited along. WhatsApp showed the message had been read but hours passed before a reply flashed up on her screen.

I didn't actually arrange any of those things, I was just invited along. I did think it was odd though, that you weren't there.

Odd? But she wasn't concerned enough to make sure Sorrell received an invitation to the next get-together, or the one after that. Audrey's blasé response hurt more than the photographs had and, too angry to reply, Sorrell turned off her phone. She still made small talk with Audrey at the gates if they ran into each other, but the hurt she felt had closed a door in her heart. Their friendship had been more important to her than it was to Audrey; the revelation made her feel small.

Since they'd moved to Lowbridge, after Finnley was made a partner at the dental surgery six years ago, she'd struggled to make any other close friends amongst the school mums. There isn't a single woman she can confide in or laugh with. There's no one in her life, other than Finnley, and a handful of old friends from St Ives that she phones weekly who accept and love her for who she is.

Audrey's confidence had balanced out Sorrell's fearfulness, her outspokenness masked her reserve, and her witty observations made her laugh like a drain. She'd seemed genuinely interested in Sorrell as a person, and that kind of attentiveness was addictive; it made her feel good.

If she accepts Victoria's invitation it gives her the opportunity to rebuild her friendship with Audrey without too bright a spotlight shining her way. She's never been a great actress, but she can be easy and breezy. She can pretend that the text message never happened, that life just got in the way.

There's just one issue. Is it safe to leave Finnley by himself?

Clutching her phone, she hurries into the house in search of her husband. Unlike yesterday, when despair had radiated off him like heat, he'd seemed much brighter all day. His side of the bed was empty when she woke, and the twins' room was deserted. She descended the stairs, trepidation weighing every step, pausing part way down when the faint notes of a jaunty pop hit, and three discordant voices, floated up from downstairs. She peered around the kitchen door and discovered Finnley standing by the oven, a child-sized apron barely covering his torso, and a frying pan in his hand. He was flipping pancakes for the twins, who were wiggling their hips to 'Happy' by Pharrell Williams and singing along. It was so unexpectedly lovely – a throwback to the life they used to share – that she backed out of the hallway before she was spotted, and sobbed in the bathroom until Scout began crying, demanding to be fed.

'You okay?' Finnley glances up at her now, then frowns, reading the expression on her face. 'Kids all right?'

'Yeah. Yeah. Fine. I'll go and collect Scout from nursery in a bit. I was just—'

'Amit texted me.'

'Really?'

'He's back from Dubai. Wants to go for a drink.'

'When?'

'Tonight. I said yes. That's okay, isn't it?'

Her excitement about her own invitation fades. Finnley hasn't seen any of his friends for months and if he's feeling well enough to go out then he must. Victoria, and Audrey, can wait.

'What is it?' Finnley asks. 'You don't think I should go?'

'No, no. Absolutely you should. It's great!'

'No, it's not.' He's picked up on the false notes in her voice. 'What's the matter? What's wrong?'

She perches on the sofa, beside him. 'Victoria texted me, inviting me to hers for drinks tonight. And Audrey will be there . . .'

Her husband's expression shifts. He looks guilty. He really wants to go out too. 'It's fine. I can arrange to see Amit another day.'

'No, Finnley. I want you to—'

'You haven't been out in forever. You need a night out.'

'But you—'

'We could get a babysitter? What's the name of that teenager we normally use? Sadie. Let's ask her. What time are you going out?'

'Victoria said to come round from six. You?'

'Eight o'clock. The Bat and Badger, that nice pub we had dinner in a million years ago, the one in the sticks.'

She remembers the pub – all dark wood, tantalising smells and roaring fires. 'Maybe I should wait around until you leave, get the kids to bed. I think Sadie might struggle to get Scout to sleep.'

Finnley raises his eyebrows, a smile playing on his lips as he clears his throat.

'What?' she asks. 'What's that look for?'

'I'm depressed, honey, not incapacitated. I know how to put the kids to bed.' His smile widens. 'Everything's going to be all right. You know that don't you?'

'I do,' she says and, in that moment, she really does.

Chapter 6

Victoria

THURSDAY

Victoria casts a critical eye over her living room, taking in the high ceiling, ceiling rose and picture rail – dust-free, sofas and cushions plumped, and a selection of Waitrose tapas artfully arranged on the coffee table.

With any luck they won't need to use the living room – the evening's 'drinks and nibbles' are due to take place in the garden. It's an unusually warm October evening, rain isn't forecast and the firepit, gazebo and throws should ensure that everyone's so warm and cosy that they'll only have to go into the house to use the loo. Victoria checks the downstairs bathroom for the third time, nods approvingly then moves through the rest of the house.

She pauses to look in at her daughter's bedroom, then her son's. She decorated them six weeks after she and Andy had sat the children down and told them that Mummy and

IT'S ALWAYS THE HUSBAND

Daddy didn't make each other happy anymore and they were going to live in different houses. The children were so distraught that their plan for Andy to move out went out of the window. They mutually agreed that he'd continue sleeping in the spare room until the children's shock had worn off.

The weekend Victoria redecorated the bedrooms, Andy was at a friend's stag do. When he returned and surveyed each child's bedroom his expression grew darker, and Victoria became more tense, with every second that passed. They had a furious low-voiced row in the kitchen ten minutes later. Andy demanded to know how much she'd spent and, when she told him, he accused her of trying to buy their children's love. She called him a tight, cold, heartless bastard. Why shouldn't she do something nice for the children? They were tearing their lives apart by splitting up, the least she could do was give them somewhere lovely to play and sleep. Half an hour later, with the children at the top of the stairs screaming at their daddy not to go, Andy moved out.

That was four months ago and, while the children still bemoan the fact that their parents aren't together, they've largely settled into a routine, splitting their time between their parents.

Satisfied that everything is as it should be upstairs, she heads back down to the kitchen – pausing en route to check her reflection in the mirror – then picks up her phone to look at her messages. Theresa still hasn't replied but, other than that, no one's cancelled, which is good. She still feels nervy and anxious though, like her insides are being twanged by a three-year-old who's just discovered a guitar. She knows her 'girls' – Dawn, Audrey, Caz, Shahina and Sara – inside out, but there will be two interlopers in the mix tonight – Jude and Sorrell – and *their* behaviour she can't predict.

If there's one thing that makes her feel secure and safe, it's knowing exactly what's going on in Lowbridge. If a family moves out of the area she needs to know where they've gone (and what their house sold for). If there's an argument between two of the mothers, she needs to know why. And if a teacher goes off long-term sick she won't rest until she's discovered their disease. If there are no unanswered questions in her world then she can't be caught off-guard. It's why she rarely reads crime novels. If someone in her book club insists on choosing one, she'll read the first few chapters, flick to the end to see what happens, then read all the rest.

If only real-life stresses were so easily circumvented. As they aren't, she's had to do the next best thing and invite two people she barely knows into the safe space that is her home.

Jude Miller and Sorrell Edwards are key in providing answers to two new mysteries that have appeared in Victoria Fitzgerald's life:

Who beat up Will Ledger?

and

Why has her dentist Finnley Edwards taken extended sick leave?

She opens the replies she was sent by Jude and Sorrell; their responses to her invitation couldn't be more different. Sorrell, who's been on the outskirts of the group for years, can't hide her surprise and delight. Jude, by contrast, replied with: **Not being weird but how did you get my number?**

Victoria had replied with a smirk on her lips.

There's nothing you can't get hold of if you know who to ask. She added a winky face at the end of her message then added, **No judgement on your friendship with Will**

Ledger but there's a lot you don't know about him. See you later. No need to bring a bottle or snacks. I will provide. The keycode for the front door is 59372 (I might be in the garden/field when you arrive).

'No judgement'. Obviously, that was a lie. And not the first thing she's lied about either.

Chapter 7

Jude

THURSDAY

The 'drinks and nibbles' evening is taking place under a gazebo in Victoria's vast garden. The other women – Dawn, Audrey, Sorrell, Sara, Shahina and Caz – are gathered around an elegant black firepit table, sitting on expensive-looking cushion-covered chairs. They'd already arrived by the time Jude rang the doorbell and, as Victoria leads her into the garden, their eyes swivel towards her like haunted dolls. She flashes a smile in their direction. The only reason she's there, that she booked a babysitter for Betsy, was to find out what Victoria knows about Will.

The moment her arse touches her seat the onslaught begins.

'Where are you from?'

'Where was Betsy at school before?'

'Why did you decide to move here in Year 5?'

'Are you single or married?'
'Does your ex live here?'
'Does Betsy see her dad?'
'What do you do?'

They're obviously questions the other mums have been dying to ask since she first appeared at the school gates – and swerved anyone who looked like they might want to talk to her – but now they're rapidly fired her way.

She patiently answers each of the questions in turn – Hertfordshire, the local state primary, because she was being bullied, divorced, ex still lives in Hertfordshire, Betsy sees him one weekend a month, every half-term and for half of the holidays, freelance copywriter. Victoria saves the most controversial question for last:

'Are you and Will Ledger having an affair?'

There's a surprised gasp from one of the women – Dawn. She's got what Jude's granny would call a 'lived-in face' that clashes with her short blue hair and the ring in her nose. In her leopard print shirt and tatty black denim jacket, with a Tubigrip around her wrist, she couldn't look more different to the other mums. That kind of wanton individuality endears her to Jude. That and the fact that her reaction to Victoria's question was very similar to her own. Not that Jude would give Victoria the satisfaction of a gasp. For now, she's keeping it to herself that she thinks she's a dick.

'Did you hurt your wrist?' she asks Dawn, swerving the question.

'Got the cast off!' Dawn sits up taller and raises her arm so everyone can see her Tubigrip in all its grubby glory. Her delight at being the centre of attention is so obvious it makes Jude wonder whether she's a little bit attention-starved. It can't be easy, suppressing your personality to bow and scrape at the feet of Victoria Routledge.

'I rang the Woodster from the hospital,' Dawn continues, her warm Brummy accent a soft hug compared to Victoria's more clipped southern tones. 'That's the hubbie by the way, Simon. Anyway, I said I'd broken it in three places and he said—'

'Not again!' Sara catches her eye and shakes her head, mock exasperated but still friendly. She's got the kindliest face in the group. Younger than the other women, she's plump and rosy-cheeked, her curly chestnut hair twisted into a messy bun on the top of her head. Whatever Dawn's about to say, Sara's heard it before.

'No, go on, Dawn,' Jude says, playing along. 'What did he say?'

'If you broke it in three places I suggest you hang out somewhere else!'

There's a collective groan from everyone but Victoria who's staring at Jude with undisguised irritation.

'Nice try deflecting,' she says tightly. 'Well? Are you? Having an affair with Will Ledger?'

'An affair? Seriously?' Jude laughs drily. 'That's a hell of a conclusion to reach because I helped him off the ground when he was beaten up.'

'Oh, come on.' Victoria leans towards her and places a hand on her arm, her expression pure 'you can tell me'. 'We've seen the two of you in the playground and going into each other's houses. You're a single woman; why wouldn't you if you get on?'

There's a pause, during which Jude tries to work out why the hell Victoria cares. Boredom, curiosity, a side career as a shit spreader?

'I take it you're not a fan.'

Victoria snorts. 'You could say that.'

'And why is that?'

'Has he told you about his relationship history?'

'He told me that Milly's mum and stepmum are both dead, yes.'

'He said that?' Victoria stares at Jude in disbelief, jaw dropped, eyes wide. 'He actually said that Ali *and* Robyn are dead?'

Her expression couldn't be more cartoonish if her tongue had dropped to the floor. As it is, the only sound in the garden is Ed Sheeran crooning from a Bluetooth speaker and Dawn slurping the last of her Long Island iced tea from a long metal straw. At the mention of Ali and Robyn's names Jude notices Caz cross her arms and turn her head sharply away from the group, as though she's mentally seeking refuge in the darkness beyond the patio. With her blunt bob and thick weighty glasses, she gives off a stern librarian vibe from the nose upwards, while her crimson lipstick, billowing leopard print dress, weighty beaded necklace and chunky black boots give her more of a fashionista vibe. No one comments on her sudden frostiness because every other woman around the table is staring at Jude as though the night's entertainment has finally begun. Dawn takes another long, noisy slurp of her drink.

'Dawn, stop that!' Audrey snaps and the slurping stops instantly. 'Get a refill! Please. I can't stand that disgusting noise.'

Dawn looks at Victoria, gauging her reaction, mortification in her eyes. But Victoria's too focused on Jude to notice. Acting more casually than she's feeling, Jude takes a sip of her vodka and Coke.

'What's wrong with Will saying that Robyn and Ali are dead?' she asks.

'Everything.' Victoria glances around the group, her eyebrows raised, seeking validation and everyone, apart from Caz, nods like good little worker bees.

'No one knows what happened to Robyn,' Shahina says from across the firepit. With her sleek shoulder-length hair, large, wide-set eyes, high cheekbones and effortless air of elegance, she reminds Jude of the actress Naomie Harris.

'Thank you, Shahina, I was coming to that.' Victoria says tightly before Jude can respond. 'What happened was— Oh, hello sweetie. Is everything okay?'

Standing directly behind Jude is a small red-haired boy. He'd first interrupted them half an hour ago, clutching a teddy bear, which he'd carefully placed on the floor next to Victoria's chair. Now, he taps it affectionately on the head then looks up at his mother.

'Please, Mummy, can I stay here with you?' The child's probably five or six years old but he's using the kind of toddler voice that older children use when there's something they desperately want. 'I don't like the babysitter, and Sophia's being mean.'

'No, sweetheart. I'm afraid you can't.' There's a kindly, yet frustrated, tone to Victoria's voice as though she suspects that the other women are judging her mothering skills. 'It's time for bed. Come on, let me tuck you in.'

She scoops up her son and cups the back of his head as he nestles his face into her neck. 'I'll be back shortly,' she tells the group. 'No talking to Jude until I get back, or there will be consequences. Just kidding,' she adds quickly, her rictus smile back in place. 'Or am I?'

'That boy walks all over her,' Caz hisses once Victoria's out of earshot. They're all still watching her as she heads back into the house with her child in her arms. 'He's nearly six and she still lets him sleep in her bed.'

'Don't judge,' Shahina snaps back. 'She lost four pregnancies after Sophia. He's always going to be her baby boy.'

Caz doesn't reply but the muscles in her jaw tighten and, as she lowers her gaze, there's a steeliness to her eyes.

An awkward pause follows, one that Jude feels a compulsion to fill.

'So, what are the consequences if you lot talk to me? Hair pulling? Nipple clamps? An invitation to join the PTA?'

There's a snort from the other side of the firepit. It's Sorrell, the woman who picked Will's violin up out of the road. She's barely said a word since Jude arrived and, with all eyes in her direction now, she flushes a fiery red. She glances at the person sitting to Jude's right – Audrey, a French woman in her late thirties with loosely waved blonde hair to her shoulders and a slash of red lipstick across her wide thin lips – then looks away again quickly.

'I've been meaning to talk to you, Sorrell,' Jude says, 'to say thank you for yesterday. It gave Will one less thing to worry about, knowing Milly would still get her violin.'

'It's fine.' Sorrell shrugs self-consciously. 'It was nothing really. We'd have all done the same.' Her eyes flick again towards Audrey, who appears to be resolutely avoiding her gaze. A spark of intrigue ignites in Jude's chest. Interesting. There's obviously an issue between these two, but what happened and why, she hasn't a clue.

'Did he say what happened?' asks Sara. She's dressed in navy dungarees with a long-sleeve blue and white stripy top underneath it. There are daubs of paint and glitter on the front of her dungarees, as though she was doing arts and crafts with her children just moments before she left the house. 'Will – did he say why he was attacked?'

Dawn, who's been crunching ice and staring at her phone since Victoria left the group, flinches as Sara gives her a nudge in the side. This is something they all want to know.

'No . . . no . . . no . . .' Victoria appears at Jude's side, gripping two jugs of Long Island iced tea like a Bavarian barmaid wielding beer. 'What did I say about waiting for me to return? Who wants a top-up?'

Dawn's first to raise her glass, then Caz and Shahina. Drinks replenished, Victoria retakes her seat and an expectant silence falls.

'Well?' She turns to look at Jude, her blue eyes sharp and demanding. 'What did he say?'

Something inside Jude contracts. It's the air of entitlement that she finds so repellent, as though Victoria's never been told no in her life. But it's tit for tat with this woman. She won't get answers without providing information of her own.

'He told the guy on the e-scooter that he shouldn't be riding on the pavement when there were children around.' She shrugs. 'It was a random attack, nothing more mysterious than that.'

Victoria gives her a long look through narrowed eyes, as though she's weighing her up. 'Did he know his attacker?'

'No. He was as shocked as we were.'

'As *you* were, maybe. None of us were surprised.' Victoria glances around the group again. For someone who radiates confidence, she can't make a statement without ensuring that everyone else feels the same.

'Anyway.' Jude suppresses a sigh. 'Back to Robyn, I take it that's . . . Will's second wife?'

'Partner. They never married. In Year 1 she started doing the school run, ferried Milly to playdates, attended PTA, chatted at the school gates, you know, the normal mum stuff.'

Jude lets the barbed comment about the PTA (she didn't bother going last night), and the school gate chats go.

'Robyn knew next to no one in Lowbridge so, naturally,

I befriended her. I hate to see anyone all on their own.' Across the firepit Sorrell raises her eyebrows as if to say, *Really?* Caz is practically vibrating with anger and Audrey is puffing on her vape like it's the only source of oxygen in an airless world. They're all leaking so many non-verbal cues that Jude feels like she's drowning in a sea of oestrogen. They might look like they're a tight-knit group of friends on the surface but she can feel the rumblings of discontent. *Someone* is going to explode.

'Anyway,' Victoria continues. 'I brought Robyn into the group—'

Chair legs scrape against tiles as Caz leaps up. She stares around the group, trembling with emotion. 'Are we doing this again, seriously? Well fuck it, because I'm not interested. Thanks for the drinks, Victoria. I'm done.'

She stalks away, disappearing into the darkness of the garden, Sara following her at a trot, frantically calling her name while Jude looks around the group, trying to work out what the hell is going on.

Nothing out of the ordinary it seems, from the way the other women look at each other knowingly, eyebrows raised, as Victoria casually refills her glass and takes a sip of her drink. The vibe around the firepit is pure *surprise, surprise, Caz has kicked off again.*

Jude glances from one woman to another, searching for someone, anyone who will meet her eye. 'Anyone want to tell me what just happened?'

Audrey holds up her arms, palms raised to the sky and blows out her lips in exasperation. 'Let's just say that Robyn made a lasting impression on most people she met.'

'Really? So did Caz fall out with—'

'If I could finish? Please?' Victoria cuts Jude off then flashes her a *Five Nights at Freddy's* rictus smile. 'Before I lose my train of thought?' she continues, before Jude, or anyone else, can object. 'Where was I? Oh yes. I took Robyn under my wing somewhat and when we knew each other a little better she told me all about Will and how she'd met him on a dating site eight months after Ali, his first wife, died.'

'Eight months,' Audrey interjects, 'can you imagine? I'd still be grieving if anything happened to my Sully.'

'Quite. But I'm not a judgemental person, especially where love is involved.'

Victoria takes a sip of her drink, her pursed lips wrapped around the straw, as tight and pink as a cat's puckered bum. She's hamming it up like a child actor drip-feeding her lines and pausing dramatically to squeeze every last bit of tension out of her role. Jude glances at her watch. It's ten pounds an hour for the babysitter. At this rate she's going to have to extend her overdraft to find out what Victoria knows about Will.

'Sorry, I couldn't convince her to stay.' Sara steps out of the gloom, grabs a blanket from the pile, wraps it around her shoulders and retakes her seat. She shoots Jude a 'what can you do?' look, which makes her shrug in response, largely because she's got no idea how else to react.

'So . . . where was I?' Victoria sets her glass back on the edge of the fireplace and crosses one lean leg over the other. For a woman in her early forties, she's ridiculously toned. 'Oh yes, Will's first wife Ali. She was a lovely woman – friendly, intelligent, adored little Milly. She hung around with Theresa mostly, but I was so shocked when she died part way through the Reception year. Why she married Will I don't know, but hell, I fell in love with Andy, so who am I to judge?'

The other women laugh politely.

'Anyway, Ali passed away three days after Milly turned five. She and Will had taken time off to redecorate the house while Milly was at school. Ali was painting the landing ceiling. You know how tall the ceilings are in Victorian living houses? Well, she had to use a really long ladder. According to Will, Ali lost her balance when she was reaching up to paint the ceiling, fell off the ladder and tumbled down the stairs. When he checked her pulse, she was dead. Or so he said.'

A cold chill seeps through Jude's cotton sweatshirt. She's probably walked over the spot where Will's first wife died. She looks around the group, gauging their reaction to Victoria's words. Dawn, Audrey and Sara are either staring at the ground, into the fire, or at their hands. None of them meet her eye. Victoria just insinuated that Will was complicit in his wife's death and none of them have anything to say? Either they're too scared to contradict her, or they believe in Will's guilt.

Jude turns to Shahina, the only woman who isn't averting her gaze. 'That's so shocking. I can't quite believe that it's true.'

'I know.' Shahina's eyes shine with compassion. Beside her, Sorrell looks on the verge of tears. 'It was such a tragedy; Ali was so young.' It's a touching sentiment but, to Jude, it rings hollow. Will no one, other than Victoria, tell her what they actually think?

'You all believe that Will . . .' She can't finish her question. She leaves it hanging in the cool, autumn air.

The mood around the firepit changes, as though the other women can sense the anger building within her, several of them fidget, uncomfortably in their seats. Even Victoria seems to have paled in the amber glow of the flames.

'None of us thought that Will killed Ali.' Sara leaps back

into the conversation, breaking the silence. Her cheeks and the base of her throat are flushed. Whether from booze, or embarrassment, Jude can't tell. 'Not after she died, anyway. It was only when Robyn disappeared that we became susp—'

'She disappeared?' Jude sits up taller. 'How? Why?'

Victoria leaps in, cutting Sara off before she can answer. 'No one knows. She was supposed to come round for a drink, texted the group chat to say that she and Will had had an argument, and she was going to be late. And then . . . she just vanished. She didn't come to the party. She didn't contact anyone. And no one's seen her since.'

'There was a police investigation' – Audrey, who's been silently puffing on her vape during Victoria's monologue, pulls her coat tighter around her shoulders – 'and it was reported in the local news, but the national press didn't pick up on it, not even after the police got a warrant to search the house and take Will's car.'

'Victoria's husband Andy was a detective on the case. Sorry . . .' Dawn casts Victoria an apologetic look '. . . ex-husband—'

'Who's now living in a grotty little flat in that new build on the high street,' Victoria says sniffily.

Dawn shifts in her seat. 'Yeah. Anyway, Andy was part of the investigation, not that he'd discuss it at the school gates with any of us. He flatly refused.'

Victoria bristles. 'How unlike my ex-husband to be a grumpy, rude bore.'

'They took Will in for questioning,' Sara adds. 'But they released him without charge.'

'Jude.' Victoria places her hand on her wrist and squeezes. 'We're only telling you this for your own protection. I don't know if you've seen that Netflix show, *The Staircase*, but there are echoes of that here. To lose one wife is a tragedy.

IT'S ALWAYS THE HUSBAND

To lose her replacement a few years later, well, questions need to be asked. And if Will is claiming that Robyn is dead . . . then I think that says everything you need to know, don't you?'

Chapter 8

Sorrell

THURSDAY

Sorrell hasn't had a drink all night (she's staying sober in case the babysitter rings with an emergency and she has to drive home), but she's never wanted one more. All the other women, apart from Jude who left two hours ago, are now riotously drunk. After a lengthy gossip about some of the other school mums, Sara's sequestered Victoria's phone so she can change the playlist and she's now vigorously twerking to 'Baby Got Back' with Shahina, while Dawn demolishes the pizza Victoria produced earlier and is laughing along. Meanwhile, Audrey and Victoria are talking loudly at each other, occasionally demonstrating their point by clapping the other woman on the arm, hand or knee. It's 10 p.m. and Sorrell's never felt more alone in her life.

She looks to her phone for company but there aren't any new messages. Nothing from the babysitter, or Finnley. If either of them had messaged, asking her to go home, she could leave without feeling like she'd failed. After Jude left, Victoria looked disappointed and bored. Her plaything had escaped her clutches; who would she toy with next?

Sorrell, as it turned out.

For half an hour Victoria cross-examined her about Finnley, asking her why he wasn't at the practice, why he didn't accompany her to school events, why none of them had seen him in so long. The intense questioning made Sorrell's skin shrivel. She wanted to crawl inside her bones and hide. In fact, the only pleasant conversation she'd had all evening was when Jude thanked her for picking up Will's dropped violin. She desperately wishes she had Jude's assuredness and self-confidence. Even when Victoria dropped a bomb on her, telling her about Ali and Robyn, and Caz ran off into the night, Jude didn't appear wrong-footed. After Victoria made the comment about *The Staircase* she said, 'Wow, Victoria. It's impossible to underestimate you. Anyway, babysitter's waiting, got to go.' Then she left.

The whole point of Sorrell putting herself through Victoria's drinks party was to patch things up with Audrey but, apart from a clipped hello when she arrived, she hasn't spoken to her all night. She'd attempted to take the empty chair beside Audrey, but Dawn had beckoned Sorrell over to the other side of the firepit, and it would have been rude to say no, particularly as Dawn had always been on the edge of the group, like her. There was no way Sorrell was going to broach her falling out with Audrey in full earshot of the other women – she needed to be seated next to her for that – but she didn't get the opportunity until Jude left. She stood, heart pounding, ready to take her seat, but Victoria had called Audrey over, and they've been deep in conversation ever since.

'You know he just let himself into the house yesterday,' Victoria says now. 'And when I confronted him about it, he gave me the finger.'

'Not the good type of finger I take it,' Audrey says drily, which makes Victoria laugh.

'Fuck no. That bastard touched me for the last time ages ago. The sooner I find the money to buy him out of this house, the better. Anyone know anyone who needs a PT?'

'Is it true . . .' Audrey leans in closer '. . . what they say about personal trainers sleeping with their clients?'

'Well . . .' A smirk plays on Victoria's lips as she reaches for her glass. Finding it empty she knocks back Audrey's drink instead. 'Let's just say that there aren't any redheads in Andy's family and the reason Noah is ginger isn't because I'm blonde.'

'Really?' Audrey sits up taller in her seat and Sorrell clocks Sara and Shahina, who've stopped twerking, exchange a blatant 'did you hear that too?' eyebrow raise.

'I mean, who knows.' Victoria shrugs nonchalantly but something's changed in her demeanour. She's relishing the attention. 'Look, I'm pretty sure Andy's cheated on me multiple times over the course of our relationship – all those late nights he had to comb through case files, all the weekends of overtime, all the pretty young detectives he was paired with. And let's not forget the fact I found a lipstick in his non-work car. Is anyone going to judge me if I do the same?'

'No, no of course not.' Audrey gives Victoria such a sycophantic look it makes Sorrell feel sick. It's obvious why her friendship with Audrey faltered – Victoria decided to claim her as her own and now she barely recognises the friend that she adored because she's changed so much.

'Um . . .' Sorrell clears her throat, having spotted a small ginger boy lurking in the gloom. He's standing by the bushes behind Victoria, watching them. God only knows how long he's been there. 'Noah is out of bed again.'

Victoria jumps as though she's been prodded.

'Sweetie! What are you doing out of bed?' There's none of the tension that was in her voice earlier. She's reached that stage of drunkenness where she doesn't give two shits what anyone else thinks of her – she's having too much fun. 'Come on then, back to the house you go.'

'When are you coming to bed, Mummy?'

'Soon.' She takes him by the hand. 'Very, very soon.'

'I should probably get going,' Audrey says as Victoria leads Noah away, and the last drop of hope in Sorrell's heart evaporates, leaving briny resentment in its place. This was their chance to talk, for Audrey to smile her way, but she doesn't so much as glance at her. All evening Sorrell's convinced herself that Audrey was too distracted, too entranced by Victoria, to talk to her, when the truth is she's being openly ignored. She must have done or said something that's made Audrey dislike her but, after this evening, she's not sure she wants to know what that is.

'One more drink!' Dawn shouts as Sorrell's phone starts ringing. 'One more drink, Audrey. Then we'll all go.'

Sorrell looks at her phone and her stomach lurches. Finnley rarely calls, preferring to text instead. Something must be wrong.

She stands up so quickly her vision darkens and she rocks, unsteadily, on her feet.

'Sorrell?' Shahina says. 'Is everything okay?'

'Fine!' She raises a hand in acknowledgement. 'Stood up too quickly, that's all. Sorry, I have to take this.'

She hurries away, towards the solitude of the house, and answers her husband's call near the side of the building, several feet from the open back door.

'Finnley? Is everything okay?'

There's no answer, but she can hear laboured breathing.

'Finnley, where are you?'

'I . . . I . . .' She hears a sob, then a loud thump, like he's hitting something with his fist.

'Where are you? Are you with Amit? Can I talk to him?'

She hears another thump and Finnley groans in frustration. She's heard that sound before, when he's upset, and he's fighting to pull himself together. 'I just . . . I just . . .'

'Breathe. Breathe,' she says, although she's barely breathing herself. Is it him? Is it the kids? What's happened? 'Take a few deep breaths and then tell me what's going on.'

Out of the corner of her eye she sees the other women heading back into the house, bottles, glasses and Noah's teddy, loaded up in their arms. She turns her back to them, and the house, hunches into herself, the phone to her ear. On the other end of the line Finnley is still breathing shakily. Each time he inhales his breath catches in the back of his throat.

'Please. Whatever it is that's happened, we can get through this together. I can't help you if you don't tell me. Finnley just—'

'I hit something.'

'Hit what? Are you hurt? What happened?'

'No . . . no . . . I'm not hurt. I didn't have the headlights on; I wasn't thinking. I was driving home from the pub. I left . . . I started having a panic attack when Amit was in the toilet. I was hyperventilating and people were looking at me and so I just left. I got in the car and I drove and it came out of nowhere . . . hit the bonnet and I . . . I . . .'

'Was it an animal? Or was it . . .' She presses a hand to her chest as a wave of nausea sweeps through her.

'I think it was an animal. I'm pretty sure . . .' Finnley's voice is strangled with regret. 'It was so sudden and—'

'Did you stop? Is it dead? Are you okay? Where are you now?'

'Finsbury Lane. I've pulled over. I'm fine. Shaken, but fine.'

She knows the road. He's still miles from home, out in the countryside – nothing for miles apart from the pub, a service station and a glamping field run by a local farmer and his wife. It's a dark, secluded road with woodland on either side.

'I—' She turns sharply, hearing a noise behind her. There's a person-shaped shadow on the patio, cast from the open kitchen door. As she watches, barely breathing, it retreats then disappears.

'Sorrell?' There's panic in her husband's voice again. 'Are you still there?'

'Yes, yes, I'm here.' She lowers her voice. 'Have you gone back to the place where it happened? Is there a badger or something, at the side of the road? If there is you need to put it out of its misery if it's badly hurt.'

'I was going to but I couldn't see anything because there's a ditch at the side of the road, full of brambles. I don't know exactly where it happened. And—'

'If it isn't on the side of the road then maybe it's okay. Maybe it ran into the brambles or the woods. You sound shaken up. Do you want me to come and help you?'

'No.' He says the word crisply. It's such a sudden change in mood – a flip from fear to irritation – that Sorrell's breath catches in her throat.

'I'll drive myself home.'

His sadness she can deal with, his despondency too, but when he swings into anger it feels like punishment, like she's getting everything wrong. She's never lived with anyone with depression before and, despite hours and hours of googling, when she gets up each morning and her feet touch the carpet, she knows she'll spend the day on unsteady ground.

'I'm sorry.' Finnley's tone has softened now. 'I'm so sorry. I know you were only trying to help.'

Sorrell says nothing. She'd feel stronger if there were an end date to his illness, or a cure that was guaranteed to work.

'I shouldn't have rung you,' Finnley continues. 'I should have just pulled myself together and I . . . I'm sorry. I'm really sorry.'

She takes a slow, steadying breath. For better for worse, that's what they promised each other, isn't it? 'It's okay,' she says softly. 'I'll see you back at home. Drive . . .' She tails off. 'Drive carefully' feels redundant right now.

'I'll see you soon,' Finnley says. 'And sorry again.'

As the phone line goes dead, Sorrell rests the side of her head against the hard brick of the house. 'You're made of strong stuff,' her brother told her, the last time she called him, but right now the only strong stuff she wants is a large gin and tonic, once she gets home.

'Everything okay?' Victoria's voice rings out behind her and she turns slowly. She's standing in the doorway to the house, little Noah clinging to her legs.

'Everything's great,' she says, as Audrey's laughter rings out from inside the house.

Chapter 9

Jude

THURSDAY

'Honestly, Emma, they're the most neurotic, uptight women I've ever met in my life.' Jude's mobile is warm against her ear. Back at home, with Betsy fast asleep upstairs, a cup of tea in one hand and her phone in the other, she feels more grounded than she's felt all evening, although she's still absolutely fuming.

'If they're not interrupting, or snapping at each other, they're acting like it's completely normal for someone to just storm off into the night. What that was about, I've got no idea because Victoria Routledge wouldn't let me get a word in edgeways. Seriously, Em, she's the most hideous excuse for a human being. I swear that if she was any stupider, she'd need watering once a day.'

Her older sister laughs. 'I'm so glad I don't have to do the school run anymore.'

'You were the one who recommended the school, you bastard.'

'Hello! I said the school was good; I didn't mention the mums.'

'Fine. I'm moving back in with my ex.'

'Should I ring him and warn him, or do you want it to be a surprise?'

She laughs then takes a sip of her tea. Talking to Emma always makes her feel better. Also, she's the only person she knows who regularly stays up past ten o'clock, and actually answers her phone.

'How are Blaine and Isla doing? Is Blaine's asthma under control?' Blaine's her sister's eldest.

Her sister sighs heavily. 'Let's hope so. The hospital sent him home with a nebuliser and a new course of drugs. He seems all right in himself, but I've given up hope that he'll grow out of it. Regular asthma checkups and steroid prescriptions are going to be in his future for a while.'

'I'm really sorry to hear that. Will you give him my love?'

'Only if you want him to die of embarrassment. He's fourteen now, remember – could you *be* any more cringe. Anyway, back to the gossip. Does that thick-as-shit school mum really believe that Will killed both women? She wasn't just winding you up?'

'Nope. It was why she invited me over. She wanted to humiliate me in front of her coven.'

'Or to warn you off . . .'

'Seriously? You're taking her side?'

'Look, the police had to have had a good reason to search his house and car.'

'Because the husband is always the prime suspect. Anyway, they didn't find anything. He'd be in prison now if they had.'

She can almost hear Emma's brain ticking over in the silence that follows. 'You sound very certain of his innocence. Are you shagging him by any chance?'

Now it's Jude's turn to pause.

'You are! I knew it! Oh my God. You've been here five minutes and you've already fucked one of the dads! No wonder they're talking about you!'

'Um, hello, Mrs Judgy. You're supposed to be on my side.'

'I am. I just . . .'

'You think he did it? No smoke without fire and all that.'

'No . . .'

'Emma . . .'

Her older sister sighs deeply. 'How well do you actually know him?'

'Well enough! He's funny, in a dry, weird, quirky kind of way. He laughs at my shit jokes, he's a good dad and . . . he's the only person in Lowbridge who wants to sleep with me.'

'Jude!'

'I was kidding. Although I'm pretty sure the seventy-something cashier in Waitrose was giving me the eye the other day.'

'But do you want to shag him again?'

'The Waitrose cashier? Nah, probably not.'

'Jude! You know who I mean!'

'It's not about sex, Emma. I want to know what happened. Women don't just disappear. Someone has to know where she is.'

'Why do you care?'

'Because either the school mums are right, and there's a double murderer offering my kid sleepovers at his house, or there's a perfectly nice bloke who's been set on by the local harpies because he's had shitty bad luck.'

'I don't think you should get involved.'

'Because you're assuming he's guilty.'

'Because you don't really know him!'

'What's he going to do – strangle me at the school gates? I'm more worried about being gored to death by Victoria. Come on, Emma. Do I have to remind you what happened to Dad?'

Her sister inhales sharply, then falls silent.

Thirty-one years earlier their dedicated, hardworking and no-nonsense dad, Brian, was accused of raping a female farmhand. She was one of a dozen workers who'd travelled from Eastern Europe to live in caravans on a neighbour's farm and pick fruit from dawn until dusk. They were all drinking in the local pub one night – the same night her dad had popped in for a pint. The woman left before her friends and headed back to the neighbour's farm, walking alone on the country roads in the dark. Brian left shortly after her, driving himself home. The woman wasn't able to describe the man who attacked her, or the car he'd been driving, but the locals put two and two together, and the police were called. Brian was arrested, tested and released, and no further arrests were made. Whoever had attacked the woman had disappeared into the night.

But still the town turned against Brian. They painted the word 'rapist' on his front door, slashed his tyres and smashed his windows. One afternoon Jude witnessed her father being attacked in his own driveway, by a local man wielding a baseball bat. Too scared to intervene, she hid in her bedroom until she heard her mother's terrified scream.

Stubborn to the core – a trait he passed on to Jude – and dedicated to the animals on his farm, Brian weathered everything the local community threw at him. He refused to be bullied out of his own home when he hadn't done anything wrong, but the situation wore him down. He grew quieter and paler, hunched and small, concertinaed by the stress. The day social services threatened to take the girls into care, after multiple tip-offs that he was a threat, the little strength he had left was also snatched from him, and he hanged himself in the barn. Jude was the one who discovered his suicide note, then his body.

Six months later, after Jude and Emma's mother had sold the farm and moved to a different town, the real rapist was arrested and charged. No one they'd known from their old town bothered to contact them. No one said: *sorry, we hounded the wrong man to his death.*

'I'm not making light of what happened,' Jude says now. 'Totally the opposite actually.'

'This is nothing like that, Jude, and you know it.' There's a tightness to Emma's voice.

'Isn't it? People passing judgement based on . . . what exactly? Coincidence? Conjecture? Gossip?'

'Dad was arrested and released!'

'And Will was taken in for questioning but no charges were pressed. Still think I should judge him?'

Her sister falls silent again.

'Look,' Jude says, 'I know you're just looking out for me, and you want me to be careful. And I will be, but I'm not going to let a bunch of gossipy bitches tell me what to think. More than that, he's Betsy's best friend's dad. You know how lonely she was at her old school. When all her friends turned on her and started bullying her because one girl decided she was weird.' Jude's voice catches at the memory. 'Do you know how hard that was? Having her come home in tears? Day after day, after day.'

'I know, Jude. I remember.'

'I felt like the shittest mum in the world because I couldn't protect her. I couldn't make things right. She was still getting over the fact that her dad had moved out and—'

'You're a good mum! And you did the right thing by moving here. You gave her a new start.'

'And she's happy now. She comes out of school smiling because of her friendship with Milly and I'm not going to take that away from her.'

'So have Milly over to your house but stay away from Will. If anything happened to Betsy you'd never forgive yourself.'

'Nothing's going to happen to Betsy, or me.'

'Please, promise me you're not going to go digging around.'

'Fine.' She crosses her fingers. 'If you're that worried, I'll leave it alone.'

But the book is open now. She's turned the pages and discovered the mystery, and she's never been the type of person to abandon a book, unread.

Chapter 10

Andy

THURSDAY

It's been over twenty-four hours since Will Ledger was attacked outside the school – if Victoria didn't make the whole thing up – and the thought still makes Andy grin. If anyone in Lowbridge deserved a good kicking, it's that arsehole. The fact he got away with murder – and Andy would bet his house on the fact that Ledger killed Robyn Lewis – makes him feel sick every time he thinks about it.

He worked on that case for *months* – he barely saw Sophie and Noah. Ledger's 'I was at home all night' alibi was as weak as they come. Neighbours had reported hearing the couple arguing and, while Robyn had disappeared with her bag, phone and purse, the phone data suggested she hadn't left Lowbridge and her bank card had never been used. Everyone on the team was certain that, other than a body, they had a cast-iron case against Ledger.

The CPS disagreed. That night Andy went home nursing a swollen hand after he'd smashed his fist into his locker and, for the longest time, he refused to do the school run (something that pissed Victoria right off). He didn't care. There was no way he could look that murdering bastard in the eye.

It's nearly midnight but, as normal, he's not sleepy. For the last three hours he's been watching captured footage, and listening to audio, with the intensity he'd normally reserve for a high-profile murder case.

He was lucky, yesterday, that Victoria hadn't come home ten minutes earlier. If she had, she'd have seen him fiddling with the fittings in the kitchen, dining room, hall and bedroom. Piling clothes up on the bed (in a faked search for his tuxedo) was his alibi for letting himself in.

He's got it down to a fine art – how quickly he can replace the SIM cards in the cameras and listening devices – the only evidence of his snooping, a handful of circuitry and plastic in the palm of his hand.

He touches a finger to a key on his laptop and fast-forwards several hours until his ex-wife and his children walk in the front door, just after 4 p.m. on Tuesday. Headphones on, he listens to their conversations as they move through the house – Victoria moaning at the children to remove their muddy shoes, Sophia trying to tell her mother about a model she's been making out of scrap materials at school, and Noah saying he's hungry (that makes Andy smile, like father like son). What he's looking, and listening for, is anything he can add to his dossier – the hardbacked notebook beside his laptop where he lists all the reasons that Victoria's an unsuitable mother, along with supporting evidence that his children's welfare and safety are at risk if they continue to live with her. He's already filled several pages detailing how much she drinks, including consumption in the evenings, when she was in charge of the children. The afternoon she took her eyes off Noah during a visit to London and he wandered off, causing a full-scale search of the museum, and the dates and times of A&E visits when the children hurt themselves in her care.

From the footage he's seen of Victoria watching late-night TV in the living room, she's upped her drinking – he's got photos of her recycling bin that back that up – but what he's searching for is something even more damning: Victoria inviting a man, or several men, into the home that should be a refuge for their children. He can look up the criminal history of anyone she dates (using the PNC at work, laying the groundwork carefully, so he's not caught), and if a domestic violence conviction comes up all he needs to do then is get social services involved.

Unfortunately for him, other than a few tradesmen, coming in to service the boiler and fix a leaky tap in the kitchen, she hasn't invited a single man home, but what's this? He turns up the volume on his laptop and as Sophia and Noah perch at the kitchen counter and devour their post-school snacks, Victoria's talking on the phone.

'Party round mine on Thursday. What do you think? . . . No, no . . . we won't go wild, it's a school night! Drinks and nibbles, that sort of thing . . . You're in? Brilliant! I look forward to seeing you then!' She ends the conversation with an obnoxious kissy sound, then puts down her phone.

'Who was that?' His daughter, who's unfortunately inherited her nosiness from her mother, takes another bite of her sandwich.

Victoria taps her own nose with her index finger. 'Wouldn't you like to know?'

'Will there be snacks?' Noah asks as Sophia says, 'Can I come?'

'Yes . . . and no!' Victoria's adopted the high-pitched playful tone she reserves for the children, and whenever she's trying to get her own way.

'I'm coming!' Noah climbs down from his stool and wraps his arms around his mother's legs. 'So's Teddy!'

Andy runs a hand through his hair, a wry smirk playing on his lips. 'Good boy, good boy.'

He knows that Noah misses him; he said as much last weekend. They were playing Mario Kart together on the sofa in his flat, shouting 'Banana!' and 'Got you!' at regular intervals while Sophia was on SnapChat with her friends in her room.

'I love this.' Noah had rested his head on Andy's shoulder. The barely-there weight of him, and the soft scent of his hair, made his heart break. 'I wish you still lived at home.'

'So do I, buddy. So do I. But I'm afraid that's not possible. Mummy doesn't want me to live there anymore.'

'I hate her! I want to live here with you.'

That was a bomb he hadn't seen coming.

'I'd love that too, mate.' He'd softly ruffled his son's ginger hair. 'Maybe that could happen . . .'

His son had stiffened with excitement. 'Can it? How?'

'With this . . .' Andy leaned forward and fished a teddy out of his rucksack.

'A teddy? Is it for me?'

'Of course it's for you. It's for you to hug, whenever you miss me. There's something special about Teddy. Do you want to know what?'

Noah nodded wildly, wrapping the toy in his arms and burying his face in his fur.

'Teddy really likes people – that's how he gets his magic.'

'Magic?' His son looked up at him with bright, unquestioning eyes. He still believed in Santa, the Easter Bunny and the tooth fairy. He was also certain that his toys were alive.

'That's right.'

There were only three places where Andy had failed to place cameras and listening devices – on the patio, in Victoria's car and on his ex-wife herself. Stripped bare of plant pots and paraphernalia (Victoria didn't like clutter), the only bits of furniture on the patio were the firepit, gazebo or chairs – none of which were good hiding places.

'Take Teddy in Mummy's car with you. You can leave him there when you go to school,' he told Noah carefully. 'And when Mummy's friends come round next take Teddy to hang out with them. See if you can find him his own chair.'

'Why?' A frown furrowed his son's brow.

'So he can be around people and charge up his magic.'

'But . . . but . . .'

'When Teddy's got enough magic, you can come and live with me here, or maybe even in the big house at home. You'd like that wouldn't you?'

'Yes, Daddy.'

'Good boy.' He kissed his son on the head. 'Don't tell anyone that Teddy's magical, because that will make his magic go away.'

'Like if you see Santa on Christmas?'

'That's right.'

'Okay.' Noah hugged the white bear tightly. 'Okay, Daddy, I won't.'

Now, Andy sits back in his chair, interweaves his fingers and stretches out his arms. It's his turn to have the kids this weekend, and he'll make sure that Noah brings along his teddy. He can't wait to hear what it has to say.

Chapter 11

Sorrell

THURSDAY

Sorrell had no idea what state Finnley would be in when she returned home from Victoria's drinks evening and, when she walked through the front door, she was braced for the worst. The children would be awake and crying, and Finnley would be catatonic, having played the last few hours over and over again until his brain had capitulated and shut down. Or it could be worse, he might not have made it home at all, but she couldn't let herself think like that.

She checked the garage the moment she parked up in the driveway, her chest loosening as the doors slid into the roof and Finnley's black BMW was revealed. He was home then – he'd made his way back to her and the kids. She spotted the damage immediately – a sizeable dent on the bumper, as though a cannonball had been dropped from a height then rolled off, leaving an imperfect circle in the crumpled metal hood. She had no idea what kind of animal would leave that kind of imprint, but she hoped to God that it had been killed on impact and wasn't lying somewhere, suffering. The thought made her want to cry but she pushed it down. One of them had to be an adult and get the car fixed and, as with every other area of their lives, it would have to be her.

She made a mental note to ask Finnley for his insurance details so she could put in a claim the next day, then headed into the house. It was quiet inside, save the burble of the TV in the living room, and she crept upstairs to check on the children, who were all sleeping soundly. They all looked so much smaller and softer at night, the hard edges of the day rubbed off by sleep. Her heart ached as she moved between rooms, checking in on Harper and Henry (still sharing a room even though they were ten), and Scout, splayed out in his baby sleeping bag. He'd almost outgrown his cot. There wasn't anything she wouldn't do for her children. She'd shoulder Finnley's mental health issues alone, a hundred times over, to keep her family together and give her children a loving, protective and stable start to their lives, to do what she'd always done, and make a sanctuary of their home.

Bed check complete, she headed downstairs to her husband. Finnley was on the sofa watching a crime drama on TV, curtains closed, lights dimmed, a blanket over his legs, and a cup of tea in his hands. She paused in the doorway and pressed a hand to the frame.

'You okay?'

'Yeah.'

'Want anything?'

'I'm good.'

'You sure?'

'I'm fine.'

There it was again, that word, but she was too tired to press him to say more. It was almost as though each time he had a breakdown, each time he made himself vulnerable, shame would rise up like a wall afterwards, blocking her out.

'Are you coming to bed?'

'Not yet.' He didn't turn to look at her. 'I'm going to finish watching this show.'

'Okay. Enjoy it.' Sadness made her voice crack and she hurried out of the room knowing that if she said another word, she'd cry.

Now, Sorrell gets out of bed and slips her feet into her slippers, then slides her dressing gown off the chair and pulls it on. The alarm clock's been taunting her sleeplessness for hours, blinking its way from just after midnight to 1 a.m., 2 a.m., to 3.17 a.m. – the time it is now. Finnley, still wrapped up in the duvet, is snoring softly. Like the children, sleep has smoothed the stress from his face.

Moving as quietly as she can, she heads down the stairs and into the kitchen then unlocks the door to the garage. Finnley might have managed to put what happened behind him the moment his head hit the pillow, but she's been tossing and turning for hours. It isn't Audrey, Victoria, or the phone call that's been haunting her. It's the shape of the dent on his car, and the fact Finnley wasn't a hundred per cent sure it was an animal he'd hit.

She turns on the light inside the garage and makes her way over to the bonnet. She perches on the edge of it then, using her arms and one foot for leverage, slides her way across the shiny paintwork until she's reached the dent in the metal. She moves her body into the gap and presses a hand to her face as despair floods her chest. Her hip perfectly fits into the gap.

Chapter 12

Jude

FRIDAY

School's over for the day and it's bitterly cold in the park, but that's not why Jude's mouth is set in a hard line and her arms are folded across her chest. Whilst Betsy and Milly take turns on the trampoline, Jude is being watched. Gathered in a witchy huddle on the other side of the play park, Victoria, Shahina and Audrey clutch cups of takeaway coffee, talking furtively, their icy gossip hanging between them like a cloud. Every now and then Victoria shoots an evil glance in Jude's direction then promptly looks away.

Jude's been making small talk with Will for the last fifteen minutes, standing beside the metal fence that rings the play park. They've discussed the school nativity (Milly is an angel; Betsy is a sheep), the Christmas fayre (*more* shit they need to buy from Tesco for the PTA to sell) and the big new show on Netflix that Jude's addicted to and Will hasn't seen (that was a one-sided conversation), and there's only so much more crap that Jude can bear to hear herself say. She can't keep skirting around the issue that kept her awake for hours last night, long after she said goodnight to Emma and put down the phone. There's no delicate way of bringing it up – God knows she's considered all possible opening gambits, and rejected them all:

'Did you get on with your late wife?'

'Have you watched *The Staircase*?'

'Know any good places to hide a body?'

She's just going to have to come out and say it. Blunt is best or 'just cut the crap and spit it out' as her dad used to say. She steadies herself, says a silent prayer that she's not about to destroy Betsy's friendship with Milly, and takes a deep breath.

'You know they think you murdered Ali and Robyn.'

She steals a glance at Will, expecting to see his jaw tighten or his eyes narrow. Instead, he sighs softly, his gaze fixed on the girls, still joyfully bouncing up and down.

'Tell me something I don't know.'

'Seriously?' She'd expected him to be angry, defensive, or irritated, but he seems like he genuinely doesn't give two shits. 'Have they said something? Openly?'

He looks at her, a bemused expression on his face. 'They've not exactly been quiet about their suspicions. Victoria's parting shot the other day was the least of it. It's ridiculous, although, if I was her husband, I'd take a murder charge over being married to her.'

Jude's laugh is a beat too slow.

'That was a joke,' Will adds, his eyes searching her face, trying to read her reaction.

'I know. It just . . .' She hears Emma's voice in her head,

telling her to be careful, to take a step back, but that's not going to happen. If he wants to joke about the accusations then she's going to too. 'It did sound a lot like the sort of joke a serial killer would make.'

'This is about the hamster funeral, isn't it?' There's genuine amusement in his eyes now. His hands are in his pockets, his shoulders are relaxed and he's breathing evenly. There's nothing in his demeanour that suggests this conversation is making him the slightest bit tense. 'You're putting two and two together and coming up with serial killers torture small animals.'

'Well, you did laugh when I told you about the hamster funeral.' She raises her eyebrows, playing along. 'Am I going to have to kidnap Milly's hamster for his own safety? Because—'

'Hi, Jude!'

She turns to see Dawn beaming at her, her blue fringe peeking out from beneath the furry hood of the oversized olive green parka that hangs from her shoulders, her cheeks pinkened from the cold. At her feet, whining impatiently, is the sweetest golden cockapoo puppy.

'Hi!' Jude says. 'Who's this?' She bends to pet the dog who excitedly jumps at her legs.

'Eddie. After Eddie Vedder from Pearl Jam.' Dawn smiles proudly. 'He had his last set of injections earlier this week. This is only his third time in the park.'

'He's adorable.' Jude stands back up as Will dips to say hello to the dog. 'Eva not with you? I bet she doesn't leave him alone.'

'Exactly! Which is why we've escaped, to give him a rest.'

'Eva didn't fancy playing with the other girls after school?'

Something in Dawn's expression shifts; there's pain in her eyes. 'She's not always invited. You know how it is with Year 5 girls. One minute they're best friends; the next someone's out in the cold.'

'I do know.' Jude touches her arm. 'Betsy was bullied at her last school, and it was heartbreaking. If Eva ever wants to come over for a playdate you know where I am. I hate to think of anyone being left out.'

'That's very kind of you but she's made of tough stuff, just like her mum.' Dawn gives her a watery smile. 'Anyway, I didn't want to interrupt, but I couldn't just walk past without saying hello, especially after Caz's little strop the other night. Talking of which, could I have a little word . . .'

Will takes the hint and drifts far enough away to give them the space to talk.

'The thing is . . .' Dawn lowers her voices and glances at Will from beneath her hood. She looks nervous, like she might be speaking out of turn, or maybe she's scared of Will – Jude can't be sure. 'I don't know if any of the others have told you this about Robyn but not everyone got along with her.'

Jude raises her eyebrows and nods, urging Dawn to continue.

'Some of the women thought she was a flirt. She was very touchy-feely with other people's husbands. Not straight away. It was obvious that she was madly in love with Will at the beginning – he was all she ever talked about, him and Milly, but later on, after she'd been at Lowbridge for a while, rumours started to fly that maybe she was . . . er . . . looking elsewhere for fun.'

'Caz's husband?' Jude ventures, stealing a glance at Will, who's scrolling through his phone.

'He was one of them! Robyn came on to him at the cricket club. Stroking his arm at the bar, flicking her hair, laughing constantly. Caz told her to back off and refused to be in the same room as her afterwards, which made nights out a bit of a mare. That's why she stormed off the other night. She hates all the Saint Robyn shit.' Dawn's gaze drifts across the playground to where Victoria, Audrey and Shahina are chatting animatedly. Sensing she's being watched, Victoria turns her head, then smiles and waves. Dawn returns the wave, her expression so joyful that Jude feels nauseous. Is there anyone who doesn't worship at Victoria Routledge's feet?

'Was Will there?' she asks Dawn. 'At the cricket club?' It's weird, talking about Will when he's only a couple of metres away but she's learning more about Robyn in this brief conversation than she did during Victoria's interminable drinks party.

'Nope, but he had to have found out about it.' Dawn shrugs. 'Lowbridge is a small place.'

'When was this?' She glances across at Will, jolting as his eyes meet hers. He looks concerned, and he's not the only one. If this happened right before Robyn disappeared, then she can see why the police might have zeroed in on him.

'About six months before she disappeared.'

'Right.' The tight knot in her stomach softens. Hardly a crime of passion then, assuming he ever found out. You said a few people didn't get on with her . . .'

'Well, Shahina had a row with her about the PTA Christmas Fayre and she pissed Audrey off by calling her husband a sugar daddy.'

'Did you get along with Robyn?'

Dawn smiles warmly. 'Course! I get on with everyone and she didn't fancy the Woodster, which helped!'

Jude laughs. 'And Victoria?'

'She really liked her, but then who doesn't love Victoria? Anyway, I just wanted you to know why it might have felt a bit—'

'Sorry, one sec, Dawn.'

Distracted by the sound of raised voices, Jude looks back towards the playground. Eloise, Gini and Sophia (Audrey, Shahina and Victoria's daughters) have abandoned the swings and are demanding that Betsy and Milly let them have a go on the trampoline. She takes a step forward, prepared to defuse the situation, but Will, suddenly beside her, puts a warning hand on her arm.

'Let them deal with it.'

'But it's three against two.' She can see the tension in her daughter's body, the stiff set of her shoulders, the dropped chin and the worry clouding her eyes.

'Let them deal with it,' Will says again as Milly takes a step towards the other girls, shielding Betsy, who looks like she'd rather be anywhere else.

'Five more minutes!' Milly shouts. 'We're playing a game, and we haven't finished yet.'

Across the playground the huddle has paused their conversation; they're watching too.

'I'll leave you to it,' Dawn says, giving a soft tug on Eddie's lead.

'You've been on there for ages!' Eloise's cry rings out. To Jude's ears she's got the same haughty tone as Audrey.

'Yeah,' chimes Gini. 'Give someone else a go.'

'Five minutes,' Milly repeats. 'Then it's your turn.'

She's so confident, so brave, that Jude can't help but feel impressed.

'If you don't let us play,' Eloise says. 'Then you can't come to my party.' She glances back towards her mother. 'Can she, Mum?'

Audrey, sipping her coffee, raises her eyebrows. Her eyes meet Jude's for a split second then she looks, hastily, away. 'Come on, Eloise, play nicely. She said you could have your turn. Just give them a little bit—'

'No!' Now firmly in the spotlight, Eloise is in too deep. If she backs down now, she'll lose face in front of her friends. 'She's not coming. Nor are you, Betsy. Enjoy your stupid little game.'

'Oh shit,' Jude mutters as her daughter folds further into herself, her face crumpled with disappointment. 'She was really looking forward to that.'

'Doesn't matter!' Milly shouts after the group of three as they stalk off, arm in arm, towards the slide. 'I wasn't going to come anyway. Betsy's coming over for a sleepover. Aren't you, Bets?'

Jude's daughter looks over at her hopefully and she, in turn, looks at Will.

'Course she can,' he says softly. 'And you're very welcome to stay for a drink yourself.'

And there it is again, the same look he gave her in the kitchen: the one that says he likes her, that they're in a bubble, the only two people in the world.

Her mouth dries as she considers his proposal. In the back of her brain Emma is screaming at her not to be an idiot. But Jude's not being stupid, and she trusts her instincts. Will isn't a murderer. He's a loner, an outcast, and he's bloody lonely, just like her.

She glances across at her daughter, pink-cheeked from the cold, lightly bouncing on her toes, still waiting for an answer. 'What would the school mums think?'

'Fuck the school mums.' The gravel in Will's voice makes her skin tingle.

'They'll talk.'

A smile pricks at the edge of his mouth as he runs a hand over his close-cropped hair. 'So, let's make it worth their while.'

Chapter 13

Victoria

FRIDAY

Victoria strides towards the home of the only person who didn't reply to her drinks party invitation – Theresa Fairchild – her anxiety increasing with each step. Theresa is a core member of Victoria's friendship group, but it's been at least a week since she's seen her at the school gates and her text – *Everything okay with you and the family? Haven't seen you on the school run for a while* – was read, but unanswered.

As she walks, her thoughts switch to Will and Jude. They're almost definitely having an affair. She could tell by their body language, even from across the play park – all smiles and little touches. Neither of them said hello, or even acknowledged her. Not that she would have expected that from Will, but Jude's attitude stunk. She'd invited the woman to her house, fed and watered her, and told her something that could potentially save her life. And what thanks had she got? Not a word! Jude had insulted her, then slunk off into the night, making an excuse about the babysitter. Well screw her and Will bloody Ledger. Jude won't be gazing at him adoringly when she's lying at the bottom of his stairs.

Seeing the two of them in the park has only added to the bad mood that's been brewing since the school run. It's the start of the weekend, which means it's Andy's turn to have the kids and she feels lost without them already. Technically she didn't actually need to turn up at the school for 3.15 p.m. but she couldn't bear the thought of Sophia and Noah standing with their teachers, the last children to leave. She knows – God knows she knows – that detectives rarely leave work on time, and that there could be a hundred reasons why Andy could be late, but she doesn't trust him to inform her. He didn't do that when they were married and he's even less likely to do that now they're on the verge of divorce. So she turned up at the school prepared to take her children home if her ex-husband was even ten minutes late.

Only Andy hadn't turned up late had he? He'd waltzed through the gates at exactly 3.15 p.m. with a shit-eating grin and a box of KFC under his arm (she rarely lets the kids have fast food but, with Andy, it's every bloody weekend). While Sophia eyed him coyly with a small smile on her face (too cool for public expressions of love now she's in Year 5), Noah couldn't have looked happier. He threw himself into his father's arms then pulled the teddy he's become surgically attached to out of his rucksack and shouted something that Victoria couldn't hear. There's a part of her – the bigger, more wholesome part of her – that's happy the children have a good relationship with their father, but there's a smaller uglier part that wishes the kids looked as delighted to see her every day; that they associated her with treats and surprises, not homework, bedtimes and being forced to finish their veg. She knows they love her – the fact they gripe and moan at her after school means they view her as their 'safe space' – but she finds it hard being their emotional punchbag, day after day.

She pauses at the edge of Anderson Avenue and takes a long, deep, cleansing breath. It's not the children's fault. It's not even Will and Jude she's pissed off with, not really. It's everything. Finances, responsibility, the house, her friends, her ex-husband. She needs a holiday from her own life.

Re-centred (or as much as she can be without a boxing bag or glass of wine), she continues to walk towards Theresa's house then stops short. There's a 'For Sale' sign outside. What the fuck? She speeds up the path and knocks twice on the front door. Theresa never said anything about moving.

She takes a step back from the doorstep and surveys the windows. The blinds are down in the living room and the curtains are closed upstairs. She knows Anthony works from home, but there aren't any lights on beyond any of the curtains, and no cars in the drive. They couldn't already have moved out, surely? Not when it's 'For Sale' and not 'Sold'.

'Are you looking for Theresa and Tony?' An elderly, well-dressed woman appears in the doorway of the house next door holding a fluffy white Bichon Frise in her arms.

'That's a lovely dog.' Victoria flashes the woman a smile. *Smile and compliment, smile and compliment* – advice her mother drummed into her from almost the moment she could speak.

'Thank you,' the woman returns a warm smile. 'This is Albert.'

'I'm a friend of Theresa's,' Victoria says. 'We have children at St Helena's, but I haven't seen her around for a while.'

'That'll be because they've moved, my dear.'

'Moved?' She stares at the woman in shock.

'Yes, they moved out last week. To Devon. I believe they're living in a rental property, or with family while they wait for the house to sell. They were keen to get the children settled in new schools.'

'What . . . why . . .' She can't make sense of it. Why the sudden desire to move to Devon? Theresa had told her she wasn't particularly close to her parents. Unless . . . 'Is she caring for relatives? Is one of them ill?'

The neighbour purses her lips and shakes her head lightly. 'No, no. Theresa said they were moving because Lowbridge had become toxic and they didn't want to be here anymore. Toxic! This lovely place. Can you believe it?'

Victoria continues to stare at her. What on earth could have happened for Theresa to call Lowbridge toxic? She got on with everyone. She was a keen member of the PTA, always up for a laugh and a drink and a gossip. She's one of the funniest women she knows.

'Did she say why?' she asks.

'What were her exact words?' The neighbour looks away, as though searching her memory. 'Oh yes! "The other school mums are a nest of vipers. There isn't a single one that I trust."' The neighbour nods to herself, satisfied with her recollection, then pets Albert on the head. 'Oh dear' – she glances back up at Victoria – 'perhaps I shouldn't have shared that with you, what with you being a school mum too. I suppose there's a reason she didn't give you her forwarding address.' A knowing smile plays on her lips as she steps back into her house and closes the door.

Chapter 14

Andy

FRIDAY

Andy climbs the stairs to his bedroom, Noah's backpack in his hand, the smell of KFC drifting up from the living room where the kids are watching some YouTuber who's screaming at the top of his voice. Leaving his bedroom door ajar to listen out for the children, he sits at his desk and pulls Noah's backpack onto his lap. He opens it, pulls out the teddy and slides a hand under the back of its T-shirt. He moves his fingers over its soft fur until he finds a small Velcro opening in the seam then he slips the voice recorder out from the toy. He presses the button on the side, hears his ex-wife moaning about something or other and grins, satisfied. Voice-activated, up to seven metres away, the device can record up to fifteen hours' worth of crystal-clear audio. Audio, he hopes, that will help him regain control of his life and ensure that he gets fifty/fifty custody of his children, and nothing less. He wouldn't put it past Victoria to try and convince the divorce court that she should be the primary caregiver and there's no way he's going to let that happen.

His plan was to wait until the kids were in bed before he listened to the recordings but waiting that long would be torturous. He had a shit day at work – meetings that dragged on unnecessarily, mountains of paperwork and the CPS giving the thumbs down to a case he's been working on for days. The thought of getting one over on Victoria was the only thing that got him through.

He plugs one end of a lead into the voice recorder, and the other into the laptop. As the files transfer across, he sits back in his seat, stretches out his arms and stares in disgust at the damp stain on the ceiling.

The flat he's living in is as poky as shit, the roof leaks whenever there's a downpour (something his landlord is taking his sweet time about fixing), and the children have to share a room. That would have been fine a couple of years ago, but Sophia is on the verge of puberty and she finds Noah increasingly irritating. She's started making noises about not wanting to stay at his flat because she can't stand sharing a room with her brother. The sooner he gets the house, or a share of the sale, the better. Then he'll be able to give Sophia the room of her dreams. One she actually wants, not the kind of room her mother thinks will impress other people.

File transfer done, he puts the listening device back in the teddy – there's still loads of space left on the SIM and he can't be arsed to wipe it. He reseals the Velcro, then puts on his headphones and presses play. He listens to a couple of minutes of the kids complaining to their mother about their days at school, the fact they're hungry, that there's nothing they want in the fridge, then fast-forwards as the inane ramblings of a YouTube presenter fills his ears. He hits play again after an hour, still YouTube. Two hours, more YouTube. Three hours and it's still playing. Does Victoria never actually talk to the kids? Yeah, sure, the kids are watching TV in his flat too, but that's just temporary. Normally it's board games, cinema trips and days out when they're with him. Unlike his ex-wife, he enjoys spending time with them. They make him smile, they entertain and distract him. His job is grim and relentless, and Sophia and Noah are beacons of light.

Irritated, he fast-forwards to bedtime and hears Noah sigh and say, 'Mummy's friends are here, Teddy. I can hear them outside. Come and meet them so you can charge up with magic.' Andy's heart twists in his chest. His son really is the loveliest, kindest, most pure little boy. What he did to deserve him, he has no idea.

He listens as Noah makes his way downstairs, the soft snuffle of his breathing and the smallest of creaks on the stairs. The sound changes as he makes his way through the kitchen – echoey, colder – then again as he makes his way into the garden. The sound of women laughing and chatting grows louder and louder until snippets of their conversation become clear.

'Has anyone heard from Theresa recently?' That's Victoria.

'No, not for ages.' Dawn's deeper, more throaty tone. He's never understood the friendship between Victoria and Dawn Wood. Dawn – whose hen-pecked husband Simon is as charismatic as a lettuce and daughter Eva has a perennially runny nose – has the vibes of someone who spent the early Nineties sitting in a field in an oversized jumper with a spliff in one hand. She was fairly dumpy when the kids started Reception but she's lost a lot of weight since and, unlike some of the snobbier women, she'll talk to anyone at the school gates, even him.

'Isn't she coming tonight?' Audrey's a cold fish. Hot as fuck, but she knows it. Husband's an aged neurosurgeon, biggest house in Lowbridge and she doesn't have to work, but she does something to do with the arts or charity every now and then, the philanthropist that she is.

'I did ask her.' Victoria again.

'Do you think she might be pregnant?' That's Caz, oldest of the group. Looks like butter wouldn't melt but is probably into ball gags, whips and all that S&M crap. 'Maybe she's avoiding us because she doesn't want us to guess. There's only so many times you can claim you're on antibiotics when you're offered a drink.'

'Doubt it. Didn't she just get a promotion?' He hates the way Sara looks up to Victoria, like she's something to aim for with her trim figure, high-achieving children and clutter-free house. Actually, he can't understand why any of them are friends with her, unless it's her gossip prowess. She's charming, he'll give her that. It was what attracted him to her in the first place, that and her incredible body, her sense of humour and the fact she respected what he did for a living and found him hilarious, hot and fascinating. But familiarity, like rust, can tarnish even the most sparkling of relationships.

'Oh my God, Noah!' Victoria's tone changes from conspiratorial to annoyed. 'When did you get out of bed? Mummy's spending some time with her friends.'

'I finished my book.'

'Did you? Well done, sweetie!' A pause then: 'He's on free reads already, and he's only six.'

There's a chorus of oohs, ahhs and well dones from the other mums, then Victoria says, 'Come on now, Noah. Let's get you back to bed.'

Andy hears the sound of a chair scraping on the patio

tiles then the group falls silent, presumably as Victoria leads Noah back into the house.

'Oh!' one of the women says. 'He's left his teddy behind.'

It's Sorrell Edwards. Bit of a hippy, surfer type from Cornwall, married to a dentist. She's attractive but she's not Andy's type with her plaits, make-up-free face and loose, floaty dresses. She always looks a bit startled, like a horse about to rear.

No one replies to Sorrell's cry and the conversation quickly turns to some shit to do with the school and the teachers. Eventually Victoria returns and suddenly someone called Jude is being cross-examined. From her carefully phrased answers to Victoria's questions he can tell that she's not his soon-to-be ex-wife's biggest fan. She's trying to mask that dislike with humour and largely getting away with it, if Victoria's reaction is anything to go by.

He sits forward in his seat when his ex-wife says, 'Are you and Will Ledger having an affair?'

Jude says something flippant in response but, suddenly feeling warm, Andy undoes the top button of his shirt. Will Ledger's dating again? That's an interesting development. He either believes the heat's off him, or he's so cocky he doesn't care what kind of reaction he gets. Andy takes a small notebook from his shirt pocket and clicks his pen against the desk.

Jude? he writes. *Possible relationship with Will Ledger. Find out her surname and who she is.*

Note written, he continues to listen as Victoria, relishing the spotlight, tells Jude about the death of Ali Ledger and the disappearance of Robyn Lewis. He grits his teeth as his own name is mentioned but it's only in passing and, for once, no one passes judgement on the police or his team. He continues to listen, laughing when Jude calls out Victoria.

Shame she decided to leave, he was enjoying someone giving his ex-wife as good as he got.

When conversation turns to Sorrell and her depressed husband, he removes one of his earphones and listens out for the kids. Downstairs YouTube is still playing and no one's screaming. Makes a nice change for the kids to get on. He replaces the headphones and listens to the rest of Sorrell's dull conversation at double speed.

He stiffens as his name's mentioned again. Victoria's pissed off with him giving her the finger, as he knew she would be and—

'Daddy? DADDY! Sophia took my drink and said it was hers!'

He swivels in his chair to discover his son – his mouth and cheeks coated with KFC gravy – standing in the doorway. He slips one of the headphones off his ears but the audio's still playing. Audrey's asking Victoria if she's ever slept with any of her clients.

He looks at Noah with his soft round face, unruly red curls and delicate features and his heart fills with pride.

'Well . . .' Victoria says into his ear as his son crosses the room, reaching for the teddy bear at his feet. Andy touches a hand to Noah's hair, feels its softness under his fingertips. He'd do anything to protect him. He'd give up his life for his children. 'Well . . .' his ex-wife's voice is a scratched record in his brain '. . . let's just say that there aren't any redheads in Andy's family and the reason Noah is ginger isn't because I'm blonde.'

He was breathing, but now he's not. He was listening; now there's white noise. He was thinking; now there's emptiness. The clock on the wall doesn't stop, but the second hand lurches as his hand slips from his son's silken hair.

Chapter 15

Sorrell

FRIDAY

Sorrell's grip tightens on the steering wheel. She's got an hour and a half to search for the animal Finnley's convinced himself that he hit, then get back to school, pick up the twins from after-school club and ferry all three kids home. Scout, in the car seat in the back, gurgles softly to himself as the next nursery rhyme on the playlist – 'Three Blind Mice' – tinkles out of the speakers. The words swim in and out of her brain – *to cut off their tails with a carving knife* – and she tries to block them out.

Harper and Henry don't normally go to after-school club but with a packed day – teaching back-to-back pottery classes then unstacking the kiln – this is the first opportunity she's had to go for a drive. As far as Finnley, at home in front of the TV, is concerned, she's in the park with the other school mums, letting the kids burn off their post-school tension, before she brings them home for tea.

Normally, when the students crowd into her studio for a class, she plays a Spotify playlist of upbeat funk and soul. Today, she kept local radio on, so she could keep an ear out for the news. Not that she heard much of it – there was always a student with a question, or a pot on the verge of collapse, or someone about to apply brown slip to white clay. At lunchtime, when she finally had half an hour to herself, she pored over local and national websites, searching for reported hit-and-runs, combing the news. She didn't find anything, not locally anyway. One woman had sustained life-changing injuries after a hit-and-run on the same night as Finnley's accident, and she was in a coma. Sorrell's heart had skipped a beat, but she read on and discovered that the woman was found an hour and a half away, much further out than Finsbury Lane.

When she'd left the house to collect Scout, Finnley had seemed more emotionally stable than he had been the previous night. He'd even apologised for calling her about the hit-and-run. He'd over-reacted, he said. He was embarrassed and he was going to visit his GP to see if she could up the dose of his meds. His calm demeanour had rippled when she'd asked when he was going to take the car to the garage and he'd snapped at her, telling her not to nag him, that he had it all in hand.

There was no point talking to him about the dent in the bonnet – she'd only have to explain how she'd discovered that it had almost exactly fitted her hip – and she was pretty sure she was over-reacting anyway. He wasn't the only one who was stressed out of their mind.

Now, driving out to the Bat and Badger with Scout in the back, she feels faintly ridiculous, but when she's not worrying about the size of the dent in the bonnet she's stressing about the thought of an animal, dying and in pain at the side of the road. The sooner she discovers the body of the unfortunate animal the sooner she'll be able to put it all behind her. It's not like she hasn't got enough to worry about as it is.

Finally reaching the pub she turns a circle in the car park and heads back along the route Finnley would have taken to get home. He'd pulled up on Finsbury Lane but she's not entirely sure if that's where he hit the animal. It's possible he hit it nearer to the pub, while his panic attack was cresting, and had continued to drive for a while longer before he pulled over and called her.

Keeping one eye on her rear-view mirror to make sure no one's behind her, she slows her speed enough that she can scan the hedgerows and verge to her left. Finnley had told her last night that there was a ditch full of brambles so he wasn't able to see what he'd hit, but there's no ditch or brambles here.

She touches her foot to the accelerator and, keeping one eye on the verge, continues on down the road. She notices a dark crumpled shape as she takes a left onto a B road but, when she slows as she approaches it, she discovers that it's nothing more than a waterlogged black plastic bag. 'Jack and Jill' starts playing on the stereo. She glances back at Scout to see how he's doing but his head's lolled, resting against the side of the car seat. He's fast asleep.

Jack fell down and broke his crown and Jill came tumbling after.

'What is it about nursery rhymes?' she says more to herself than her son. 'That they're all so dark? If animals aren't being murdered, children are hurting themselves and dying of the plague or babies are being dropped.'

She resolves to buy a new CD for Scout – something more cheery – then spots a bramble-filled ditch out of the corner of her eye. There's a lay-by too, about fifty feet further down the road. She pulls into it and turns off the engine. She glances back at her sleeping son and deliberates. Should she leave him where he is or take him out of the car seat and carry him back to the brambles? They're in the middle of nowhere and the roads are quiet.

Moving quickly and quietly so as not to wake him, she slips out of the car, leaving the driver side door open so she can hear him if he cries, and hurries back the way she just came, moving from one side of the road to the other, looking for anything that shouldn't be there. But there's nothing – no skid marks, no crumpled foliage, and no body. Whatever Finnley hit either dragged itself somewhere else to die, or it was disposed of by another animal. She takes a long, deep breath of cool, country air and moves her head towards one shoulder, then the other, stretching out the tension in her neck. She's come all this way for nothing – the best kind of nothing – and she might actually sleep tonight.

There's a lightness to her step as she makes her way back to the car. She glances towards the back seat as she opens the driver's side door – Scout's still fast asleep – then slips inside and reaches for her phone, lying on the passenger side seat. There's a message alert – a text has arrived. She opens it idly, expecting it to be from her dentist or hairdresser – everyone she knows uses WhatsApp to contact her – but there's no name attached, just a phone number.

Probably a scammer, she thinks as she opens it. But what she reads is no missed Evri parcel, inheritance claim or urgent request from 'her bank'.

IT'S ALWAYS THE HUSBAND

I know for a fact that your husband was involved in a hit-and-run. He's probably told you that it was an animal. It wasn't. Pay me £20,000 or I'll contact the police.

Chapter 16

Jude

FRIDAY

The flirtation in Will's voice earlier has all but vanished now he's dishing up oven chips, fish fingers and beans for the girls, but his eyes keep returning to Jude, signalling that the promise of their conversation in the park still stands. It's been half an hour since she walked into the house but she can almost feel the weight of Will's hand on her shoulder – solid, lingering – after he'd helped her out of her coat.

She watches him as he moves around the pristine kitchen – stacking the dishwasher, wiping the work surfaces, getting drinks for the girls. Everything he does is utterly pedestrian. Even his fridge contains a mixture of healthy food and processed crap. Nothing about him says, 'I've killed two women', but what does a man like that look like? They can certainly be attractive – Ted Bundy proved that. And no one was neater and tidier than Dexter. *Although he was fictional, Jude notes, and Will isn't a serial killer until he's killed three people.*

Not that he's killed anyone, she reminds herself as she pushes out Emma's voice, screaming that she'll be his third victim. She takes a sip of tea and tries to tune in to Betsy and Milly's dinner table conversation about how it's not fair that the boys always get to use the school court for football when they want to play netball at break time. But listening to the girls does little to distract her. She's still watching Will out of the corner of her eye. He rarely stands still, but when he does, a lost expression floods his eyes for a split second, then it's gone and he's off again, finding something new to busy himself with. He's the same in the play park, or at the school gates; he's incapable of being still. If he isn't shifting his weight from foot to foot, he's wringing his hands or fiddling with the zip on his coat.

She can imagine him in his art history lectures, striding back and forth across the theatre, getting passionate about culture and philosophy, styles and techniques. The male students probably admire his presence and his knowledge, while the female students are entranced by his broad shoulders, gravelly voice and piercing blue—

'Holy crap!' She jolts, spilling tea onto her lap, as Will touches her shoulder. She was so lost in thought she hadn't noticed him cross the kitchen.

'Mum!' Betsy says, her eyes wide with horror as she exchanges a look with Milly. 'You're so embarrassing!'

Not as embarrassed as you'd be if you knew what I was thinking, replies the voice in Jude's head.

'Sorry.' She glances up at Will who's looking at her with a mixture of amusement and concern. 'I was miles away. I'm not normally so jumpy. I . . .' She tails off as he hands her a tea towel. Heat rises from her throat to her cheeks as she presses the tea towel against the tea stains on her jeans.

He thinks I'm jumpy because I'm worried he might kill me next.

'I just wanted to know if you fancied something to eat.' He opens the fridge as though to demonstrate *here be food*. 'I haven't got that much in, but I could make you an omelette or cheese on toast.' He rummages around. 'There's some lasagne left over from last night or a slice of cheesecake if you fancy something sw—'

'That's Robyn's.' Milly's chair scrapes on the kitchen tiles as she jumps to her feet.

The room falls silent, and Jude tenses. Even Will, with his back to her, stops foraging in the fridge. The silence stretches and, desperate to break it, Jude says, 'I'm not actually that hungry, Will.'

'No? That's cool.' He extricates himself from the fridge and closes the door. 'Let me know if you change your mind.'

He flashes her a smile but there's a wariness in his eyes that wasn't there before. Feeling the weight of someone else's gaze, Jude turns to look at Milly, who's sat back down but is staring intently at her from the other side of the table.

'You've got the same wonky teeth as Robyn,' the girl says, as their eyes meet.

'Milly!' There's a warning shot in Will's voice. 'Don't be rude. Jude's our guest.'

'I'm not being rude!' Milly's voice quavers. 'It's true. She's got the same . . .' she touches her own teeth with a finger '. . . tooth crossover. Here! Robyn got a brace to make them straight. Didn't she, Dad?'

He nods silently.

'Robyn was perfect.' The glare Milly casts in Jude's

direction is loaded. *Don't even think about going anywhere near my dad.*

Will clears his throat. 'Why don't you and Betsy go and play upstairs, if you've both finished your dinner?'

Betsy immediately pushes her chair away from the table and bounces to her feet. After a pause Milly does the same then the two girls rush out of the kitchen, chasing each other down the hallway, their socked feet lightly pounding the wooden boards. As they disappear upstairs, Will removes the plates and crockery from the table and carries them to the dishwasher.

Jude shifts in her seat and, for the second time that day, she's unsure what to say.

'Sorry about that,' Will says as he places the plates in the dishwasher's racks.

'It's fine, honestly. I know what kids are like. If they think of something it comes straight out of their mouths. I can relate.'

It's supposed to be a joke, but Will doesn't laugh. Instead, he closes the dishwasher and remains bent over it, his hands gripping the countertop.

'She misses her,' he says softly. 'It's been eighteen months but she's still unsettled. Talking about Robyn helps her cope.'

'I get it,' Jude says, as he adds, 'Is it too early for wine?'

'Never.'

She doesn't normally drink this early in the day but she can sense the request is more for Will than for her.

'Red okay?'

'Yeah, lovely, thanks.'

He takes a bottle from the rack on top of one of the cupboards, then a corkscrew from a drawer. 'The truth is,' he says as he uncorks the bottle, 'neither of us particularly like cheesecake but Milly insists that I buy it so there's something nice for Robyn to eat, when she comes back.'

The sorrow that sweeps through Jude is so sudden, so powerful, that it brings tears to her eyes. Heartbreaking is too small a word for a young girl who lost not one mum but two. And Jude knows all about keepsakes and symbols. The day after her dad's death the sight of his muddy wellies in the porch tore something within her. The boots are in her shed now, carefully stuffed with newspaper and protected from the damp and the cold by a waterproof bag, but she can't bring herself to look at them. Just thinking about them is physically painful. The wound's still there.

'Thanks.' She takes the glass that Will hands her and takes a long sip. The wine catches at the back of her throat – oaky and earthy – then travels down to her chest, warming her, taking the chill from the memory.

'Sorry.' Will sits down and places his glass on the table. 'That was all a bit heavy.'

Jude gives him a long look. 'I think it's important to talk about, not just for Milly.'

'Yeah.' His gaze drifts to the table and rests there, his wine untouched.

'If it isn't too delicate a question . . . what makes you assume Robyn's dead?'

His sigh is so long and anguished it's obvious that this isn't something he talks about often, if at all.

'Her silence.' He looks up at her. 'It's been eighteen months and, regardless of how she felt about me when she left, she never stopped loving Milly. There's no way she'd just drop out of her life. I can only assume that there was a terrible accident, or she drank too much or something happened to her, health wise, when she was alone and miles from home. Or maybe she took herself off somewhere remote to . . .' He swallows, leaving the sentence unfinished but the inference is clear.

'You weren't happy?' Jude asks. *Regardless of how she felt about me.* There's a weight to that phrase that she can't ignore.

'We were, especially for the first six months or so after she moved to Lowbridge. It shouldn't have worked because we were so different but she was clever, inquisitive, one of life's optimists. The opposite of me. I'd been in such a low place for so long and suddenly there was life in the house again, real joy . . .' He passes a hand through his hair. 'Things were good, until they weren't.'

'What happened? The night she disappeared?'

Will sits back in his chair and blows out his cheeks. His gaze drifts to the left, as though he's dredging up the memory. 'We argued about the fact that she was going out and wouldn't tell me where. I'm not a possessive man . . .' He shakes his head lightly. 'Not jealous, never have been . . .' his gaze swings back towards Jude, as though seeking her validation '. . . but she was literally never home. Maybe a Sunday night, maybe the odd night during the week, but the rest of the time . . .' he shrugs '. . . she was either out with the school mums, or going to the cinema with someone, or going to some fitness bootcamp, or roller-skating derby. She even joined the choir. Couldn't sing a note though.' He laughs drily. 'Hobbies are great. Time to follow your own passions or see your own friends is important in a relationship, but it had started to feel like she was doing all these things to avoid spending time with me.' His expression darkens. 'I felt like she'd agree to do anything, or go anywhere, just to get out of the house.'

'Did you talk to her? Ask why?' She pauses, wondering if this is where he mentions the flirtation Dawn told her about.

'Of course! Multiple times.' There's anguish in his eyes

now. 'But she kept claiming there wasn't an issue. She said she was happy, but I wasn't. Milly wasn't either because Robyn was so rarely home. I hadn't meant to fall in love again so soon after Ali's death, and I definitely hadn't planned to introduce my daughter to someone so soon. I'd only joined a dating site because the house felt so quiet in the evenings, after Milly had gone to bed. I just wanted someone to talk to. Most of the conversations I had were surface level and I was going to cancel my membership but then Robyn messaged me and she was different, right from the start. She was witty and clever and flirtatious. She kept me on my toes, intellectually and emotionally. It was exactly the kind of distraction I needed from my grief. Because that's what I thought it was at first, a bit of fun, but then I found myself refreshing my emails hourly, in the hope she'd replied. It was addictive, that hit of excitement.' He pauses, his eyes roaming Jude's face uncertainly. 'Am I saying too much?'

'No, not at all,' Jude's response sounds light and airy but there's a tightness to her chest that wasn't there five minutes earlier. Envy – at the intensity of Will's feelings for Robyn – is making her feel lesser, which is bloody ridiculous considering she once felt as intensely about her ex as Will did about Robyn, and she's not even in a relationship with the man. 'You said Milly wasn't happy,' she says, awkwardly shifting the conversation back to safer territory, 'when Robyn started going out so much . . .'

'Yeah. Milly really missed her, all those nights she went out, because it was so out of character for Robyn. Those two were as thick as thieves within a few months of them meeting. I mean, obviously Milly was reserved at first, and Robyn was uncertain how to be around her, but then they discovered that they both loved crafting and fashion and dance, and suddenly they were doing TikTok dance routines in the kitchen or covering the living room in glitter and I'd hear their laughter from wherever they were in the house. Robyn wasn't naturally maternal but she put a lot of effort into making Milly feel comfortable in those first few months before she moved in, and for a good six months afterwards. I don't know if the grind of the day-to-day routine got to her, or if she felt she'd lost something of herself by mothering someone else's child but . . .' His chin drops and he shrugs. 'That's why I was so supportive of her doing her own thing, at first anyway. It felt like she'd lost some of her sparkle and I felt responsible.'

Jude looks at the slumped shape of his body and his eyes, dulled by failure, and can't help but wonder how many relationships would be saved if people just talked instead of second-guessing each other all the time.

'So, the argument . . .' she says, '. . . the night she disappeared. You were pissed off because she wouldn't tell you where she was going?'

'That . . .' Will takes a long slug of his wine then nurses the glass, rolling it back and forth against his lips '. . . and the fact it was my birthday.'

'And she wanted to go out? Without you?'

'Pretty much.'

'That's rough.'

'She stormed out while we were arguing, and I didn't go after her. I sat there – here actually – and realised I had to end things when she got back. I still loved her, but it wasn't working. The only reason I'd let it drag on for so long was because of Milly. She'd already lost her mum and if she lost Robyn too then . . .' He tails off and rubs a hand over his face. 'Sorry, this is . . . I don't want to say too much and push you away.'

His words ignite sparks in Jude's belly, but she pushes

them down and reaches across the table, laying her hand over his. 'You've got nothing to be sorry about. I appreciate you being so honest.' *That's if he is actually telling you the truth,* whispers the voice in her head. 'If it's not too painful, can I ask how your first wife die—'

'Can we play a board game?' Milly bursts into the kitchen with Betsy in tow. 'I don't want to play Switch anymore and we never get to play Monopoly because it's just the two of us. Please, Dad, please can we? The three of us.' Her gaze shifts towards Jude, only for a second but long enough for her to clock the wariness and fear in the young girl's eyes.

Will glances at Jude who minutely nods her head. There'll be time for more questions later, once the girls are both tucked up in bed. 'We'll all play,' he says. 'All four of us.' The emphasis on *four.*

Jude braces herself as Milly processes the suggestion, her brow furrowed, eyes narrowed, gaze fixed on her father's face. She's trying to read him, predict how he'll react to her answer.

'Okay . . .' she says slowly, hesitantly. 'But I'm the banker. Can I be? Please?'

When Will nods, she speeds away again then stops halfway down the hallway and turns back. 'Can we have popcorn too? Just as a treat? Because Betsy's here.'

'Sure!' Will smiles at Jude, his face relaxed and open now the weight of their previous conversation has lifted. 'As long as we can have some too.'

He said *'we'* again. She meets his gaze. It's a throwaway word but there's an intimacy to it that reignites the sparks in her belly. She's getting in too deep, but she's not sure she wants to get out.

It's 11 p.m. and the girls are finally asleep. It's later than either of them go to bed normally but, for now, Jude's calling it a victory. Between the Monopoly arguments, the popcorn fight, and the stomping up and down the stairs, she hasn't had time to reintroduce the conversation about Will's first wife, but she's too mentally exhausted to bring it up now.

'I'm shattered.' She slumps back against the sofa, a glass of wine in her hand. 'I don't know how people have more than one child.'

'Tranquillisers probably.' Will sits down too, his shoulder brushing, then resting against hers. 'For the kids, not the parents.'

She takes a large sip of her wine then, feigning seriousness, says, 'Darts or in their food?'

'Darts definitely – moving targets, more fun.'

She laughs. His sense of humour is even darker than hers, and she loves how he just comes out with this stuff, like he doesn't give a crap.

'You all right there?' he says as inhaled wine makes her cough.

Unable to talk she touches her back, signalling to him to hit her between the shoulder blades.

'You want me to take your bra off?' His delivery is so deadpan that a strangled laugh escapes in the gap between coughs.

'Sorry, sorry.' He slaps her on the back with the flat of his palm until she stops coughing.

She slumps back on the sofa and flashes him a 'thank you' smile. He returns the grin but says nothing. And there it is again, the sexual tension, like a mist or a smoke, winding itself around them, lifting the hairs on the back of her neck. She lets her knees rest against Will's and he puts a heavy hand on her thigh.

'Would this be a mistake?' His voice is deep and gravelly.

She holds his gaze, as though the truth might lie somewhere beyond the amber of his irises and the dark pits of his pupils, but all she can see is desire.

'You'd better not slope off afterwards.'

'I can't. I live here.'

'You're trapped.'

'Or maybe you are.'

He reaches for her, his hand cupping the back of her head as he pulls her in for a kiss.

Saturday morning. Jude rolls over, the duvet soft against her naked shoulder, the pillow plump beneath her cheek. As sleep ebbs away, confusion takes its place, then clarity. She's sleeping in Will Ledger's bed! Her eyes fly open, and she spots Will, dressed only in boxers, quietly opening and closing the drawers of the bureau on the other side of the bed. Sensing her watching, he turns and smiles widely then presses a finger to his mouth.

The bed sags under his weight as he sits down beside her.

'The girls will be awake soon,' he whispers as he leans towards her. Before she can respond he touches his mouth to hers and she loses herself in the soft brush of his lips. Last night couldn't have been more different to the first time they slept together. They had sex multiple times, collapsing against each other, satiated and exhausted, before a single touch started it all over again. But what was different, what hadn't happened the first time, was the tenderness that interspersed the moments when they lost themselves, a caress, a slowing of their breathing and eye contact that locked them together more tightly than their limbs.

'You're kicking me out,' she says now as he eases himself away from her and the kiss ends.

'Yeah, sorry.' There's amusement in his eyes.

IT'S ALWAYS THE HUSBAND

She fakes objection but her heart's not in it. He's right, of course; she has to leave before either of the girls discovers her lying, naked, in Will's bed. Explaining *that* is something neither of them want to face right now.

'I'm going to have a shower.' He kisses her again.

'I'll be gone by the time you get out.'

'Like sweat,' he says, and she laughs.

'Romantic to the core.'

He gives her one last, lingering kiss then gets up from the bed. He pauses when he reaches the bedroom door and, for a second, she thinks he's about to turn back and say something, but the moment passes and he leaves the room, closing the door behind him.

Gripped by a sense of urgency, Jude sits up and throws back the duvet. She swears softly as the fabric moves across the bedroom table and sweeps her phone, watch and earrings to the floor. She gets out of bed and picks up the phone, her watch and one of the tiny diamond earrings that were a present from her parents for her eighteenth birthday. Over the years she's lost loads of jewellery, but never the earrings. They were the last present she received from both her mum *and* her dad.

Please, girls, don't walk in now. Fear sings a new song as, still naked, she drops to her hands and knees, and peers under the bed. Like the rest of Will's house, the space is clean and clutter-free, apart from one thing. Sitting beside her lost earring is a grey leather box labelled 'Robyn's stuff'. She plucks at her earring and puts it on her phone with its twin and her watch. Heart racing, she glances across at the closed bedroom door, then back at the box. She shouldn't, she really shouldn't. Will's been honest with her about Robyn. He opened his heart to her last night. He had sex with her; he looked at her lovingly for God's sake but what if . . .

she hates herself even as she thinks it . . . what if she's wrong about him and Emma's right?

She sinks back onto her hands and knees and then, almost as though her hand has a mind of its own, she reaches for the box and pulls it out from beneath the bed.

She lifts the lid carefully, as though it could contain a hand grenade or a bomb, then swiftly shoves the whole thing back under the bed as a floorboard creaks beyond the closed bedroom door. She grabs her jumper from the floor and pulls it over her head then waits, heart pounding, for one of the girls, or Will, to walk in. Nothing happens. No one comes in. Will's in the shower. It's an old house and she can hear the pipes clanking as the hot water comes on.

'Screw it!' She pulls the box out again and removes the lid, hastily this time. Inside are packets of printed photographs, curled with age, some postcards and a small plastic container that she's pretty sure contains, or once contained, a brace. There's also some jewellery – necklaces, some cheap, some that look like gold – a couple of books, some little essential oil bottles and a burner. She sorts through it, carefully moving things out of the way to get a look at the rest, listening out for footsteps, her gaze continually returning to the closed bedroom door.

'A diary!' In the quiet of the bedroom her excited whisper sounds like a roar.

Why would Robyn leave something so personal behind? Will must be right – she left after an argument then something happened, and she never returned. Unless . . . unless she never left the house at all.

Jude lifts the book out of the box reverentially, feeling its weight in her hands. There's a year and the word 'diary' on the cover, but she doesn't pause to look at the spine or the back. She flips it open and speed-reads the first few pages, missing a word here, a phrase there. What she's looking for is a mention of Will, that Robyn's scared, that she needs to leave him, but it's all about the other school mums and—

She slams the book shut, sensing someone watching her, but when she turns sharply, the bedroom door's still shut and there's no one there. She's never believed in ghosts but she can't shake the feeling that there's someone else in the room, watching, judging, willing her to leave. Unsettled, she returns the diary to the box, replaces the lid and squirrels it back under the bed. Then she pulls on the rest of her clothes, shoves her earrings, watch and phone in her pocket and hurries out of the bedroom and down the stairs She's pretty sure it was her own guilty conscience, urging her to stop reading Robyn's diary, but right now all she wants to do is get home, drink a coffee, and shower.

Chapter 17

ROBYN'S DIARY

Things are still no better with the other women on the school run. On the surface they're friendly enough. They smile when they see me. They wave, they stop for a chat, but it's all surface-level stuff. If I just randomly disappeared they wouldn't even notice. And if they did, it would become something else to gossip about, not because they actually cared.

It's so painful, watching them all head off together in twos and threes after we've waved off our kids. I force a smile when they say, 'See you later!' and wander off to each other's houses, or a coffee shop, but each time it happens something in me breaks.

I don't understand how they've bonded with each other so well and I haven't. I don't know if it's my chat, my dress sense or my sense of humour, but if I make a joke they look at me blankly, or they fake a laugh. The other week I plucked up the courage to ask a couple of them if they'd like to come for a coffee at mine, but they made excuses and said, 'Next time for sure.' Neither of them have mentioned it since and I can't face rejection twice so I haven't asked them again.

It's really getting me down.

I've tried talking to W about it, but that doesn't help. I just get: 'Ask them again! If you don't ask you don't get' – *like I'm asking for ten per cent off a bill or for a second helping of roast potatoes. It's not as easy as that.*

I'm starting to dread the school run now. I hate how it makes me feel, being on the periphery, but I don't know how to change that. I don't know what else I can try.

Chapter 18

Victoria

SATURDAY

Victoria drags the trolley containing her training equipment – weights, skipping ropes, kettlebells, battle rope and boxing gloves and pads – across the park, then packs it all into the boot of her car. She's not as exhausted as her client but there's sweat on her brow and the hair below her ponytail is wet. Normally she's a 'demonstrate then observe' type of personal trainer but today she decided to join her client in his workout, matching him rep for rep, jump for jump and lap for lap, dissipating yesterday's anger when Theresa's neighbour intimated that she was part of the reason why Theresa had moved to Devon.

She shuts the boot of her car then slides into the driver's seat, takes out her phone and brings up the Rightmove website. Theresa's house has been on the market for a month – a whole month! She clicks through the photos on the listing but there's nothing weird or unusual about them. Not that she's got anything to compare them against. Theresa was one of the few women not to invite her to her home – something that frustrated and infuriated her. What made Theresa so special that she'd refuse her and the others a glimpse into her décor, her taste and her life?

Curious to see where Theresa and Tony are living now, she opens Facebook and searches for Theresa Fairchild. A list of women with the same name appear on screen but none of them are the Theresa she knows. Has she been blocked? They were definitely Facebook friends before. Irritated, she searches for Theresa's husband, Anthony Fairchild, and hits the jackpot. Not only is his profile still clickable but he's made all his posts public – the absolute tool. Her excitement builds as she clicks on his most recent video, posted earlier that day. It's him, doing a walking tour of their new rented house.

'All the boxes unpacked and everything where it should be,' he says proudly as he moves from the kitchen to the living room. He always was a massive show-off.

It's smaller than their Lowbridge home, but more characterful, all low beams and original stone walls. Victoria turns up the volume on her phone as he mumbles something about the kids being settled into their new schools. No mention of Lowbridge though, or how toxic it supposedly is. He walks upstairs and goes into the master bedroom. He drifts towards the window, waffling on about the views. Items of furniture appear in shot as he pans around. There are books artfully arranged on one nightstand and there's a cluster of perfume bottles on a dressing table as well as a small cardboard box containing—

'What the fuck?!' Victoria jabs at the screen.

That's her gold-leaf Eames bird! Given to her by Andy

for her birthday several years ago, during a good patch in their marriage. It was a limited edition. Now, because they're so rare, it's worth around two thousand pounds at auction. She knows that because, when hers went missing a year ago, she looked online to see if she could find a replacement and nearly fell off her chair.

She set out to discover what had happened to it, which sparked a new argument with Andy. If the cleaner didn't know anything about it, and the kids swore they hadn't broken it, then it had to be him. He swore he hadn't touched it, then he swore *at her* when she wouldn't let it drop. It was only a bloody ornament. Yes, it was an expensive one, but it wasn't the end of the world.

It was to her. It was a symbol of hope, that their marriage was repairable. A sign that if it had been good once it could be good again.

And now that bird's in Theresa fucking Fairchild's fucking house.

She clicks on the WhatsApp group 'St Helena's Mamas' where she always chats with the girls.

Am I the only one who didn't know that THERESA AND FAMILY HAVE LEFT LOWBRIDGE?! Their house is on the market, and they've got a new place in Devon already!

She pauses, waiting for the double ticks to appear beside her message. It's Saturday and none of her friends are at work. Someone's bound to reply straight away. Sure enough, at the top of the screen, *Dawn typing . . .* appears.

No way! I had no idea. Can't believe she didn't tell us.

A muscle twitches in Victoria's cheek. *And . . . wait for this . . . she told her neighbour that she thinks we're a NEST OF VIPERS and that Lowbridge is toxic.*

Dawn's reply appears in seconds. *What the actual fuck!!!*

Dots appear on the screen as Caz and Shanina reply.

Victoria feels a flush of pleasure as their horrified reactions appear on her screen.

There's more . . . she types. *Watch the video on Anthony Fairchild's Facebook page.* She pastes in the link then adds, *You know I lost my gold Eames bird a while ago? Look closely at the cardboard box on the dressing table after he walks into the master bedroom. She fucking stole it!!! No wonder she stopped replying to my texts.*

You're kidding! Dawn types back.

Shahina fills a quarter of the screen with shocked face and head-exploding emojis, whilst Caz replies, *I can't believe that! She actually replied to you at the time saying that you had such lovely taste in ornaments, and she hoped it would turn up soon!*

There's a lull in the chattering while her friends disappear off to check out the link, then they all start typing again.

OMG! I never told any of you, but I lost a beautiful Tiffany penguin ornament last Christmas, Caz types. *It was a present for my 40th from my sister who lives in NYC – the closest I'm ever going to get to going to Tiffany's! I noticed it was missing a couple of days after I had you all round for drinks. GUESS WHAT I JUST SPOTTED IN THE BOX!*

Dawn posts a message. *Ali lost a rare first-edition copy of The Handmaid's Tale when the kids were in Reception. Anyone else remember? Weren't she and Theresa really close? Maybe T stole that too!*

Then Shahina. *I can't see anything in the box, but I had a £100 restaurant gift card that my boss gave me as part of my Christmas bonus last year. It was propped up on the mantelpiece when I hosted book club. I assumed it must have slipped behind the mantelpiece and gave it up* as lost. Now I'm thinking that it must have been her. She went to all our houses, but we never went to hers!

Audrey: *I see my blue Venetian thumb bowl in that box too. I bought it when I was on honeymoon with Sully in Italy.*

Caz: *We need to contact the police. That video is evidence of theft. It doesn't matter if she doesn't live in Lowbridge anymore. I'm guessing you don't want Andy involved.*

Victoria types back, her lips a thin, straight line. There's nothing like a mention of her ex-husband to ruin her mood. *You guessed right. Who's happy for me to give the police their names?*

There's a pause, and for at least a minute no one types anything. Then a message from Shahina appears.

I can't swear for sure that she took my gift card, not without removing our mantelpiece. Go ahead and report her, but maybe don't mention my name.

Sara's typing something now.

Late to the party as always.

Audrey and Caz? You in? Victoria types. She presses send just as Sara's message appears on the screen.

Girls, I know this is really shocking and appalling behaviour on Theresa's part, and I know you're all angry, but maybe there's another way to deal with it without involving the police?

Dawn: *We all turn up to her house with baseball bats. Ha ha ha!*

Sara: *No. Let me call her. She hasn't stolen anything from me and I'll ask her to send everything back.*

Victoria's jaw tightens. It's all well and good to take the softly, softly approach if you didn't have something stolen that cost nearly two grand!

Did she tell you she was leaving? She asks.

Sara continues to type.

The three dots vanish.

She starts typing again.

Victoria breathes deeply through her nose then holds her breath before she exhales. If her blood pressure is up the next time she visits the GP then it's down to Sara.

Sara: *Yes. She sent me a message on the day she left, telling me that it was all a bit sudden but they were moving to Devon for family reasons. She thanked me for being a good friend and asked me not to say anything to the rest of you for a while. She said she wasn't ready to deal with an avalanche of 'Why have you gone?' messages.*

Shahina: *You kept that quiet.*

Dawn: *I thought the mamas didn't have any secrets from each other.*

What family reasons? Victoria asks.

Sara: *I don't know. I didn't ask. I figured she would have told me if she wanted me to know.*

Victoria rolls her eyes. *I still want to go to the police. This isn't a one-off theft. We thought she was a friend, and she went into our homes and stole from us. She can't just get away with it.*

Sara: *She works with special needs children, don't forget.*

Victoria: *Maybe she should have remembered that when she stole from us!*

Sara: *If she gets a police conviction she'll lose her job and we NEED people like her. My niece has Down's syndrome and my sister had to FIGHT to get her the kind of support she requires.*

Victoria screams into her hands. How the hell is she supposed to write a comeback to that?

Caz starts typing and Victoria waits, impatiently, for her message to appear. It was her idea to call the police in the first place. If anyone's going to take on Sara it's her.

Caz: *Just spoke to the hubster about it and he's talked me down. Still pissed off but I'll let the police thing go if she sends my Tiffany penguin back with a grovelling apology. Obviously I'll never actually speak to the bitch again but . . .*

Victoria thumps the steering wheel with her closed fist. What did Caz have to go and get her husband involved for? She *never* makes a decision without consulting him first.

Audrey? she types. **Just you and me?**

Actually . . . comes the return reply. *I can't be 100 per cent sure that the blue bowl is mine.*

'Spineless bitches!' Victoria swipes out of WhatsApp and throws her phone onto the passenger seat. 'I'll just deal with it myself, shall I?'

A couple of seconds later she snatches the phone up again as Andy's name and a message appears on the screen.

Bringing the kids back now.

What the hell? He's supposed to have them until 5 p.m. tomorrow and it's . . . she glances at the clock in the corner of the screen . . . not even lunchtime on Saturday. No explanation, no sorry, no attempt to find a time that might work for her. He's just going to turn up at the house and drop off the kids without even checking to see if she's in. What if she had clients in the afternoon? How would she manage then?

She pulls on her seatbelt and starts up the engine.

She'd cancel the clients obviously because nothing's more important than her kids.

* * *

Fifteen minutes later Victoria is still pissed off as she pulls into her driveway and parks up the car. She's annoyed with Andy, with Theresa, and with each and every one of her so-called friends. They all leap into action when there's an opportunity to gossip, have a nose around her house, and drink all her booze, but when she *really* needs their help suddenly they don't want to get involved.

She lets herself into the house, puts a capsule in the coffee maker, taps the button on the top, then brings up Google on her phone. She's typing in, 'maximum sentence for theft' when the doorbell rings repeatedly. Smiling to herself, she heads to the front door.

'Mummy!' Her son throws himself into her arms, his teddy bear dangling from his hand.

'Hi, Mum!' Sophia slips past her, her overnight bag in her hand. 'I'm going upstairs to play Minecraft. Bye!'

'Missed you too, sweetheart.' Victoria reaches out a hand to touch her daughter's hair, but she deftly ducks out of the way.

She shifts Noah's weight in her arms, then kicks the door shut with her foot. She doesn't bother to look for her ex-husband. He'll be parked up on the road as he always is. If she walks over to confront him, he'll only give her the finger and drive off. It's more important to her that the children are okay.

'How was it at Daddy's?' she asks Noah.

'Good.' He wriggles for her to put him back down.

'What did you do?'

'Not much. Can I go and play with my Switch now?' He shifts from foot to foot. 'Sophia's already gone upstairs.'

'Of course you can. Oh, hang on!' she shouts after him. 'Did Daddy say why he dropped you off early?'

'He said he was ill,' her son shouts as he thunders up the steps.

'Ill with what? I hope it's not Covid.'

Noah's face appears over the top of the banister. 'At breakfast his eyes were all red and puffy and Sophia asked if he'd been crying. He said no. That he'd stroked a cat yesterday and he was al . . . al-something . . .'

'Allergic?'

'Yeah.' He taps the banister impatiently. 'Can I go now?'

'Course.' As Noah disappears into his room Victoria shakes her head slowly. Andy's not allergic to cats. She had one when they first met, and he was all over it. So why would he lie to the kids? He's hiding something, and not for the first time. The sooner she gets the money to buy him out of the house, the sooner she won't have to deal with his shit.

Chapter 19

Sorrell

SATURDAY

With Harper and Henry playing in their rooms, and Scout napping in his, it's now or never. She *has* to tell her husband about the text she received yesterday. It's been eating away at her for nearly twenty-four hours. Perched on the edge of their bed she opens her phone and looks through the messages she's exchanged with her blackmailer so far:

> *I know for a fact that your husband was involved in a hit-and-run. He's probably told you that it was an animal. It wasn't. Pay me £20,000 or I'll contact the police.*

After the shock had worn off, she rang the number but it went to voicemail. A couple of seconds later a new text arrived:

You don't get to talk to me, Sorrell. I call the shots here.
– Who is this?
Someone who has evidence that proves what your husband did.
– He hasn't done anything
Tell that to the woman in intensive care.

She knows exactly who they're talking about. It's the woman she found on the news site, the one who was the subject of a hit-and-run on the outskirts of Mallow. If the blackmailer really does have footage of it happening then not only has Finnley hit a woman and driven off, he's also lied to her about his movements that night. If he wasn't at the Bat and Badger seeing Amit then what was he doing and why did he lie? Her breathing grows shallower as she continues to read.

– He had nothing to do with that.
Are you sure about that, Sorrell? Absoluteley sure? Because I'm pretty sure you know what I'm talking about.
– How did you get this number?
– It's on your website. How's the ceramics business going? And how are Harper, Henry and Scout? Do they know what Daddy did?

She feels sick that this stranger knows the names of her children. It makes her want to scoop them up and run as far away as she can.

– I don't have £20,000
Okay I'll go to the police then.
– Show me the evidence.

IT'S ALWAYS THE HUSBAND

You don't get to call the shots, Sorrell. Pay up, or I'll go to the police. Transfer the cash via PayPal to missunderstanding851@gmail.com and it's done. I'll never contact you again. You have seven days.

Sorrell stopped responding and turned to Google instead. If the blackmailer wanted money transferred to their PayPal account surely they'd be laying down a digital footprint that would lead to their bank account, and their real name. She was mistaken. According to the PayPal website no bank account is required to open an account, just an email address. She searched *missunderstanding851@gmail.com* but no results were returned. Chances were it was disposable, set up for exactly this purpose. Whoever was texting her, they'd covered their tracks well.

Now, she focuses on the blackmailer's claim to have evidence. If it does exist, then it has to be dashcam footage or CCTV from a Ring doorbell nearby. She searches Google again, this time for articles and discussions around the hit-and-run. She needs to know exactly where the victim was found; that way she'll be able to find out if there were any houses nearby.

She skim-reads several news articles but the information's too vague, so she logs onto Facebook instead. It doesn't take her long to find exactly what she's looking for on a local community group. One of the locals has posted about the accident, pinpointing the exact place where the injured woman was found. Feeling sick, Sorrell opens Google Street View, types in the name of the road and slowly travels along it, looking for the blind bend before the bridge. According to the local on Facebook, the woman's body was discovered in bushes, just after that spot. He also speculates that she either set off on foot to meet her husband in the nearby pub or she was taking her dog for its last walk of the night.

After a couple of minutes of clicking and dragging, Sorrell locates a bridge, with a blind bend just before it. She clicks slowly now, looking either side of the road for houses and buildings, but finds none. There isn't a single house within two hundred metres of the hit-and-run, in either direction. There are a couple of houses, one presumably the victim's, that are up little lanes that peel off the road, but none of them are close enough to the impact site to be able to record doorbell CCTV.

That just leaves her dashcam footage theory. She's got no way of finding out who else was on the road that night, but it all feels a bit too coincidental. What are the chances that the person who happened to be following Finnley down the road, or travelling in the other direction a) recognised him and b) just happened to be a blackmailer? If something like that happened in a film she was watching she'd probably turn it off in disgust.

Someone is lying to her. Either the blackmailer, or Finnley, or both. If the blackmailer is telling the truth, it would take them seconds to send her a screenshot or a couple of seconds of video to back up their claim. There's also a hip-shaped dent in the bonnet of Finnley's car, still hidden away in the garage, and a badly injured woman in hospital. As far as coincidences go, that's not one she can overlook. She needs to verify whether Finnley met Amit or not.

Amit Banerjee. She looks him up on Facebook. They're not friends but she can still message him. She just has to hope that he sees it.

Hi, Amit . . .

IT'S ALWAYS THE HUSBAND

She stops typing. If she asks him outright whether he met up with Finnley recently, and he hasn't, he'll know something is up and he might leave the message unanswered, contact Finnley and ask him what's going on. She needs to be more subtle.

Hi Amit, with Finnley's 40th birthday just around the corner I'd love to collect some stories and memories from his friends if there's anything you'd like to contribute. When did you two last see each other? Feels like it's been a while? Love to your family, Sorrell

She hits send. If Amit *hasn't* seen Finn recently, he'll reply and say, 'I know it's been ages' but if he *did* see him he'll say something like, 'We had drinks in the Bat and Badger. Didn't he tell you?'

But what if the person who's trying to blackmail her isn't someone who witnessed the accident but someone who's been told about it? She's pretty sure Finnley hasn't told anyone else because he could barely talk when he rang her that night and she hasn't breathed a word about—

An image flashes into her mind: Victoria and Noah, framed in the light of their open kitchen door as she took Finnley's call. How much did Victoria overhear before she called out and asked if everything was okay? Long enough to hear: 'What did you hit?' and 'Have you called the police?'

Earlier in the evening, Victoria had admitted that she didn't have enough money to buy Andy out of the house. She even, half-jokingly, asked if anyone knew someone who needed a PT. The more Sorrell thinks about it, the more sense it makes. Victoria overhearing her conversation totally explains why she's not forthcoming with evidence. There isn't any. She's skint, needs money for her house, and she overheard a conversation she shouldn't. She knows Sorrell's dad was a successful author who left her his estate in his will and that Finnley's a co-owner of a private dental surgery. She proved in the conversation about Noah's father that she's capable of deception. She must think Sorrell and Finnley have money to burn, so why not take some for herself?

All the fear Sorrell was feeling just five minutes earlier has vanished. In its place a slow, rumbling fury fills her chest. There's no need for her to say a word to Finnley about the blackmail. She's going to deal with Victoria herself.

Chapter 20

Andy

SATURDAY

It's nine o'clock at night and, out in the darkness of the countryside, the roads are quiet and the air is still. Lowbridge doesn't have a thriving nightlife during the week, but every Friday and Saturday, the streets become busier and the pubs fill up.

Andy left all that – and his mobile phone – behind him half an hour ago when he slipped out of his flat and merged in with the crowd. Now he's sitting in his car in a lay-by, the lights and engine off, and he's pulling a black balaclava down over his face.

He hasn't slept in thirty-eight hours; he hasn't eaten since lunchtime yesterday and, while he gave both kids a big hug when he dropped them off at Victoria's, he struggled to look Noah in the eye. Sophia is his firstborn, his princess, his little girl, but there's something about his bond with his son that he can't explain. He loves that boy so much, still loves him, even after everything that he's heard. He cuddled him as a baby, ran around with him as a toddler, taught him how to play football, took him swimming, read him stories, made him food, cleaned bloodied knees, laughed with him, chatted to him and held him in his arms. He didn't love him from the moment he was born; it was much, much earlier than that.

The first time Victoria fell pregnant she'd insisted they find out Sophia's gender. She wanted to prepare the nursery and buy the right clothes, but Andy disagreed. There were no surprises left in life; why couldn't they just wait and see. Victoria won the argument – the fact she was carrying the baby trumped anything he could say – and they found out Sophia's gender at the twenty-week scan. Victoria was so delighted any thoughts he'd had about waiting and surprises evaporated in the cloud of their mutual joy.

Four years later, when she fell pregnant with Noah, they didn't discuss finding out the gender of their unborn child. Victoria said yes before the sonographer had finished asking the question. 'Yes! Yes, definitely. We both want to know if it's a girl or a boy.'

Andy didn't object. All that mattered was a healthy baby that survived to full term. There were no good surprises, only bad. All three of Victoria's pregnancies after Sophia had ended in miscarriage. The last time it had happened he only had to glimpse the pained expression on the sonographer's face to know what had happened. Again, their baby was gone.

The news that this baby, this healthy child with a strong heartbeat, was a boy helped heal the grief that had haunted him. A son! A brother for Sophia. A mini me. A buddy. A boy! He'd been holding his breath for a healthy child for twenty weeks, but there was no breathing easy now. He wouldn't be able to relax until this child was born, pink and pudgy, screaming the fluid from his lungs, flailing his limbs in the air.

Right now, as he pulls on black leather gloves and opens the door to his car, Andy's not thinking about Noah. Anger, resentment and injustice have displaced the love in his heart. All day he's been simmering and stewing, his rage building, his heart pounding. It took all his self-control to fire off a single sentence to Victoria – *Bringing the kids back early* – when every part of him wanted to find her and shake her, to scream his fury in her face.

When he returned home, he ordered a paternity test on the internet, then he pulled on his workout gear, left his flat, and headed for the boxing gym. For an hour he skipped, lifted weights and pounded the punch bags, then he spent half an hour in a ring sparring with a bloke he'd only ever said hello to. By the time he returned home his tears had dried and his body was exhausted, but his mind was clear. Regardless of the results of the paternity test he knew what he needed to do to feel better. He needed to smash the shit out of someone. He needed to drive his fist right into their face.

A cold calm settled within him as he drew up his plan. He'd need to avoid traffic cams (not an issue considering his target's house was out of town), and doorbell cams (unknown, but he'd park out of sight). He'd dress in black with no identifying logos or designs on his clothes or trainers, wear a balaclava to hide his face, and gloves to avoid leaving his DNA at the scene. If he sustained any injuries he'd put them down to the sparring he did at the gym, or a suspect who'd resisted arrest. The only thing he didn't have was an alibi, but he'd leave his mobile at home and a show on

Netflix playing (he's already turned off 'Are you still watching?' because who wants to feel like a couch potato when they're just trying to unwind?).

Now everything's in place, he's out of the car, walking down a track to the five-bedroomed detached house that belongs to Lowbridge's 'premier estate agent', Rob Freeman, the ginger fucking arsehole whose fortieth birthday he went to seven years ago. A party he didn't want to go to because he didn't even know the guy, but Victoria convinced him by telling him that he was a really important client who knew everyone and could provide excellent word of mouth. Was that some kind of sick joke – word of fucking mouth? Bile rises in the back of his throat as an image flashes through his mind – of Rob Freeman's head between Victoria's legs, of his—

He shakes the thought away, his breathing growing shallower, his hands clenching into fists at his sides. Were they shagging even then? Was it their idea of a sick joke to invite him along, to allay suspicion, to parade him – her cuckolded husband – in front of the town? He got a bad vibe from the bloke the minute he met him: smarmy, fake, handsy, the kind of man who'll put his arm around a stranger's shoulders, or in the flat of their back so he can move them around. He was good-looking, if you like a chiselled jaw and high cheekbones, but it was his confidence that had all the women at the party tossing back their hair and laughing uproariously at his jokes. Andy stayed for half an hour, then made his excuses to Victoria and left.

He hastens his pace, the house in his sights. It's eight o'clock at night and, while it's dark on the first floor with the curtains drawn, there are lights on downstairs. There's only one car in the driveway: a black Mercedes. Anyone living this far out of town needs a car, so there's unlikely to be a live-in girlfriend. This 'eternal bachelor' still lives alone. Andy hasn't been able to check his relationship status to make sure – only an idiot would leave that kind of a digital paper trail – and he'd rather avoid involving a witness, but it's a calculated risk. Any man worth his salt isn't going to tell his partner to answer a knock at the front door at this time of night. And if she hears a commotion and comes running? All she'll see is a man dressed in black speeding away, and her ginger arsehole of a boyfriend or fuck buddy, lying bleeding and battered on the floor.

The thought – *Andy you're police for fuck's sake* – flashes through his mind as he raises his fist to pound on the door. He pushes it away. He knows a dozen coppers who'd do the same thing, or at least fantasise about it, if they were in the same situation as him.

Bang – bang – bang. He thumps the door with an urgency, and authority he normally reserves for arrests or searches. There's movement inside the house; he can feel it, rather than hear it and a light switches on in the porch. His chest rises and falls as he waits for the door to swing open. He bounces lightly on the balls of his feet in a boxer's stance, grounded, ready, and clenches and unclenches his hands. As the door inches open, he raises them up to his chin.

A tall dark shape appears in the doorway, ginger hair, flecked with grey. 'Hell—' the word freezes in Robert Freeman's mouth. His eyes widen as he takes in the masked figure on his doorstep and fear flashes across his face.

In the space between heartbeats, Andy pivots on his back foot and smashes his gloved right hand into his wife's lover's face. The shock and the force of the blow knock him off balance and he stumbles back into the porch, his fingers wrapped around the door handle, opening the door wide.

A grim smile lifts the edges of Andy's mouth. It's almost as though Rob just invited him in.

Chapter 21

Jude

SATURDAY

They're on their third bottle of wine – Jude and Emma – and neither of them can sit up straight. They're both slumped either side of Emma's IKEA sofa, curled into the armrests, wine glasses dangling precariously from their hands. It's like the force of gravity generated by the Ektorp is stronger than the sun's gravitational pull. Getting herself off it and walking down the hallway to the toilet might as well be a spacewalk, given how clumsy and cumbersome Jude feels.

It's Betsy's second sleepover in as many nights, this time with her twelve-year-old cousin, Isla. A little after eleven o'clock a grumpy Betsy traipsed down the stairs, complaining that Isla was snoring and she couldn't sleep. A quick switch around – moving her bed into Emma's study – and she was soon out for the count.

'Hello, hello. Couldn't help but overhear some of your

conversation.' The lanky shape of Emma's husband Angus appears in the living room door. He's the sensible adult for the evening, the only one not drinking. When he hasn't been telling the kids to keep the noise down, he's been playing electric guitar with headphones on, in the room next door.

'You're getting some action then are you, Jude? Congratulations! Why aren't I getting any shagging?' He side-eyes his wife. 'I was kidding!' he adds, before she can protest, then drops into the armchair and drapes his long legs over the arm. 'Who is it then? Anyone we know?'

'Well, he might be on *Crimewatch* at some point, if the rumours are true.'

Jude raises her eyebrows at her sister. 'Not cool.'

The promise she made to herself earlier, when she was traipsing down the street to Emma's house with Betsy, was that she would *not* tell her sister about the fact she'd crawled out of Will Ledger's bed that morning. That promise, along with her inhibitions, flew straight out of the window when they were halfway through the second bottle of wine. Emma's reaction was predictable – shock, horror, then a disappointed shake of the head.

'*Crimewatch*?' Angus repeats. 'Found yourself a local thug then, Jude?'

'No,' Jude gets in there before Emma can. 'He's an art history lecturer who just happens to have lost his last partner, and his first wife.'

'Has he looked down the back of the sofa?'

'Angus!'

'Sorry, sorry. Go on then, spill. I want all the details.'

He listens attentively as she tells him about Will's first wife and the accident, the argument with Robyn, the attack by the e-scooter driver, and the rumours that are doing the rounds. When she draws to a close, her brother-in-law looks at his wife, his eyes wide.

'You didn't think to tell me about any of this?'

'Why would I?' She shrugs. 'You don't like gossip.'

'This isn't gossip!' He looks back at Jude. 'So go on then, share your theory. What happened to Robyn? Where has she gone?'

'No one knows. That's the thing. Will thinks she up and left him and then had an accident or something and died. The school mums think he murdered her.'

'Wow! What do *you* think happened?'

'I don't think he killed her but there's . . .' Jude shifts her weight onto her elbow and awkwardly moves into a more upright position '. . . other stuff I haven't told you. It's probably grief but it's . . . unusual.'

Angus and Emma listen, open-mouthed, as she tells them about the special Robyn cheesecake in the fridge, Milly fixating on her teeth, the box under the bed and the diary.

Emma raises her glass to her mouth but seems to change her mind as the wine hits her lips. She puts the glass on a side table, a weary expression on her face. 'This just gets weirder. Jude, how many times do I have to tell you – just stay away.'

'Steal the diary and read the rest of it!' Angus bounces in his chair like a forty-two-year-old schoolboy. 'Seriously. Use the excuse about your earring, go back in there, and take it. Find out the truth!'

Jude shakes her head. As curious as she is about what happened to Robyn, that would be crossing a line. And what if Will caught her? How would she explain what she was doing? He'd never let her – or Betsy – step foot in his house ever again and her daughter would lose the only friend she's got in Lowbridge.

'That's a stupid idea, Angus,' Emma says, 'even for you! The police would have seized the diary when they searched his house. If there was any evidence that Robyn was scared, or Will had threatened her, they'd have built a case around it. You know they can prosecute people for murder without a body? If they really thought he'd killed her he'd be locked up by now.'

'So you *don't* think he killed her.' Jude shoots her sister a triumphant look.

'That's not what I said. I said there won't be anything incriminating in the diary.'

'But there might be other clues.' Angus still looks hopeful.

'What? Clues that the police missed? You think Jude's more likely to solve this mystery than them?'

'Maybe?' He shrugs. 'I don't know. But it would put her mind at rest, wouldn't it, if she reads the diary and it backs up his story: that Robyn went out loads, they argued. That there's nothing more to it than that. Jude?' He looks back at her. 'What do you think?'

'I think you've read too many Agatha Christies. Make yourself useful, Miss Marple, two coffees please.'

'Fine, fine.' Angus unfolds himself from the chair and gets up. 'I'll put the coffee on. But I know you, Jude. You're not going to be able to resist taking another peek at the diary the next time you stay over. Why torture yourself like that, reading little dribs and drabs? Just take it, read it, put it back, then it's all done.' He holds out his hands, shrugs, then ambles away.

'Don't.' Emma stares at her from across the room. 'Jude, don't listen to him. This isn't one of his stupid computer games where you go around stealing things from monsters so you can progress further in the game. This is real. That diary contains someone's private thoughts. Someone who never meant for them to be read.'

IT'S ALWAYS THE HUSBAND

'I know,' Jude says. 'I get it.' But even as she nods her head in agreement, she's pretty sure that it's Angus who's right, not her sister. She will torture herself, not knowing what's in the rest of Robyn's diary, and the only way to end that torment is to read it from the first page to the last.

Chapter 22

ROBYN'S DIARY

Well, surprise, surprise! So much has happened since I last wrote in here. It's always been the way when I keep a diary – I only write in it when I'm miserable. When life's good I'm too busy enjoying myself to even think about my diary. I just need somewhere to spill my feelings without being judged. Not that W ever judges me, but there's only so many times you can tell someone about your problems without turning into a complete bore. Anyway, big update . . .

I've infiltrated the ranks of the clique! Okay, so I'm still on the periphery but they've started inviting me to join them for coffee after the school run and the odd night out (although I'm still not part of the inner sanctum that gets to go to the Queen Bee's house!). It's still awkward as fuck when they share in-jokes or talk about the HILARIOUS drinks evening that I wasn't invited to or give each other coded looks when another mum's name is mentioned. Don't get me wrong, they're not complete bitches, other than the Queen Bee who totally dominates every conversation and turns every discussion into a story about her. The rest of them are funny, interesting, intelligent women who've lived really varied and fascinating lives. I can't help but feel lesser in comparison though – growing up my whole life in the same town until I moved here, going on bog-standard package holiday trips while everyone else seems to have been backpacking around Thailand or Australia or Outer Mongolia. It's like they all come from a different world.

Being around them makes me feel insecure. There I said it. I don't feel good enough to be part of their group. I'm not enough. I'd get therapy to get over myself if I could afford it, but it looks like I'll have to dig out my old Paul McKenna 'I Can Make You Confident' CD instead. Ha ha!

Chapter 23

Sorrell

MONDAY

It's been three days since Sorrell sent a message to Amit and he still hasn't replied. She's not sure whether to read into that or if he's someone who barely looks at Facebook. Either way, there's something more pressing on her mind. Today, if everything goes plan, she'll have evidence that proves Victoria is her blackmailer and that part of the nightmare will be over. She's halfway out the front door, having retrieved Scout's lost sock, rubbed Nutella off his cheek and convinced the twins that yes, they *do* need a coat when it's raining, when Finnley calls out from behind her.

'Did I tell you I'm going into work, today?'

And there he is, her husband, in a shirt and trousers, clean-shaven with his hair neatly combed. The scent of shower gel and shampoo fills her nose.

'James begged me,' he adds, before she can say a word. 'A patient needs an urgent extraction with sedation and their freelance anaesthesiologist is off sick. It's Andy Routledge and we can't have our police force in pain.'

'But . . .' She stares at him in astonishment, vaguely aware that Scout, in his pushchair, has started to grumble in frustration. 'I thought . . . I thought . . .'

'So did I.' His shrug, and the unreadable expression on his face, only adds to her confusion. He's been off work with stress for a month, and just days ago, she found him in her studio, having a breakdown. Yet magically he's ready to go back?

'I can tell by the look on your face that you think I'm not ready, but it's a one-off, an extraction with sedation to do James a favour; in and out.'

'Are you sure . . .' The words dry in her mouth. There isn't time for a protracted discussion about whether this is a good idea. Buried in the folds of the buggy hood, hidden in a blue plastic bag, is her secret weapon that *should*, if all goes according to plan, expose Victoria as the blackmailing bitch that she is. But if she doesn't get the kids to the park in the next half an hour, she's going to miss her chance.

'Okay! Good luck.' She shoots Finnley a tight smile. 'I'll see you when you get back.'

Out of the corner of her eye, as she turns back to the children, she registers a switch in her husband's expression – from nonchalance to irritation – but she ignores it. If Finnley needs her to pander to him, today really isn't the day.

It's a little after 8 a.m. when Sorrell, Henry and Harper arrive at the park that they cut through en route to school.

Some mothers, with children who get up at the crack of dawn, let their children play for an hour or so to burn off their excess energy before school. Sorrell is not one of those mothers. Normally they're running so late that she has to chivvy the children past the play area, ignoring their cries of, 'Please, Mummy, just five minutes on the swings!' But today is not a normal day and when she tells Harper and Henry that they can play for a little while they take off immediately, whooping with the kind of excitement and energy she can only dream of possessing. Distracted by the beautiful spiderwebs that adorn the fence, Sorrell pauses. Droplets of dew sparkle like jewels on each silken thread.

When she looks up again, she spots Victoria, dressed in a black bomber jacket, multicoloured leggings and trainers, on the other side of the play park. She's chatting away, gesticulating wildly, while Caz and Audrey, bookending her like bodyguards, give the occasional nod or shrug. At her feet is an oversized bag.

Sorrell feels sick, seeing her blackmailer's confident wide-legged stance and the upward tilt of her chin, while she feels weak-kneed with fear. 'Mum! Mum! Look at this.' Henry's shout carries towards her on the cool October air. He's clambered to the top of the climbing frame and is hanging upside down, his knees hugging a bar. It's something Harper's done a hundred times, but he's always been too scared to lean back and let go.

'That's brilliant, Henry. Well done!' She makes a big show of clapping her hands above her head, not caring who sees.

Of her three children he's the one who's most like her now. As a child, and into her twenties, she was a wild child like Harper: bold, confident and silly – a free spirit without a care in the world. But she's changed since she moved to

Lowbridge. Without a tribe of close friends who know her inside out she's unmoored, adrift and fearful. While she's outwardly chatty and happy whilst teaching her pottery students, inside she's so anxious that she doesn't recognise herself anymore.

'Hi, Sorrell.' She jumps at the sound of Sara's voice. She was so lost in thought she hadn't noticed her sidle up beside her and, as Sara's pale green eyes roam her face, she feels like her emotions are being MRI-scanned.

'One more lap around the park,' Sara shouts after her son and daughter as they zoom past her on scooters, 'then we need to get off to school!' She's ditched her normal uniform of dungarees and long-sleeved tops for a faded denim jacket over a black dress that's patterned with large, multicoloured flowers. A neon yellow handbag crosses her body and there's an empty-looking Tesco bag for life in her hand.

'Everything okay?' she asks Sorrell.

'Yes, yes, fine.' Sorrell forces a smile. The last thing she wants is for a rumour to start up that she was hanging around the park acting weirdly. And she likes Sara. She's always so upbeat and friendly she can't help but wish she'd had the courage to invite her for a coffee back in Reception, instead of falling into a friendship with Audrey. She'll be braver in the future, she tells herself – once all the blackmail and Finnley's mental health stuff is over. Maybe it's not too late to make a good friend.

'Just lost in my own world,' she adds. 'That's a lovely dress. Is it new?'

'Charity shop find!' Sara plucks at the material. There's the briefest flash of shame on her face before she thrusts her hands into the sides of the dress. 'And it's got pockets, look!'

She gasps loudly before Sorrell can respond, her body angled towards the far corner of the park where her daughter was scooting. 'She's fallen off, better comfort her before the screaming starts.'

She gives Sorrell's arm a squeeze then hurries away at a trot, raising a hand in hello to Victoria, Caz and Audrey as she passes them. Out of the corner of her eye Sorrell spots someone moving around, behind the bushes, but when she looks properly, they're gone.

She checks her watch. She needs to get this over and done with before she loses her nerve. Sorrell of old would have marched up to Victoria and Audrey and had it out with them, but she's not that fearless anymore. Glancing behind her to check that her children are okay, she slips into the copse of trees that separate the playground from the dog walking field and digs around in the hood of Scout's buggy, registering every snapped twig, every whistle and every shout of excitement in the park. She withdraws the blue plastic bag and peers inside. On first glance it appears that there are three, not insubstantial bundles of twenty-pound notes. A quick flick through each bundle would confirm that yes, there's approximately three thousand pounds. That's all she hopes Victoria has time for because, on closer inspection, she'd realise that each pack of 'cash' only contains forty pounds of actual currency – one at the top, one at the bottom, with printed, ever so slightly crumpled pieces of paper in between.

Sorrell spent three hours in her studio last night – printing, cutting and texturising the fake money. After the children were in bed she told Finnley that she'd had a last-minute order from one of her gift shop clients for two dozen hand-thrown mugs. As she hovered in the living room doorway she braced herself for his questions – 'So late on a Sunday?'

'Don't they realise you have a personal life?' or 'Can't they wait an extra day?' – but he didn't ask her a single thing. He just shrugged.

Carrying the bag, she takes a few steps away from the 'toilet tree' – so named by the children because of the potty-shaped rotten indent where the trunk splits into two – and crouches beside a dense, prickly shrub. Her hope, by tucking the bag into the bush's undergrowth, is that it won't be discovered by a dog walker picking up poo, or a child who makes a mad dash into the bushes to climb the tree.

She's only been out of sight of her children for a minute, maybe two, but the moment they realise she's vanished, all hell will break loose. She leaves a corner of the bag poking out from beneath the bush then props up her phone against a tree root, far enough away from the money that the blackmailer won't notice it but close enough that it should still catch them in the act. She sets it to record to video then ducks out of the copse of trees, pushing the buggy back onto the path. Her children are still climbing and shouting excitedly, seemingly unaware she'd temporarily disappeared. Victoria's still on the other side of the play park, staring down at her phone. Audrey, on the other hand, is staring straight at her, a frown creasing her brow.

Sorrell's stomach hollows. If Audrey mentions to Victoria that she saw her disappearing into the bushes, then the game's up. It was hard enough to get her blackmailer to agree to a secret cash drop instead of a PayPal transfer in the first place. They text-battled last night – the blackmailer demanding a transfer and Sorrell pretending that she was too scared to do it in case Finn noticed the money disappear from their savings. When they reached a stalemate Sorrell said that there was another way for her to get some cash together, but it would take several days. She had three thousand in cash, she told her blackmailer; that was all she could give her for now. Several minutes later her blackmailer suggested a drop point, and a time.

The park struck Sorrell as a very public place to leave three thousand pounds. Not only would it be difficult for her to drop off the money unnoticed, it would be equally tricky for Victoria to retrieve it without being spotted by one of her many mummy pals.

Now, as a jogger speeds towards her, Sorrell angles the buggy out of his way. It's only as the man passes her that she realises it's Andy Routledge. She looks at her watch again: 8.25 a.m. The school gates will open in five minutes, ready for the school day to begin at 8.45 a.m. The sooner she drops off Henry and Harper, the quicker she can return to the park, grab her phone, and text Victoria the video showing her pulling the bag of 'money' from the bush. She glances across at her blackmailer and her eyes widen. Victoria's foisting her kids onto Caz – getting her to do the school run for her – so she can stay behind in the park to grab herself three thousand pounds.

'Henry! Harper! Time for school!' Sorrell beckons her children from the play equipment then shepherds them towards the park gates. They chatter, whine and bicker as they approach the school but Sorrell's only half-listening. All she can think about is the look on Victoria's face when she opens the blue plastic bag, flicks through the notes, and realises that she's been had.

Children deposited at school, kisses and hugs dispensed, Sorrell speeds back to the park. She passes Will Ledger and his daughter, both running. As their paths cross, she hears him say, 'Milly, we're going to be late. I told you you should have gone to the toilet before we left home.'

IT'S ALWAYS THE HUSBAND

Empty of parents and children, the park feels deserted. It's just Sorrell, a couple of dog walkers – one of them frantically calling out to a cream-coloured Labradoodle, joyfully speeding around the field – and Audrey. She's tapping away at her phone while Eloise, the only child in the playground, swings back and forth on the swings. Sorrell watches her, confused. Why isn't she in school? More to the point, was Victoria able to retrieve the bag, with Audrey still standing there?

Not caring whether Audrey sees her or not, Sorrell rounds the play park and steps into the copse of trees. Excitement sparks in her belly as her gaze flicks towards the bush. There's no blue, just green. She crouches down to make sure and sweeps her hand beneath the branches and leaves. It's gone! Victoria stepped straight into her trap and took the bag; now all she needs is the evidence to shame her. She heads for the tree root, where she propped up her phone and swears quietly. It's fallen face down. She snatches it up and taps the screen but it's stopped recording. Shit. Did it capture anything before it fell? She taps on the recorded video, sees a close-up of her face after she hit the record button and watches herself, and the buggy, disappear. Then it's just bush, bush, bush and then nothing – a blurry shot of dark, grainy earth. She fast-forwards through the rest of the video but it's more of the same.

Angry, dirty and frustrated, she gets back to her feet and makes her way out of the copse. As she straightens up, she spots Victoria strolling along the pathway towards Audrey, two disposable coffee cups in her hands, her large tote bag swinging from her shoulder. A bag that now looks heavier and bulkier. A bag that, more than likely, contains a blue plastic bag weighed down with dozens of pieces of paper and six twenty-pound notes. Something inside Sorrell snaps and shatters. For the last month she's been holding herself, and her family together. She's been a provider, a mother, a teacher, a cook, a cleaner and a taxi driver. She's been a therapist, a life coach and a sounding board. She's not going to be a victim too.

Rage and injustice propel her down the path and up to Victoria and Audrey, relaxed, smug, nursing coffees, staring at her as though she's crawled out from under a rock.

'What's in the bag?' The question bursts out of her and Audrey, startled, steps back.

Victoria gives Sorrell a look that, if she weren't so angry, would have withered her. 'I'm sorry, what?'

'The bag.' Sorrell tugs on it. 'Show me what's inside.'

Victoria raises her eyebrows at Audrey as if to say: *What the fuck's going on? She's gone absolutely mental,* which only enrages Sorrell more.

'Stop pretending you don't know what I'm talking about. Open the bag.'

Victoria holds out a hand, palm exposed. 'Are you . . . are you okay? Feeling all right there, Sorrell?'

A snort of amusement from Audrey snaps any self-restraint Sorrell may have had left and she yanks the bag from Victoria's shoulder. There's a shocked gasp as she upends the contents onto the ground and then nothing – silence – before her ears ring with shame. Lying open on its side is a large, clear Tupperware container, and strewn across the path are a dozen misshapen cupcakes, grit and dirt embedded in their pink and white frosted tops.

She's tricked me and hidden the money, says a small voice in the back of Sorrell's head, but a louder voice is screaming, *Fuuuuuckkkkkkk.* She got it wrong. She put two and two

IT'S ALWAYS THE HUSBAND

together and made *you've just embarrassed yourself for the rest of your life.*

Cheeks burning, she scrabbles around picking up the cupcakes. One by one she places them back in the container, acutely aware of the horrified silence emanating from the two women looming above her, watching every frantic move she makes.

'I . . . I . . .' She stands slowly, willing a freak lightning bolt to put her out of her misery. 'I'm so . . . I'm so, so sorry, Victoria. I don't know . . . I don't know what came over me. I . . . I . . . I'll make you some more cakes. I'll buy some. I'll give you the—'

'It's Caz you need to apologise to,' Victoria snaps. 'She stayed up late to make those for the PTA sale this afternoon. When she's got so much on her plate too. You know her dad's just gone into a nursing home?'

'No I . . .' Sorrell curls into herself. 'I didn't. I had no idea.'

She moves to hand the Tupperware box of squashed and dirty cupcakes to Victoria who shakes her head sharply. 'What am I supposed to do with them now?'

A thought burns through Sorrell's shame and her breath catches in her throat. Victoria's going to tell everyone what just happened. By the time she returns to the school for pick-up at 3.15 p.m. they'll all be staring at her, smirking and whispering. *Sorrell had some kind of nervous breakdown in the park and tried to steal the PTA cupcakes.* Gossip's like wildfire; the smallest spark is enough for one person's life to go up in flames.

'Please don't mention this to anyone.' She can't bring herself to look Victoria or Audrey in the eye. 'I'm so, so sorry. I got confused. I promise nothing like that will ever happen again.'

With tears spilling down her cheeks, and still clutching the box of battered cupcakes, she walks as quickly as she can towards the gates, without actually breaking into a run.

Chapter 24

Victoria

MONDAY

Victoria stares after Sorrell as she sprints out of the park in tears. Her brain, so full of thoughts, plans, and ideas when she was chatting to Audrey fifteen minutes ago, has turned itself off. Now it's just white noise and chaos. What the hell did Sorrell just do?

'Victoria?' A hand on her shoulder makes her jump, but it's just Audrey, a concerned expression on her face. 'Are you okay?'

'Yeah, yeah, fine.' She forces a smile, places her hand over Audrey's and taps it briskly to signal: *You don't have to touch me anymore.*

'What the hell was that all about?' There's excitement in Audrey's bright eyes, the same shock and fascination Victoria saw all around her when Will Ledger was knocked to the ground outside school. No one wants to experience anything awful but, when it happens to other people, there's a thrill to being a bystander, a witness with a new story to tell.

'A psychotic breakdown?' She tries to make light of it but her quip fails. The light in Audrey's eyes has died. She thinks she's serious; she's working out how best to respond. 'Maybe she was hungry?' Her second attempt at a joke lands and the tight line of Audrey's mouth lifts into a smile. 'Whatever the reason, she looked mortified. Let's change the subject shall we?'

'Wow,' Audrey says. 'That's not like you.'

'I'm sorry?'

'I thought you'd be all over that.'

'In what way?'

'Any reason to bitch!'

Now it's Victoria who's raising her eyebrows. *Seriously*, that's what Audrey thinks of her? Do the others think that too? That she's a massive grade-A bitch? Absolute hypocrites the lot of them. She's the first person they ring when they're desperate to find out about an argument at the school gates or whether the whispers about a certain teacher are true. She's not a bitch, she's a source of information – like Google – but with a ponytail and a rock-hard arse.

She forces a false laugh. 'I'm having a day off.' A second later she adds, 'I've got a lot on my mind.'

Audrey readjusts her scarf then shouts something in French to Eloise who's hanging off the roundabout, her hair whipping the ground. 'Such as?'

'Theresa.'

'Ah, the video. You had no joy?'

On Saturday night, after she'd put the kids to bed, Victoria returned to her mobile, and Tony Fairchild's Facebook profile, ready to screenshot the stolen items, and found that it'd gone. Not only that but the privacy settings had been changed so that all she could see was Tony's profile picture and a photo of the football team Plymouth Argyle as the page's header. Frantic, she messaged the mamas. Had anyone taken a screenshot of any of the items in the video? Were any of them able to see Tony's profile, or was she the only one who was blocked? The replies came thick and fast. No one had taken a screenshot, and none of them could see his full profile. Reasons and possible explanations for the disappearance of his profile flew around the group but the only one that made sense to Victoria was that Theresa has spotted what was in the video, panicked, and made Tony take down the video and lock his profile. Infuriated, Victoria had hurled almost all of the sofa cushions across the room, and screamed into the one that remained. Why the *hell* hadn't she screenshotted the video when she first saw it? The only evidence she had that Theresa had stolen from her had disappeared in the blink of an eye.

'No,' she says to Audrey now. 'No joy getting hold of a screenshot. But I'm still going to the police.'

'Oh really? I would offer to come with you, but I've got to get Eloise to the dentist, and then back to school. If you can wait until tomorrow, I could maybe come but—'

'It's fine. It's fine.' She ducks down to pick up the tote bag, now empty of cupcakes. 'If you want something done properly, do it yourself.'

'What was that?' Audrey says from above her.

'Nothing.' She takes a deep steadying breath. 'Nothing at all.'

Victoria didn't think it was possible for her mood to get any darker than it was when Sorrell wrestled the bag from her shoulder earlier that morning but, after her encounter with the local constabulary just now, it's reached an all-time low. Not only was the officer at reception too busy playing online poker on his phone to notice her, but he couldn't have looked more bored when she told him the details of the theft. When she'd asked if she could speak to a detective she was told that there weren't any available and, when she asked if she could book in an appointment to see someone, he'd actually sighed.

'If you don't have photographs of the ornament from before you lost it, and an accompanying receipt, then there's no audit trail of you buying it. It'd be your word against hers.'

She pressed on, asking if he could arrange for someone from Devon constabulary to search Theresa's home for the stolen items. He shook his head.

'The DI won't authorise a search warrant from the local magistrate because said JP is a pernickety bastard. If all the boxes aren't ticked, you've got no chance, I'm afraid.'

She'd stared at him, the red mist of her frustration rising. It was the police equivalent of 'computer says no'.

Now, outside the police station, she sits on a low wall and rests her head in her hands. It's not the theft of the bird that's rankling her – as nice as it was – it's Theresa's deceit and her own loss of control. The fact she managed to steal from her, and then sneak off to Devon, without her noticing makes her feel unnerved and wrong-footed. The women in her social circle are there for a reason – she allows them to be. After what happened to her in primary school, she won't befriend anyone who doesn't make her feel good about herself. She also won't let them get close. As much as she might enjoy the company of the 'mamas' she's swimming alongside them in an emotionally shallow pool. She identified their dominant personality traits early on: Audrey – sharp-tongued; Shahina – strong-minded; Dawn – eccentric; Sara

– people pleaser; Caz – clever. She felt she could confidently predict their behaviour in most situations. More importantly, she could predict their behaviour towards her.

She'd hung the 'feisty' label on Theresa and had enjoyed watching from a distance each time she'd explode. She hadn't pegged her for deceitful, sneaky and duplicitous too. The revelation that she'd made a mistake and inadvertently allowed a cuckoo into her nest has shaken her. Add to that Audrey's comment about her being a bitch, and she's wondering how many other cuckoos there are.

She lifts her head from her hands as her phone bleeps, then sighs as Andy's name appears on the screen. What's he messaging her about this time? He'd better not be changing their childcare arrangements again. If the police won't go to Theresa's to confront her about the theft, then she's going to do it herself.

Karma has no menu; you get served what you deserve.

What the hell? Is he drunk? She rereads the message then opens Google, runs a search and taps out a message. If he thinks he can fuck around with her today he's chosen the wrong person.

Karma sleeps lightly before it takes its revenge.

Chapter 25

Andy

MONDAY

As Andy approaches the white, glossy door of Bright White Dental Clinic he pauses to check the heart rate reading on his Google watch: 141 bpm. Not good. His resting heart rate rarely rises above 56 bpm and, even after a half-hour run, it rarely goes any higher than 130–135. He's in good shape, physically at least. Mentally, he's absolutely terrified. Dentists are his Achilles heel, his kryptonite, and his worst nightmare all rolled into one.

His fear developed aged fourteen thanks to a cold and unkind orthodontist who chastised him for complaining when his braces were tightened, or the wires cut into his cheek, then crescendoed aged twenty-nine when he had four wisdom teeth removed without sedation. The CRACK sound, as first one tooth, then another, then another, were ripped from his gums, made his feet fly off the chair and tears well in his eyes. The experience was so horrific he couldn't even talk about dentists for years without his pulse pounding and sweat beading on his forehead. He'd leave the room or change the subject and, if he couldn't do either of those things, he'd think of the catchiest song he knew and sing the words to himself in his head until the conversation moved on to something entirely less fraught.

Now, every nerve, every cell, every knotted muscle in his body is screaming at him to escape, to get back in his car, drive home, and anaesthetise himself with whisky. Not for the first time he's considering taking a hammer to the fractured tooth and smashing it out of his mouth himself but he can't ignore the excruciating pain that's stretches from the left side of his jaw to his eye and skull.

Saturday night's plan to beat the shit out of Rob Freeman didn't exactly pan out. While Andy had the advantage of surprise, unfooting Rob with a blow to his nose within seconds of stepping through his front door, he hadn't predicted how strong, or how resilient, the other man was. He'd only been able to rain half a dozen punches into Freeman's face and body before he'd regained his footing and his faculties and landed a thump to Andy's jaw.

At the time, it had glanced off him. He was too focused, too full of fury, to feel pain, but later, when he'd left Rob lying battered and bleeding on the polished tiles of his porchway, his jaw began to throb. He tried to ignore the pain, numbing it with whisky and ibuprofen, drinking until he eventually passed out.

He woke on Sunday morning with a temperature and a bad taste in his mouth. His gums were bright red, his cheek and jaw were swollen, and he couldn't eat without pain. Contortions with a mirror confirmed what he suspected; he'd fractured a molar that was eighty per cent filling.

A visit to the emergency dentist took every ounce of bravery he had, and he'd perched on the chair, hands quivering between his knees, as a mask-covered dentist perched on a stool beside him and asked him what had happened. He lied and said there'd been an altercation during an arrest the day before. The dentist had nodded sagely and peered into his mouth, his eyebrows rising as he'd tapped first one tooth, then another with the metallic tool in his hand.

'I'm sorry to say that's going to have to come out.'

He'd begged for sedation and the dentist took one look at his pale, clammy face and took pity on him. 'I'll ring Finnley Edwards. See if there's any way he can come in. He's trained in conscious sedation. You'll be awake but you'll be so relaxed it won't bother you. Afterwards you'll suffer amnesia. You won't remember a thing.'

Before Andy could respond, the dentist added, 'Even if he says yes, it'll be tomorrow at the earliest, but I can write you a prescription for the pain in the interim. Are you sure you don't want me to take it out now? Get it over and done with?' Like a bullet, Andy shot out of the chair.

A phone call, several hours later, confirmed the appointment on Monday. He thanked the receptionist profusely then washed down his painkillers with a whisky. The bottle was empty by the end of the night.

Now, still outside the surgery, convincing himself to go in, he turns sharply. He just felt the skin on the back of his neck prickle, as though someone was watching him, but when he scans the street there's no one he recognises, just a few random shoppers, cars parked up and empty, and a woman standing outside a tattoo shop, puffing away on a vape. Earlier, he went for a run around the park. His jaw and hungover brain were throbbing, but it was either go for a run or wear a bald spot in the carpet by pacing back and forth.

It was as if the whole of Lowbridge was in the park too. He'd spotted Victoria, Audrey, Caz and, drifting around by herself, Sorrell Edwards. He knew there would be questions – then gossip – if anyone spotted the bruise on his jawline, so he'd kept his distance the best he could, sprinting faster than normal, hugging the edge of the park. As he'd rounded a hedge he'd caught sight of a tall man with ginger hair, walking a dog. He couldn't be sure it was Rob Freeman, but just in case, he'd changed direction, sprinting past Sorrell to get out of the park as fast as he could. The last thing he needed was for Freeman to spot the bruising on his face and put two and two together.

'Andy Routledge?' He turns back towards the dental surgery and sees Finnley Edwards in green scrubs standing in the doorway, a tight smile on his face. 'I saw you from the window upstairs. You're my next patient. Shall we go in?'

'I won't lose my inhibitions, will I? Start saying ridiculous things, or have some kind of meltdown?' Somehow Andy's made it into the dentist's chair and he's gripping the armrest like it's about to take off. 'I know I shouldn't, but I googled dental sedation yesterday and I was reading about people who either spill their guts and all their secrets or completely lose it and start smashing the place up.'

He's speaking quickly now, the words rushing out of him like a river. He's just signed the consent form for the extraction and sedation, and the list of all the things that could possibly go wrong have taken his stress levels from unbearable to insufferable.

'You shouldn't worry about either of those things. Sedation

makes most patients calm, compliant and composed. I can't see you being any different.'

Andy tries to focus on the angle-poise lamp that's thirty centimetres or so above his head as the dentist fits a blood pressure cuff to his arm. He takes a slow deep breath in, and then out.

'If there were any issues,' Finnley continues, 'and I stress that they're highly unusual, your lift home is waiting for you in reception, yes?'

'Yeah, should be Lee, from work.' He was told by the dentist he saw yesterday that he'd need someone to wait for him during the extraction and drive him home afterwards. He'd assumed it was to do with the effect of the sedation, and not because Finnley might have to call for reinforcements if the sedation turned him into a violent lunatic, instead of a meek little lamb.

'Your blood pressure's a little raised' – Finnley undoes the cuff – 'but that's not unusual in this scenario. I promise you'll feel more relaxed after the first injection. I like to describe it as a little gin and tonic, before the main course. Do you feel ready to begin?'

Not trusting himself to answer, Andy just nods.

'Okay then.' The dental nurse hands Andy a pair of sunglasses. He puts them on, hands shaking, then closes his eyes as Finnley leans closer with a syringe.

'Bite down on this, Andy. Okay, you're done.'

Andy blinks, trying to make sense of what's happening. He remembers Finnley administering the first injection, and feeling worried that it hadn't taken the edge off his nerves like a gin and tonic. He remembers the second injection going into his arm and then . . . nothing. It wasn't like a general anaesthetic. His world hadn't faded to black, but when he racks his brain, trying to remember the extraction, there's nothing. He can't even remember opening his mouth.

He frowns as the nurse gestures for him to remove his sunglasses. 'Why haven't you done it yet?'

'It's over.' Finnley has his back turned, placing what looks like bloodied cotton wool tampons in a cardboard bedpan.

'Are you sure?'

'Absolutely. How are you feeling?'

'Weird. I can't remember anything after you put the second injection in.'

'Perfectly normal.' He proceeds to reel off everything Andy needs to do to look after the extraction site once he returns home.

The words wash over Andy like a sound bath. It's too much to take in. 'I'm not sure I'll remember all that.'

'Which is why we give all our patients this.' The nurse hands him a printed piece of paper. 'It's all on here.'

Finnley, who's over by the bin now, turns to look at him. 'Let's get you downstairs to your friend. I'll hold your arm.'

In the passenger seat of Lee's car, Andy pulls on his seatbelt and waits for his mate to start the engine. After what feels like an age, with the car still stationary, he turns to look at him.

'Everything okay?'

Lee makes a low *Mmmm* sound in his throat then sits back in his seat, his hands falling from the steering wheel. 'When I came to pick you up the receptionist asked me if I was police.'

'Right.'

'And when I said I was, she commented that it's a dangerous job. Asked me if I'd ever lost any teeth.'

'Right,' Andy says again, not sure where the conversation is going.

'She told me you'd been punched by someone you were arresting on Saturday.' Lee gives him a sideways look. 'You weren't on shift.'

'I—' Before Andy can say any more Lee holds up a hand.

'I don't want to know. If this comes up, I know nothing. All right?'

'Thanks, thanks, mate. Appreciate it.'

Lee nods curtly but the judgement in his narrowed eyes makes Andy feel sick.

Chapter 26

Jude

MONDAY

It's almost as though Will knows Jude's come to his house with Betsy under false pretences. He greets her, not with a smile but a frown.

'Jude?' There's a question mark in his voice. 'Did we . . .' His gaze flits towards Betsy and the furrow in his brow deepens. 'Is there a playdate I've forgotten about? I didn't see you at pick-up.'

'No, no playdate.' Jude's throat dries and she has to clear it to get the words out. She's not one of life's natural liars and she's pretty sure the only way she'd look shiftier was if she'd turned up wearing a full-face balaclava. 'The thing is Will, I'm um . . . I'm missing one of my earrings – it's very sentimental, part of a pair my parents gave me – and I thought it might be in your bedroom from er . . . from when you gave me a guided tour the other day.'

Her daughter's nose wrinkles in disdain. 'It's not a museum, Mum. It's Milly's house and we've been here loads of times. Why are you being so weird?'

The befuddled expression on Will's face switches to amusement, and he gives Jude a loaded look that can only mean he's running the night of the 'tour' through his mind. She crosses her arms over her chest, suddenly feeling naked.

'Your mum's not weird,' Will says, still smiling, 'she's a writer. They use words to describe things that the rest of us don't.'

'No.' Betsy takes a step forwards. Milly's appeared in the living room doorway and is beckoning her in. 'She's definitely weird.'

Will moves to one side to let her into the house. His gaze returns to Jude as both girls go into the living room and the door slams shut behind them. 'I've got dinner on, but I can make it stretch to four. It's only casserole but—'

'I love casserole.' The statement, so quick to come out of her mouth, so earnest and utterly banal, makes her anxiety quicken. What the hell is she saying? Betsy's right – she's definitely weird.

'Wow.' Will flattens himself against the wall to let her pass him in the narrow hallway, his eyes shining with amusement. 'I've never had such an enthusiastic response to a bit of beef and some spuds and carrots before. I'll have to cook it more often and . . .' His words fall away as Jude steps into the tight space between his body and the other wall. They're face to face now, less than six inches separating them, and the air feels heavier, warmer, charged with possibility. Her gaze flicks from Will's eyes to his full lips, to his broad shoulders and strong arms, to the solidity and strength of his chest beneath his white shirt, top button undone, the tie loosened. He looks so undone, so dishevelled, that her fingers dance at her sides, desperate to touch him.

Will's not smiling anymore. There's an intensity to his gaze that makes something inside her hollow. His lips part as his chest rises and falls. He's breathing faster, as is she, as though there's not enough air between them. Time slows, then speeds up again as Will moves towards her, then his body's pressed against hers, his mouth on hers. She gasps into him as her back hits the wall.

They move against each other, desperate and hungry and Jude disappears into the darkness behind her closed eyelids, into the feel of him, the smell of him, the weight of his body against hers. She isn't aware of the cool breeze from the open front door or the bag strap cutting into her shoulder; she's lost in the feel of his lips on her neck, the prickle of his cropped hair beneath her fingertips, the warmth of his skin.

'I'll tell my mum!' The shout yanks her back to reality, and she twists her head from Will's. He leaps away from her, his eyes on the slowly opening living room door.

'Mum.' Betsy leans her body into the hallway, keeping hold of the door. 'Milly said that I'm not allowed to have a go on Roblox until she's finished her game and I've already been waiting ages.' She draws out the last word.

'I . . . I . . .' Jude looks from her daughter to Will – wide-eyed, panting lightly, his tie askew. 'I'm sure you won't have to wait very long.'

'Yeah, but I've already—'

'Milly!' Will heads for the living room. 'What did I tell you about sharing when you have guests over?'

'Whatever!' His daughter's voice carries from deep inside the room.

There's a weight to Will's sigh, which isn't just a reaction to his daughter's rudeness and, when he turns to look at

Jude, there's frustration, and longing, in his eyes. 'Do you want to go and look for the earring? I'll deal with this.'

She touches a hand to her lips. They feel bruised, the skin around her mouth singing from the prickle of his stubble. 'Yeah.' She flashes him a smile that reflects his frustration. 'Yeah sure, if you don't mind.'

She hurries up the stairs, catching Milly's plaintive 'It's so unfair!' wail from the living room as she crosses the landing and hurries into Will's room. She heads for the bed and drops to her knees.

What's the worst that can happen if she takes Robyn's diary? Her fingers brush the edge of the box. If Will finds out that she stole it he might ban Milly from having anything to do with Betsy, and her daughter would lose her best friend.

Her hand falls away from the box.

She couldn't do that to Betsy. But what if she doesn't read the diary? Could she honestly keep sleeping with Will with that whisper of suspicion at the back of her mind? Could she leave Betsy alone with a man who'd potentially murdered two people? In her heart she doesn't believe it. It's noise and bluster, whispers and gossip. An innocent man has been accused of something he didn't do – just like her dad. Reading Robyn's diary could put everything to bed. It might answer unanswered questions, shed light on why she left him or where she is now. It might explain why the police closed the investigation. It might give her the ammo she needs to tell Victoria Routledge to shut the fuck up, and stop another man from being hounded to his death.

Before she can change her mind again, Jude pulls out the box, removes the diary and shoves it deep into the black hole of her handbag. The stomp-stomp of small feet charging up the stairs startles her and she shoves the lid back onto the box. The door to the bedroom flies open just as she's shoved it back under the bed.

'What are you doing?' The indignant shape of Milly Ledger is an angry little painting in the centre of the doorframe.

'Looking for my earring.' Still on her hands and knees Jude smiles tightly, a trapped nerve pulsating beneath her eye.

'I told you!' Betsy appears beside her friend. 'I said Mum was just looking for her earring.'

'This isn't her room. It's Dad and Robyn's room. She shouldn't be in here.'

Jude shifts back onto her haunches, startled by the anger in the young girl's eyes. It's been eighteen months since Robyn disappeared and Milly's obviously still grieving. The thoughts, dreams and fears of the woman she loved are in the bottom of Jude's leather bag. The weight of the theft rests heavily. This isn't about sleeping with Will, Betsy's friendships or proving Victoria wrong. It's about Robyn, and what happened to her. It's about giving this little girl peace.

'I'm sorry, Milly.' She gets to her feet and crosses the room. 'I didn't mean to upset you. I couldn't find my earring; it wasn't there.'

Milly steps back from the doorway to let Jude through, her arms still firmly crossed over her chest. 'Don't go in there again.'

'Or what?' Betsy says, but Jude takes her by the hand and whispers in her ear, 'Time to go. Please don't make a fuss.'

The scent of stewed beef and carrots envelops Jude as she reaches the hallway, scoops up Betsy's discarded coat and hisses at her to quickly put it on.

'Jude?' Will, in a black and white chef's apron has appeared in the open kitchen door. 'Did I tell you I saw Andy Routledge coming out of the park earlier, looking like he'd been punched in the face? About time someone did that. I've never met someone more in need of a—' He breaks off, his eyes clouding with confusion as Betsy pulls on her coat. 'You're not off, are you? I was about to serve up.'

Jude searches for a plausible reason for their hasty exit but, where once there was a working brain, now there's porridge.

'Milly shouted at her,' Betsy says indignantly. 'She said she shouldn't be in your and Robyn's bed—'

'Betsy, shh.' Jude yanks on her hand.

'God, she didn't did she?' Will runs a hand over his hair then takes a step into the hallway and shouts up the stairs. 'Milly, get down here now!'

'Oh, no. Please don't tell her off!' Jude lets go of Betsy's hand and rushes to Will's side. She touches a hand to his arm and lowers her voice. 'She's still grieving. It's why she still likes you to buy Robyn's favourite foods. It's really not my place but I think you should take her to see someone. It's important to talk—' Her hand falls away from his arm. His whole demeanour has changed. It's as though he's turned to stone.

'Don't tell me how to parent my child.' There's a warning tone to his whisper, a low growl in his throat.

She takes a step away from him, chastised and unsettled. 'Sure, sure. Absolutely. Like I said, it's not my place—'

Before she can finish her sentence, he turns away, stalks back into the kitchen, and closes the door.

Chapter 27

ROBYN'S DIARY

Just a quick one today because I'm about to do the school run and I'm making a bit of extra effort with my hair and make-up because, like the absolute twat that I am, I've got a crush on one of the dads. ARRRRGGGGGH. So embarrassing. I mean, if the other women are more interested in talking to each other than to me, who else am I supposed to talk to but random dads standing all by themselves?

Anyway, somehow, I've become ridiculously obsessed with A. I don't know if it's the fact that he's a policeman, so he's got that air of authority that makes me feel a bit giddy, the fact he's got piercing Paul Hollywood eyes that seem to look straight through me, or the way he's really focused on me when we talk, not looking over my shoulder to see who else is about. Anyway, like I said, it's just a stupid crush and I'm pretty sure he'd never make a move, being married and everything. Although, if the Queen Bee is to be believed, he's had his head turned before (and so has she!). I'm not stupid, or self-obsessed enough to think I'm the only one he flirts with. I've seen the way he looks at some of the other mums – mums who are beautiful, charming, sexy and confident. Basically, everything I'm not . . .

There's another husband who gives off major ladykiller vibes but more about that another time. Lowbridge is definitely full of secrets, and I intend to uncover them all . . .

Chapter 28

Victoria

MONDAY

'Where are we going, Mum?'

'How much longer is it going to take?'

'Are there any more snacks?'

'I need the loo.'

The questions from the back seat keep on coming, each one a sharp poke in Victoria's brain. She's not, and has never been, a spontaneous person. In her world safety lies in keeping a schedule, writing lists, and checking the calendar, but she was so frustrated, so infuriated, after her visit to the police station earlier that, when she arrived in the playground for pick-up she headed for Sara like a heat-seeking missile, then gathered her children and loaded them into the car.

'Where even *is* Devon?' comes Sophia's wail from the back.

'It's where thieves run away to when they're too gutless to admit to their crimes.' The words are out of her mouth before her brain's had a chance to filter them.

'What thieves?' *Now* Noah is interested. He's obsessed with the *Girl Called Justice* books by Elly Griffiths and anything that sounds even remotely crime-like makes his ears prick up.

'Smugglers.' She's got no clue whether Devon has a history of smuggling or not but it's by the coast, so it feels like a safe bet. Safer than telling him the truth about her real mission, which is to confront Theresa Fairchild face to face. Sara was loath to give up Theresa's address but when the other women gathered around them, attracted by the whiff of conflict in the playground air, she swiftly backed down and forwarded a text.

'Are we going to explore some smugglers' caves?' There's so much excitement in Noah's voice that Victoria feels like the worst mum in the world.

'Not this time, darling. There's someone I need to talk to. Theresa,' she says, over Noah's disappointed moan. 'You'll remember her, Sophia. She's Pixie's mum.'

Her ten-year-old daughter shrugs noncommittally. Anyone outside her immediate circle of friends doesn't really exist.

'Anyway,' Victoria says as Google Maps updates to reveal that they're one minute away from their destination. 'We're there now. I want you both to stay in the car while I go and have a quick chat with Theresa.'

This time both the children groan.

Victoria views Theresa and Tony Fairchild's new house with a critical eye. She'd expected an upgrade from their Lowbridge house but, whilst the home is detached, with a large driveway and bucolic countryside setting, it lacks

IT'S ALWAYS THE HUSBAND

character. The cream, pebble-dashed exterior looks tired and dated. The windows are small and in need of replacing and the extension, tacked onto the side, above the garage, suggests that there isn't much space in the main body of the house.

She heads for the front door, the knot in her stomach tightening. She was all fire and brimstone when she left the police station earlier but now she's getting nervous. She knows Theresa well enough to anticipate some bite-back if she goes in hard on her, and she's not so bulletproof that it doesn't hurt when she's verbally attacked. Bullied for most of Year 7 at secondary school, it wasn't until she proved herself to be quite the athlete, picked for all the school teams, that she was able to pull a tribe around herself for protection. Deep down she's as shit-scared as everyone else.

She knocks, sharply, three times, on the weathered front door, then takes a step back. Whatever Theresa comes at her with she'll go harder. She's not the thief here. She didn't steal from her friends.

She waits for thirty seconds, forty, looking and listening for any sign of movement from within the house, then she knocks again, louder this time. Still, nothing. Did Theresa spot her pulling into the driveway? Is she hiding away from the windows, pretending that there's no one at home? There's no other car on the driveway but that doesn't mean it isn't locked away in the garage. Victoria knocks a third time then steps onto the patio and peers in at the first window. What she sees is a surprisingly light and airy modern living room with the same bold yellow leather sofa she'd seen in the online photos of the Fairchild's Lowbridge home, a crushed velvet turquoise sofa, laminate flooring and a squared archway leading through to a modern kitchen. The previous owners must have extended not just the side of the house, but the back as well. She leans closer to the glass, examining the bookcases and alcoves for any sign of her beautiful Eames bird but, other than a couple of framed photographs of the family, the room is devoid of ornaments and trinkets. No doubt Victoria's prized possession is still hidden away in a box in the bedroom, along with Caz's ornament and Audrey's glass bowl.

Anger washes away her uncertainty and she moves on to the second window on the ground floor of the house, only to jolt in terror when a male voice calls out, 'You there, can I help you?'

She turns to see a grey-haired man with a sizeable nose and a large liver spot on his right cheek, peering at her from above the long line of the fence.

Feeling herself pinken she flashes him her most dazzling smile then says, 'Yes. I'm a friend of Theresa's. She asked me to pop by but there doesn't appear to be anyone in.'

'That'll be because they've taken themselves off to the pub, my dear. She was only telling me yesterday that the children have a sleepover tonight, so she and Tony decided to make the most of it and go out.' He pauses, his brow wrinkling above his bushy eyebrows. 'Odd that she didn't mention anything to you though, inviting you over and all.'

'It must have slipped her mind. Happens to the best of us.' Aware of movement from the car, restless children, probably punching each other in the back seat, Victoria gets straight to the point. 'I don't suppose you know which pub they've gone to?'

'Sure I do. It'll be the Doe and Farrow.' The man's eyes narrow as he studies her reaction. 'You not from round here? I'm good with faces and I can't place you at all.'

'No,' Victoria says tightly. 'I'm not. Anyway, I really must get back to my—'

'Surprise is it? This visit? Stopping round to visit an old friend?'

IT'S ALWAYS THE HUSBAND

Her lips tighten over her teeth. 'Something like that. I'll certainly be a surprise.'

The Doe and Farrow looks exactly as Victoria imagined it to be: thatched roof, stonework, low beams, log-burning fires and the scent of ale and history, hanging in the air. Sophia and Noah trail after her as she steps into the belly of the pub and surveys the clientele. Having the children witness her confrontation with Theresa was *not* part of her plan but there is no way she can leave them in the car for a second time, not if she wants both of them to remain alive by the time she gets back.

'Can I have a Coke?' Noah says from behind her.

'And crisps,' Sophia adds.

'No. Yes. Maybe.' She's too preoccupied with her search for Theresa to work out the logistics of feeding and watering the children.

'Which one is it?' her daughter whines as, out of the corner of her eye, Victoria spots the squat, rotund shapes of Theresa and Anthony Fairchild sitting at a table near the open log fire. The pub is warm and stuffy, and Theresa's cheeks are pink and shiny as she surveys the menu in her hands, a glass of red wine nearby.

'Here.' Victoria rummages around in her bag for her purse then presses a twenty-pound note into her daughter's hand. 'Take your brother to the bar and order what you want. Don't go anywhere. Stay by the bar. I'm going to talk to Theresa and then I'll be back.' She takes a step then stops and turns back. 'Not alcohol, obviously.'

Sophia rolls her eyes in that special display of exasperation she saves solely for her mother, and mutters, 'As if.' Before either child can complain about anything else, Victoria heads across the room towards Tony and Theresa.

Several of the older, male customers stare at her as she walks past them, but it takes a good ten or twenty seconds before Theresa senses her presence and looks up. Her grip on the menu doesn't loosen and her cheeks remain rosy, but Victoria catches the flash of fear in her eyes.

'Victoria?' Tony fills the silence then gazes behind her. 'Andy not with you?'

She gives him a *what the actual fuck* look then her gaze swings back to Theresa. 'You left Lowbridge suddenly. Any particular reason?' She can hear the sharpening to her tone, knows she's giving off Queen Bitch vibes, but her indignation and anger are so heightened that she really doesn't care.

Tony sits up taller in his seat, his Labrador eagerness still buoyant. 'Lowbridge was wonderful, but we wanted to move closer to T's par—'

Theresa cuts him off. 'What are you doing here?'

'More to the point, why are you a thief?'

'Oh, come on now,' says Tony, his docile expression gone. 'You can't just come over here and start accusing—'

'You took my Eames bird,' Victoria talks over him like his monotone voice is just background noise. 'And you took Audrey's Venetian bowl and Caz's Tiffany ornament. We're pretty sure you took Shahina's gift card too. Don't bother denying it – we've got proof.' The last bit is a lie but when has she let that stop her before?

'I'm not having this conversation.' Theresa gets to her feet in such a hurry that she knocks against the table, sending both glasses of red wine flying. Tony leaps up from his seat as red wine splashes over his pale blue jumper and beige chino slacks.

'I want our things back, and I want an apology. Otherwise, I'm going to the police.' Victoria body-checks Theresa as she tries to pass her but the other woman, whilst shorter and less fit, is considerably heavier and when she barrels towards her, barking, 'Move!' her shoulder barge knocks Victoria out of the way.

'T!' Tony calls after her. 'Don't leave. We haven't ordered yet.'

'I'm going to the toilet. Make sure that bitch is gone by the time I get back.'

The other diners react with raised eyebrows, smirks and unimpressed headshakes, but Victoria's too far gone to care.

'Your wife is a thief,' she says to Tony, staring after his wife, still dripping with red wine. 'She came into our homes, as our guest, and she stole from us, then she crept off to Devon. Don't bother denying it because I saw the video you posted to Facebook, all our stolen stuff in a box.'

'I . . . I . . .' He gawps at her. 'I don't know what—'

'A gold bird, a blue glass bowl, a penguin ornament, a gift card. Ring any bells?'

'Um . . .' He blinks rapidly, sweat dampening the salt and pepper hair at his temples. 'Um . . .' His gaze shifts away from Victoria to the space behind her. She twists around, following his gaze. Sophia is standing at the bar, Noah beside her, chewing on his thumb. There's no sign of Theresa. She hasn't returned to save her husband. He's going to have to deal with this alone.

'There's no point you lying.' She looks back at him. 'I know you know what I'm talking about. I took a screenshot.'

Tony swallows and rubs a hand over his face. 'We had several boxes of knick-knacks that we donated to a charity shop recently.'

'A charity shop! The bird alone was worth two *thousand* pounds. Tell me you're joking?'

'I'm afraid not.'

'Which charity shop?'

'I don't know.'

'Well maybe the police can help jog your memory. Let's ring them now shall we? See what they have to say?' She slips her phone out of her pocket but, before she can touch the screen with her thumb, he lays a warning hand on her arm.

'Please, don't.' There's desperation in his eyes now. Aware of the other diners still watching them, he steps closer to her and lowers his voice. 'She's not well. She's not been well for a while. The stealing, it's a . . . it's a symptom. It resurfaces when she's mentally suffering.'

Victoria frowns, trying to process what she's hearing. Theresa's a kleptomaniac. Really? Or is Tony just telling her that to try and gain her sympathy, and get his wife off the hook?

'She's been battling it for years,' he adds, as though he can read the scepticism on Victoria's face. 'It started when she was a child, during her parents' divorce, and grew out of control when she was a student, sitting her final ex—' He breaks off, his eyes wide and startled.

'She's behind me, isn't she?' Victoria spins around to find Theresa's face inches from hers.

'What have you told her?' Theresa glares, accusingly, at her husband. 'I thought I told you to get rid of her.'

'Darling . . .' Tony steps around Victoria to reach his wife but when he tries to lay a hand on her arm she snatches it away.

'Get out.' The snarl is aimed at Victoria.

'Not until you apologise for what you've done.'

'What *I've* done? Fuck you.'

She tries to read the other woman's face to make sense of the words that are coming out of her mouth and fails. She thought she knew her but it's like looking at a stranger. 'I don't know what you're talking about.'

IT'S ALWAYS THE HUSBAND

Theresa's laugh is a short, sharp bark of disbelief. 'You always were a lying bitch.'

Her eyes are shining, her cheeks are flushed and she's twisting her hands together as though she's frantically washing them. In the whole time she's known Theresa, Victoria has never seen her so wired, so unhinged, so utterly disconnected from reality and it terrifies her. She looks back at Tony, but there's no fear or confusion in his eyes when he meets her gaze. Instead he looks exhausted, a man desperate to escape but too tired to run.

'Tony!' Victoria snaps, checking on her children who are drink-free and waving desperately at her from the bar. The barman's looking at her too and shaking his head. Shit, he won't let them buy a drink.

'What's Theresa talking about?' she asks Tony, torn between finding out the truth and getting to the children before they have a huge meltdown.

Tony glances back at his wife, as though checking for her permission, then sighs heavily. 'The blackmail.'

'What?'

'Someone in Lowbridge was blackmailing her about her . . .' he coughs lightly then lowers his voice '. . . kleptomania. They said they'd go to the police if she didn't pay them twenty thousand pounds.'

Victoria stares at him, her mind clouded with shock as Theresa hovers in her peripheral vision like a ghoul.

'I told her to just ignore it,' Tony continues, 'but they wouldn't leave her alone. They kept on and on, saying they'd go to the police and ruin her career if she didn't pay up. Eventually it got so bad I told her that we should go to the police ourselves – blackmail's a serious crime – but she was terrified she'd be revealed as a thief and hounded out of Lowbridge. She just wanted to get out of there and never go back. Please, please just leave us alone. She's not well. I'm taking her to Cornwall tomorrow for a couple of days. Please, never come here again.'

Victoria glances back at Theresa but she's stalked off and is halfway to the front door. 'Did she tell anyone?' she asks Tony. 'Anyone in our friendship group about the blackmail? Sara, maybe. Did she tell her?'

Tony laughs drily. 'God no. She didn't tell anyone. She thought the blackmailer was you.'

Chapter 29

Sorrell

MONDAY

With the two eldest children arguing over which YouTube video to watch in the living room, and Scout napping upstairs, Sorrell turns on the radio in the kitchen, opens the fridge and looks inside. It's 4 p.m. Too early for wine? The school run was as horrific as she'd anticipated. There was no sign of Victoria in the playground, but the other women were gathered around Audrey, listening intently as she held court, their eyes wide, their mouths agape. Dawn spotted Sorrell first then the rest all followed, swivelling on the spot like weird mechanical figures. Only Sara shot her a sympathetic look. Sorrell put her head down, avoided eye contact and dragged Henry and Harper from their friends, promising ice-creams if they left the playground quickly, without a fuss. Miraculously they complied; ice-cream in October was an unusual and magical treat.

She closes the fridge. As tempting as wine is – and as much as she needs it – she's home alone with the children because Finnley still isn't back from work. She also needs to be sober when she goes into her studio. She's done the bare minimum over the last couple of days and guilt's been nagging at her. Wyrethorpe Fayre – the biggest craft fair in the area – is on in three weeks' time, and she's barely got anything to sell there. Normally her stall would be piled high with jugs, mugs, vases and wall plaques, but she's looking at half a dozen mugs, a handful of seconds and her students' pots unless she gets a move on. No matter how scary and unpredictable her life's become, she's still got to provide for her family and her work won't throw itself.

But first, dinner. She reopens the fridge and takes out an onion, some mince, mushrooms and a red pepper and puts them on the kitchen counter. Then she takes a packet of spaghetti and some Bolognese sauce from the cupboard. Simple, easy, the kids like it, and she hasn't got the brain space to do anything else. As she peels and chops the onion, she pauses to turn up the radio. The news has just come on.

'. . . news just in about the hit-and-run victim who was taken to Mallhampton General after an incident just outside Mallow.' Sorrell freezes as the newsreader's authoritative voice fills her kitchen. 'The police have reported that the victim, Sherri Toser, forty-seven, died at 7.13 this morning. Her family were by her side. The police are increasing their efforts to find the individual responsible and are asking that anyone who was in the area between 9 p.m. and 11.30 p.m. and saw anything suspicious, or has dashcam footage that may be useful, to please get in touch.'

The newsreader moves on to the next topic – the House of Lords delaying Government legislation – but Sorrell is no longer listening. She's pinned in place, staring at the radio. Amit *still* hasn't confirmed whether he was at the Bat and Badger with Finnley the night Sherri Toser was hit by a car and now she's not just worried that Finnley hit someone and drove off, she's also terrified that he killed her. She's going to have to talk to him. She can't deal with this alone anymore.

Her phone vibrates on the countertop, making her jump. There's a message but no name, just a jumble of numbers, a contact that she hasn't saved. Her blackmailer has been suspiciously quiet all day.

Think you're clever do you? the text says.

'Fuck off!' the words explode from her but in the next breath she's glancing guiltily behind her, listening for the children. But they're still arguing in the living room, her cry lost to the noise of their shouts.

Her phone pings again. *You don't get to play games with me, Sorrell.*

Ping! *Try that shit again and just wait and see what happens. I know where you live.*

Ping! *Finnley will get more time in jail now that poor woman is dead.*

Ping! *You have until midnight to transfer the money to my PayPal account or I'll hand over the evidence to the police.*

Sorrell's thumbs fly over the screen as she bangs out a response. *You do that and I'll show them this text thread as evidence that you're blackmailing me.*

Ping! *They'll have to find me first. And your husband will be in jail for five years. Make sure the kids give him a kiss before they go to bed because it's the last time they're going to be able to do that for a very long time.*

She wishes the blackmailer would show up at her door.

She doesn't care if they're male or female, scrawny or a bodybuilder. The rage that's boiling inside her has given her the strength of a dozen people. If anyone comes for her family, she'll destroy them.

There's no evidence that Finnley hit ANYONE, she types back. *He wasn't anywhere near where the accident happened. I'm not falling for your bullshit anymore. After this message I'm blocking your number. You say you know where I live but you're too gutless to turn up at the door. Well, the game's over. I'M DONE.*

Her thumb slides over the screen but, before she can hit 'Block & report spam' her phone pings with another message.

Oh, I've got evidence, Sorrell.

A voice note appears and, bracing herself, she hits play.

'Where are you? Pick up your phone!' It's Finnley, sounding frantic. *'I just hit something. They came out of nowhere and I slammed on the brakes but there . . . there . . . there was a thump. I definitely hit them. Please, please pick up. I don't know what to do. You have to help me. Robyn, please!'*

Chapter 30

Andy

MONDAY

Andy's stretched out on the sofa, a blanket over his body and *Raging Bull* playing on the TV (comfort viewing, he's watched it so many times). He's been in pretty much the same position since Lee dropped him off and, now the local anaesthetic in his gums is wearing off, the extraction site is throbbing like hell. The combination of the pain in his mouth, his sluggishness post-sedation and the emptiness of his two-bedroom flat have had an effect on his mood. He just wants to see his kids. What he'd give for a hug from Sophia and the unfiltered excitement on little Noah's face.

His heart constricts as his gaze drifts towards the DNA paternity test on the coffee table. It was waiting for him in his mailbox when he got back from the dentist. He's opened it and read the instruction sheet, but he feels sick just looking at it. The next time he sees Noah he'll have to swab the inside of his mouth and lie about why he's doing it. He could kill Victoria for what she's putting him through but he's lashed out once already – at the man she cheated on him with – but he has to be more careful now. If Noah is his, and he prays to God that he is, he's going to do everything he can to ensure that he's always a part of both children's lives. He can't risk losing them forever by doing something he'll live to regret. And if Noah isn't his? That's something he's trying hard not to think about.

Tap, tap, tap. The knocking at the front door makes him start. Could it be Victoria, bringing the children to see him? Has Sophia shown her the message he sent her? Maybe, by thinking about his children he manifested a bit of compassion in his ex-wife's cold and bitter heart?

Grunting, he throws off the blanket and eases himself up off the sofa, leaves the living room and, still a little off balance from the sedation, gingerly makes his way down the hall. He unlocks the door, opens it, and gawps at the person in front of him.

It's someone he never, ever, thought he'd see at his door.

Chapter 31

Sorrell

MONDAY

At the sound of a key turning in the front door Sorrell grips the edge of the kitchen table and fights to control her breathing as waves of adrenaline course through her body.

Finnley is home.

She listens, breathing shallowly, as he removes his shoes at the front door, pads into the living room and asks the children about school. It's been half an hour since the last text from her blackmailer arrived, but she quelled the urge to ring her husband. She needs to look him in the eye when she asks him about Robyn. That way she can analyse every twitch, shift and tightening in the muscles of his face.

'Hello, love.' He strolls into the kitchen, his tone casual – but there's tension in his body – and he flips the switch of the kettle. 'I'm just going upstairs to get changed and then—'

'Sit down.'

He starts at the sharp edge to her voice and there's a flash of fear in his eyes.

'Finnley.' She gestures at the chair across the table from her. It's where he's sat, many times for family dinners, but from his pained expression as he moves across the kitchen, it may as well be an electric chair.

'What's up?' he says, feigning ignorance as he sits down and it's all Sorrell can do not to throw her phone at his face. 'Are the kids—'

'The kids are fine.' She doesn't recognise her own voice. She's speaking quietly, so as not to alert the children, but there's a power to her words that she hasn't heard before. The adrenaline that made her so fearful is now preparing her for a fight. 'This is about you . . . and Robyn.'

And there it is again – the shocked widening of his eyes – along with a sharp intake of breath. 'I—'

She holds up a hand, interrupting him. 'Don't even bother to lie. I know everything. I've heard the voicemail you sent Robyn about the hit-and-run.'

That's all she's got on him, but she's not going to let him know that. There's no way she's going to give him the space to wriggle into a lie. She looks at him steadily, expecting a shift from shocked to defensiveness and is surprised to see relief in his eyes. He rests an elbow on the table, drops his chin to his hand and lowers his gaze. 'How long have you known?'

'Long enough.'

She can see the beginning of a bald spot on the crown of his head, a pink patch of skin with sparse dark hairs, circling the whirlpool of his scalp. It's something she's never noticed before. How long has she been asleep?

'I . . . I . . .' Still he can't bring himself to look at her. 'I never meant to fall in love.'

IT'S ALWAYS THE HUSBAND

His words pierce the armour of her anger, and she presses a hand to her chest, instinctively protecting her heart. A one-night stand or a fling she was prepared for, but not love.

There are so many questions she could ask him, about Robyn's disappearance, about Will, about the police investigation, about the lies Finnley told on their doorstep, but they're all secondary to the pain that's pulsing through her.

'How long?' is all she can say.

'A while.' He risks a glimpse at her face then guiltily lowers his head. 'Nearly two years if you count her disappearance.'

'Two years!' A dagger she hadn't been expecting. 'Scout is nine months old!'

'I'm sorry.' Finnley cradles his head in his hands and croaks something she can't hear.

'What was that?' She pulls at his wrist, forcing him to look at her. 'What did you just say?'

He raises his head slowly. 'I thought Robyn was dead. I was . . . I was trying to move on.'

Sorrell stares at her husband, too stunned to speak.

'We had an affair,' Finnley mumbles, 'for several months but she called it off, about a month before she vanished. She said she had to because she was scared of Will and what he would do if he found out about us. She said he was already suspicious of her creeping out all the time to meet me and we couldn't start a new life together because—'

'You were going to leave me, for Robyn? You were going to leave *our children* . . .' something breaks in her voice as she says 'children' '. . . for her?'

Finnley rubs his hands over his eyes as they fill with fat, self-pitying tears. 'I didn't mean to fall in love with her. You have to believe me—'

'Believe you? Fuck off, Finn!'

'I wasn't looking for an affair, I swear, but Robyn and I got on so well and I was . . . I don't know if it was family life or getting older or being a bit bored—'

'Bored! Could you not have taken up golf like a normal man? Or bought a motorbike or painted Warhammer figures in the shed, you fucking arsehole! Bored! Don't you *dare* use that as an excuse.'

'I know. I know.' He shakes his head so pathetically that Sorrell imagines the sharp sting of his cheek beneath the flat of her palm.

'Did you help her disappear? Was that the plan you cooked up together? To get her away from Will?'

'No! I swear. I was as shocked as everyone else when she disappeared. I . . . I . . . was terrified that she and Will had argued and he'd killed her, that everything she was worried about had happened.'

'You lied to the police on our doorstep when they asked you how well you knew her.'

'I panicked because you were right there beside me. I couldn't tell them the truth. I planned on going to see them separately but when they arrested Will I figured I didn't need to. I was grieving her loss. I didn't know what to think and—'

'You grieved for Robyn, while you were lying next to me in our bed?' She's never hated anyone in her life as much as she hates Finnley right now. 'That's why you didn't go to work for ten days after she disappeared, isn't it? You didn't have a virus at all. So . . .' she stares intently at him, the noise in her brain quietening '. . . the depression. Recently. Was that all bullshit too?'

'It was fear . . . and frustration. She sent me a message six months ago – out of the blue. She made me swear not to tell anyone that she was alive, that she'd fled Lowbridge after a blazing row with Will. She said she was struggling, that she missed me, that ending things was the worst mistake of her life. I tried to get her to meet up with me but she was too scared. She thought I might be followed, that somehow Will might find out. And it got . . . it got too much for me, her constantly cancelling on me. I just wanted to help her, to make sure she was safe and—'

'When you said *I don't want to be here anymore* I thought you were talking about killing yourself. Do you know how scared I was? That you'd leave our children without a father, and me alone? No, you don't because what you actually meant was that you wanted to be with her instead of us, you absolute piece of shit.'

The tears reappear, rolling down his cheeks as the sound of Harper and Henry arguing drifts into the kitchen from the living room. She eyes the tears dispassionately, her heart an icy rock in her chest. Finnley's not her husband anymore. He's the most miserable, pathetic self-serving, selfish prick she's ever met.

'You weren't in the Bull and Badger with Amit, were you?' Sorrell says, everything suddenly clear. 'And you didn't have a panic attack, did you? At least not for the reason you told me. It was because Robyn didn't show up, wasn't it? You left in a tizzy, hit an animal and rang her and when she didn't pick up, you called me.' Her lips form a thin, tight line as anger surges through her body. 'Because I'll always pick up the pieces, won't I? I'll hug you and console you and sleep with you, and take care of the children and pay the bills and buy food, and organise our holidays and buy the birthday and Christmas presents and every other fucking thing that holds this family together. I'm reliable and stable even though I'm a bit boring and—'

'Please. Please don't.' Finnley reaches for her hand but she snatches her arm away.

'Get out.' The words are a low growl between gritted teeth. 'Get the fuck out of my house, RIGHT NOW.'

Chapter 32

Jude

TUESDAY

She doesn't know if it was a reaction to Will's coldness yesterday afternoon, some 'off' red wine she picked up from the corner shop on her way home with Betsy, or the one day out of date M&S prawns with cocktail sauce that she scoffed after dinner, but *something* (and she's pretty sure it was the prawns) kept her up with the worst upset stomach of her life. She'd only managed to read three entries in Robyn's diary in the stretch of time between Betsy going to bed and the food poisoning beginning and, as tempting as it was to take Robyn's diary into the toilet with her at 10 p.m., 12 a.m., 3 a.m., and 5 a.m., it just felt wrong. Besides, she was terrified of damaging it in such a way that, when she did eventually return it, Will would suspect that something was up.

Not that Will's even speaking to her at the moment, so

it's not a case of *when* she returns the book but *if*. It hurt more than she'd expect it to when he'd blanked her on the school run just now. Their eyes had met across a crowded playground then, almost as though she was a complete stranger, he'd turned his back on her. She hadn't been *that* critical of his parenting style had she? What had she even said to him? That he shouldn't shout at Milly because the child was still grieving. It was true. Okay, so maybe it *wasn't* her place to say those things – even if they were true – but she couldn't bear listening to Will chastising his daughter when she was the one who'd been sneaking about.

She'll give him a bit more time to cool off, she tells herself as she heads home from the school run, then give him a ring and apologise (hoping to God that he doesn't cancel Betsy and Milly's playdate tomorrow). She hears her sister's voice in her ear as she walks: *how many times do I have to tell you – just stay the hell away.*

As strong as their sexual attraction is, and how compatible their sense of humour is, the truth is they hardly know each other at all. Emma might see things in black and white but she doesn't have a child who cried herself to sleep because she doesn't have any friends, and she's pretty sure (from a few indiscreet comments her sister made once when they were drunk) that Angus isn't the type of man to push her up against a wall and kiss her like the world is ending.

There aren't many entries in Robyn's diary – and when Jude flicked through it she discovered the last few pages had been ripped out. From the snippets she's read so far, she's learned that Robyn didn't feel able to fully open up to Will about how lonely she was after her move to Lowbridge or how she'd struggled to make friends with the other school mums. And she's pretty sure she didn't tell him about her crush on Andy Routledge.

IT'S ALWAYS THE HUSBAND

Yesterday, after Jude had stolen the diary and was helping Betsy into her coat, Will had shouted from the kitchen that he'd seen Andy jogging around the park and that the man deserved a punch in the face. She didn't give it much thought at the time – assuming his dislike of the man was to do with the police investigation – but now, in the light of what she's read in the diary there's another possible reason for his hatred. Maybe Robyn and Andy did have an affair, and Will found out.

More worrying is the thought that Will could be capable of violence. In the short time she's known him he's seemed so measured – more cerebral than physical – but if he could imagine himself punching Andy in the face then perhaps she's got him wrong. Maybe he did have something to do with Robyn's disappearance after all. Or maybe Andy did? Maybe Robyn threatened to tell Victoria, so he killed her? It would certainly explain why the police investigation found nothing and then stalled.

Jude feels certain that, if Robyn's diary can't answer her questions, then maybe Andy can.

Only, he was nowhere to be seen during school drop-off. She overheard Sara and Dawn talking about the fact he'd had a tooth extracted on Monday. Sara's friend, a receptionist at the dentist, had gossiped to her about the fact Andy looked like he'd gone ten rounds with Anthony Joshua. An arrest gone wrong, he'd said.

But what if that was a lie . . .

Chapter 33

Sorrell

TUESDAY

Sorrell stands outside Will Ledger's front door, her mind in free fall, repeatedly thumping the painted wood with her fist. She'd missed him on the school run and had practically run to his house afterwards. She's been knocking for five minutes now and, wherever he is, he's definitely not in.

Yesterday afternoon, after she'd hissed at Finnley to get out, she'd remained in the kitchen, head in her hands, as the stairs creaked under the weight of her husband as he went upstairs to pack a bag. He didn't return to the kitchen to speak to her before he left, but he did pop into the living room and loudly declare to the children that he was going away to a conference and he'd be gone for a week. More lies. She was pretty sure he was heading straight to Robyn.

When the front door had clicked shut behind him, Sorrell snatched up her phone and called her blackmailer. She was going to let that bitch know exactly what she thought of her. But she ended the call before it could connect. Why give Robyn the satisfaction of knowing how much she'd hurt her when she could get her revenge instead?

The one thing she hadn't confronted Finnley with was the fact that Robyn had been blackmailing her. That would have wiped the morose, self-pitying expression from his face. Well, he'd find out when the police turned up to arrest her, only there was the small matter of telling Robyn's husband first.

Only Will's not at home and the thought of sitting alone in an airless police interview room terrifies her. She's not the one who should be under the microscope and questioned. Robyn's the one who should be afraid.

She turns away from Will's front door, trying to find the courage to go to the police station alone, when a face flashes up in her mind – the brow low and heavy, above the palest blue eyes; eyes that narrow for those he can't stand, but the biggest, most charming smile for those that he likes. Sorrell's been on the receiving end of Andy's smile; she's shared the occasional school gate chat with him about their children. Instinctively she feels that he's the right person to talk to. God knows he's been looking for Robyn long enough.

She knows where Andy lives. She overheard Victoria describing his new-build flat at her drinks party. She'll go and pay him a visit. A smile pricks at the corner of her mouth as she heads down the street to the bus stop. For the first time since she listened to Finnley's voicemail to Robyn, she finally feels in control. Robyn's probably wondering why she hasn't replied to her last message, but she'll find out soon. Very, very soon.

Chapter 34

Victoria

TUESDAY

Victoria views the other school mums with new eyes as she ushers Sophia and Noah along the pavement, through the gates and into the school. She says hello to Caz, Dawn, Sara, Audrey and Shahina as she passes them, but her smile doesn't quite reach her eyes. What she is looking for, in those brief exchanges, is signs of tension beneath their bright, friendly demeanours. Whoever has been blackmailing Theresa has to be secretly terrified that, one day, their dark secret will be brought into the light. And who better to do that, than her?

Morning school run over, it takes her less than ten minutes to drive into the centre of Lowbridge but, when she parks up in a side street, she takes a few seconds to gather her thoughts before she opens the door.

IT'S ALWAYS THE HUSBAND

She's kicking herself for not getting more information out of Theresa and Tony before she left Devon, but the children were desperate for food and something to drink and, as priorities go, the children always come first. By the time they arrived back in Lowbridge, via McDonald's, Sophia and Noah were happier and settled, but Victoria felt anything but. Whoever had blackmailed Theresa had been in her house or caught her stealing. As far as she knows, the only person Theresa's ever invited round is Sara, but she obviously doesn't suspect her, otherwise she wouldn't have told her she was leaving. So, either someone else went to Theresa's house and kept quiet about it, or she was caught in the act. But if the latter was true she'd know the identity of her blackmailer.

Last night, when she got home, Victoria logged onto Facebook and searched for Tony Fairchild's page in the hope she could message him for more information, but of course, she was blocked. After Sophia and Noah had changed into their pyjamas, she'd messaged Andy instead. As loath as she was to contact him for help, he was the only person who could help her solve the mystery:

Hyperthetically, if someone was being blackmailed because they'd been caught stealing, and they went to the police, could they be arrested for being a thief? Or would the police let the thief bit slide because blackmail is a more serious crime?

She paused, knowing how much of a pedant he was about grammar, checked the spelling of *hypothetically* on Google, corrected it and then continued. *NB: No one knows that the thief is a thief and if they were charged and convicted they'd have a lot to loose.*

Satisfied with her message, she clicked send.

Would he tell her to keep her stupid questions to herself? Or – worse than that – ignore her completely?

Thirty seconds later, three dots appeared on appeared at the top of the screen as he typed his reply and she girded herself for his reaction, desperately hoping that, for once in his life, he'd be reasonable and just answer her question.

The dots disappeared from the screen.

Sighing, she carried the phone into the kitchen, opened the fridge and, her gaze continually flicking back to the screen, poured herself a glass of white wine.

The dots reappeared.

She glugged at the wine, heard small feet running back and forth across the landing.

He was still typing.

She took another sip. Was he writing an essay? She bounced on her toes, nervous energy flowing through her. What would he say?

The word is 'Lose'.

She stared at what he'd written. What had she lost? Her gaze flicked up to the message she'd sent him, then she hurled her phone at the floor.

Now, cracked phone in her hand, she gets out of the car, and lightly jogs down the street. Andy might be able to ignore her text messages but he can't ignore her if she turns up. She'll make out it's something to do with the children then casually slip the blackmail question into the conversation. As much as she hates herself for doing it, she's not afraid to use charm to get what she wants. Even if it does mean being within one metre of her soon-to-be-ex.

She cuts through a back alley, pops out on the high street, and makes her way to the new-build apartment block. She's been there multiple times before to pick up the children, but she's never been inside. She normally buzzes Andy's flat, asks for Sophia and Noah, then waits for the kids to come flying down the stairs and out of the front door. This time she's going to have to go in. She knows Andy's in his flat because he texted Sophia earlier with a photo of him holding his jaw and the message: *Daddy had a tooth out today! I'm okay but no work for me tomorrow. Will pick you up after school as normal.*

But Victoria's not going to risk him refusing to let her in so she presses a finger to the buzzer labelled Mrs M Squire instead. If she can get into the building she can knock on Andy's door and there's only so long he'll be able to ignore *that*.

Mrs Squire is Andy's elderly neighbour. She's also the only person, other than Andy, to possess a key to his flat. He flatly refused to let Victoria have a key of her own, even though he knows the keycode to enter *her* house (she'd change it, but she hasn't got the first idea how). After a lot of cajoling and arguing about potential fires, accidents or heart attacks, he eventually agreed to give a key to his neighbour. That way, if he was ever late returning the children, and Victoria couldn't contact him, *someone* had access to his flat.

'Hello?' There's suspicion, or maybe weariness, in the voice that crackles through the speaker. 'Can I help you?'

Victoria smiles winningly at the CCTV camera above the buttons then, remembering that she's supposed to be worried about Andy, changes her expression accordingly.

'Hello, Mrs Squire,' she says, with just the right note of worry in her voice. 'I've popped round with some pain meds for Andy after he had a tooth extracted and he's not answering his buzzer. I'm worried about him. Could you let me in please so I can check he's okay?'

Mrs Squire, who obviously has no idea how acrimonious things are between the two of them, clucks sympathetically, then the buzzer sounds and the front door clicks open. She's in!

Chapter 35

Sorrell

TUESDAY

Sorrell is so lost in her own world as she gets off the bus and scurries down the high street that she doesn't notice Jude until she's only a couple of metres from Andy's apartment block. Jude is speaking into the door entry system, her back bent, her hair slicked to her head from the rain.

Before Sorrell can run away, Jude takes her finger from the button, straightens up and turns to look at her. Her jaw drops as their eyes meet.

'Oh my God! Sorrell! You're not here to see Andy as well, are you?'

Too shocked for her brain to come up with an alternative explanation she can only reply 'Yeah.'

They stare at each other, frozen by surprise until Jude laughs lightly, nervously. 'Mysterious. I'm guessing you have some sort of police enquiry too.'

'Something like that.' Sorrell can tell by the expression on Jude's face that she's acting weirdly – again – but she can't help herself. Running into one of the other school mums is so unexpected it's completely thrown her.

'Weird, that we'd both turn up at the same time,' Jude says and Sorrell nods. Surely she hasn't realised that Robyn's alive too? No, that's impossible. Unless Robyn and Finnley have told Will already, there's no way she could know. She's probably come to talk to Andy about something else, Sorrell decides, but it's still a hell of a coincidence that they've turned up to see him at the same time.

'I'm pretty sure he's number seven,' Jude says, turning back to the block of buzzers. 'His initials are A.R. right? He didn't answer so I tried number six. She said she's pretty sure that he's in.'

'She wouldn't let you in though?'

'Nope, she said they weren't allowed to buzz in visitors for other flats. Something about the tenancy agreement.'

Annoying.

As Jude nods, awkwardness steps in. They barely know each other and, other than their conversation about Milly's violin case, and a brief chat at Victoria's garden party, they haven't really spoken. Yes, there have been smiles and nods of acknowledgement at the school gates but neither of them has initiated conversation. Sorrell wanted to, but with her brain so preoccupied with Finnley, the hit-and-run and her blackmailer, she couldn't think of anything to say.

'Have you tried pizza?' She suggests now. 'Pretending you're a pizza delivery driver, I mean. Try one of the other flats. Tell them it's for Andy's flat, but he's not answering.'

Jude looks doubtful. 'I'll give it a try.'

She presses her thumb against the button for number three and delivers her pizza spiel. Ten seconds later there's a clicking sound and when Sorrell pushes at the front door it swings open.

Jude runs a hand over the back of her neck as they step inside the building. 'Okay, do you want to go up and see him first or should I? We can't both go up, unless you're having an affair with him too. I was joking!' she adds hastily. 'Sorry, I don't know why I said that. If you want to go up, I'm happy to wait.'

'I don't mind going second,' A smile creeps onto Sorrell's lips. 'To talk to him that is.'

She's not sure where risqué Sorrell has surfaced from. Maybe it's Jude. She's so quick to laugh, so relaxed in herself that Sorrell can't help but match her energy. It's like the ghost of her twenties has risen again. Finnley doesn't like 'gauche' women. He made that clear when they first started dating. Thinking about him deflates her. She's not here to banter with Jude, she's here to tell Andy that Robyn's still alive and she's turned her whole life upside down.

'You all right?' Jude asks.

'I'm fine.' Sorrell says tightly. 'You go first,' she adds. 'I don't mind waiting. Honestly. I'll be fine down here.'

Chapter 36

Jude

TUESDAY

Jude slows her pace, taking the stairs one at a time. Her initial burst of energy – to get her chat with Andy over and done with before she loses her nerve – has been replaced with confusion. She couldn't have been more surprised to find Sorrell standing outside Andy's flat too. It was the strangest coincidence and she'd tried to smother the awkwardness with banter. It hadn't worked. Instead she'd nearly given away the reason why she'd come to see Andy – to find out if Robyn's flirtation with him had become an affair.

She rounds the last set of steps, pauses to catch her breath (she really needs to start running again), then freezes as a haunting scream fills the air. It came from the other end of the landing, where a door is ajar.

'Jude! Jude!' Sorrell appears beside her, breathing heavily, having run up the stairs. 'Are you okay? I heard you scream!'

IT'S ALWAYS THE HUSBAND

'That wasn't me. It—'

'Did you hear that noise?' A diminutive woman in her late sixties or early seventies, dressed in a tweed skirt and navy jumper, her blonde hair held back from her face with an Alice band, appears at the door of flat six. She looks from Jude to Sorrell.

'It came from that flat.' Jude points at flat seven and they all listen intently, braced for another ear-splitting scream but the only noise on the landing, other than their laboured breathing, is the faintest of sobs from across the hall.

She drifts towards the sound, stepping lightly on the brown and beige stripy carpet, as though in a dream. It's only when she reaches the doors that she registers the presence of the neighbour just behind her. She stops, turns and holds out a warning hand.

'I think you should stay here.' She's not sure why she's whispering but the notes of the scream were so shrill, so anguished that there can only be something worrying behind the door.

The neighbour opens her mouth in objection then seems to think the better of it and nods in agreement.

Jude glances at Sorrell and sees her trepidation reflected straight back at her. 'You can stay here too if you want?'

'No, you're not going in there alone.'

Comforted by the strength in the other woman's voice, Jude gently pushes at the door so it opens another couple of inches. 'Hello?' she says softly. In the gap between the door and the frame she can see a slice of Andy's living room – closed curtains, cream leather sofa, squat white coffee table and a section of a galley kitchen at the back of the room. Wherever the sobbing is coming from, it's further into the flat.

Somewhat reassured by the ordinary living room scene,

she opens the door wide enough to step into the flat. Sorrell, breathing heavily again, follows behind her.

'Hello?' She says it louder this time.

'Help!' A woman's voice rings out. 'Please! Please, help me!' Wherever she is she's not far away.

Heart pounding, Jude takes a left out of the living room into a short corridor then stops short outside the bathroom. Inside, soaking wet and crouched into a ball on the floor, is a blonde-haired woman, her face buried in her knees. In the bath, fully clothed, unmoving, his hair fanned around his head, with just his nose and forehead – deathly pale – visible above the waterline, is a man she's almost certain is Andy Routledge.

'We've got to get him out of there!' While Jude is still processing what she's seeing, Sorrell charges past her and bursts into the bathroom. The woman on the floor gives a shrill, shocked shriek and jumps to her feet. It's only then that Jude realises that the woman she heard screaming – the woman now staring in horror at her, dripping water onto the bathroom mat, as Sorrell reaches into the bathtub – is Victoria.

'Help me, someone! Quickly!' Sorrell plunges her arms into the water and grapples with Andy's body, trying to hook her hands under his arms. 'Jude, grab his feet!'

Jude rushes forward and does as she's told but, even as she wraps her hands around Andy's ankles and grips the wet fabric of his jeans, she knows getting him out is going to be a struggle. He has to weigh at least fourteen or fifteen stone and Sorrell can't be more than eight or nine stone. She's pretty sure he's not breathing, if he's not already dead.

'Victoria!' She turns to the grief-stricken woman, pressed up against the bathroom wall, her fingers gripping the tiles.

IT'S ALWAYS THE HUSBAND

She looks cemented in place. 'You need to help us get him out of the bath. We can't lift him by ourselves.'

Victoria doesn't respond. She's not even looking at her; she's staring straight ahead, her eyes fixed and glassy, as though an invisible movie is playing out on the wall above Jude's head. From the state of her she's obviously already tried to get Andy out of the bath. Either that or she held him under the water. Jude pushes the thought out of her head. The scream she heard was pure pain. She drops Andy's legs back into the water as an exhausted Sorrell struggles to keep his head out of the water.

'Victoria!' She shakes her by the shoulders, but it's as though she's made of rock. 'We have to get him out of the bath. Lift his feet. I'll help Sorrell. Victoria!' Still, the other woman looks at her vacantly as though she doesn't even exist.

'Oh my God!' the neighbour says from the doorway. She's gripping the doorframe, her face drained of colour, horror filling her eyes. 'Has anyone called an ambulance?'

All eyes turn towards Victoria, who doesn't respond.

'Do it!' Sorrell shouts. 'Quickly!'

The neighbour gives a small, juddering gasp, then disappears.

Jude returns her attention to Victoria and gives her another strong shake. 'You have to help us! We can't do it alone. Please, please! For your children!'

The words shake Victoria from her stupor and she blinks rapidly, shock replacing the vacuity in her eyes. Silently she moves to the end of the bathtub and, as Jude and Sorrell wrestle with Andy's arms, weaving and bending around each other to try and hold on, Victoria scoops her arms beneath his legs. But Andy's dead weight and, try as she might, Jude can't get a good a good grip on his right arm from this side of the bath.

'I'll get in,' Sorrell says, panting. 'If I push him into a sitting position and you grab his right arm and Victoria grabs his right leg, we can tip him over the side of the bath.'

Jude shrugs.

Bath water leaps over the side of the tub and soaks Jude's feet as Sorrell climbs in. Jude and Victoria, who still isn't speaking, pull on his arms while Sorrell squeezes behind him and, teeth gritted, pushes at his back. Somehow, they get him into an unstable sitting position, his head tilted backwards, chin raised. As Jude reaches for his right arm she knocks against him. She stifles a scream as his head lolls to one side.

'Ready?' Sorrell says. 'Three, two, one . . . pull!'

Wet hands wrapped around Andy's right wrist, Jude puts one foot up against the side of the bathtub and leans her weight back. Beside her, Victoria, stronger and more athletic, lifts his right leg clear out of the water. Sorrell grunts loudly, there's a bang as Andy's chest and head hit the side of the tub then, like they've landed the heftiest fish in the ocean, he's out of the bath, face down and on the cold bathroom tiles.

Water surges over the side of the bathtub as Sorrell clambers out. 'Flip him over, flip him over!'

Breathing heavily, they haul Andy over so he's lying on his back and the spell that's rendered Victoria mute shatters.

'I've got this.' She kneels beside her ex-husband, tilts his head back and lifts his chin. She pumps at his chest with her clasped hands then covers his mouth with hers and breathes into him. His chest inflates. She breathes into him again, then continues pounding at his chest.

Jude watches, waiting, hoping, her arms and legs shaking, adrenaline still coursing through her veins.

She glances across at Sorrell, perched on the closed toilet

lid with her arms wrapped around her knees. She's watching Victoria intently, barely blinking, tears cascading down her cheeks.

This time, Jude tells herself as Victoria moves like clockwork – chest, mouth, chest, mouth. *This time, this time, this time.* But Andy doesn't move, he doesn't judder or tremble. His eyes remain closed.

She doesn't know if minutes, or hours, have passed since they dragged him out of the bathtub. They're trapped in a stasis – a cold, tiled vacuum. As long as Victoria continues to push her weight, and her breath, into Andy's supine body, then he isn't officially dead. The sound of footsteps and voices snap Jude out of her reverie and when two paramedics – one male, one female, in their dark green shirts and trousers – burst into the bathroom she gasps with relief. An authoritative voice says, 'If we could please have some space,' and her legs carry her out of the room.

She's joined by Sorrell and the neighbour in the living room. They stand apart, shell-shocked islands in a sea of beige and cream. The neighbour's speaking but Jude lets the words wash over her. She's tuned in to the sounds from the bathroom, to the paramedics pleading with Victoria to let them take over. Her gaze drifts to the table, to the whisky, the glass, the bottle, the phone, the pen, and the DNA test instructions, then her vision blurs and she's sitting in a barn, straw scratching at her ankles and calves, clutching her father's suicide note and she's staring up at the beams. She's too late. She should have got home earlier. She could have talked him out of it, stopped him, cut him down before it was too late.

'Jude . . . Jude . . .' She feels a hand on her shoulder, smells the faintest whiff of pachouli. 'Jude, please open your hand.'

'No, no.' She snatches her arm away. 'It's all I've got left. It's the last thing he wrote!'

'Jude. The police are here and they need to see the DNA kit instructions. Jude? Jude, can you hear me? Can you open your hand? The police are here. Andy is dead.'

Chapter 37

Victoria

TUESDAY

Victoria is alone on her sofa, slumped over, her arms wrapped around a cushion, her head bent low.

She can't remember who took the phone from her and organised for the children to be collected from school by Sara. Sorrell maybe, possibly Jude. Someone used the phrase 'there's been some bad news' then 'she's obviously very shocked' and 'the police need her to go to the station but she doesn't want anyone to go with her'. Then she was on a hard chair in a beige windowless interview room and she can't remember how she got there. Or how she got home.

There have been phone calls – dozens of them – WhatsApp messages too. Her phone vibrating and ringing; each bleep, each ping, her cheery ringtone, like needles piercing her skin. The jungle telegraph has begun drumming, spreading the news of her loss far and wide. She leaves almost all the messages unread. She doesn't want to read, 'How are you?' 'Oh my God' 'I'm so sorry, those poor children' or hints of 'I'll hug my family closer tonight.' She doesn't want anyone to hug her, sit with her or console her. She's counting the minutes until Sara brings her children back home.

She wants Noah to rush in demanding snacks, drinks or cuddles. For Sophia to give her the briefest of hugs then run up to her room. She wants them to get on with their lives, to feel safe, secure and adored no matter whether they're in Andy's home or hers. Because that's something she could never accuse him of doing – withholding love from his children. They were his absolute world. For years before they separated she bitched and moaned at him about overtime, for missing sports days and presentations, for forcing her to fit her job around the children, for shouldering most of the childcare burden alone. But when he was at home, when they were a family, his love for his children radiated out of every smile, cuddle, game and joke.

But that's all over. It's gone. He's gone. And he's never coming back.

Soon, Sophia and Noah will walk through the front door – innocent, happy, unknowing – and Victoria will wrap them in her arms. She built a world for them that was safe, secure and protective, but her words, the soft words she'll choose so carefully, will land like a hammer and smash their hearts to bits.

She hurls the cushion she's been hugging away from her. It clips the mantelpiece, sending a vase of white lilies and roses crashing to the floor. 'Fuck! Fuck! FUCK!'

They told her not to look at the piece of paper in the police officer's hand. – Jude and Sorrell, they begged her to 'please, please don't look at it now' – but she snatched it anyway, drinking in the words.

Paternity test requiring the DNA from the alleged father and child.

Alleged – just one word – but it may as well have been a bullet, the way her legs gave way beneath her, and she tumbled to the floor.

It's been an hour since she left the police station, since she perched on a hard seat in a characterless room and answered question after question, the kindly-faced DS waiting patiently as she sobbed and shuddered and buried her face in her hands.

'What was Andy's state of mind the last time you saw him? When was that?'

'Would you say Andy was depressed?'

'Can you think of any reason he might take his own life?'

'No. Never.'

'But the paternity test,' the DS said gently. 'Might that have been—'

'Noah's his!' she screamed. 'I didn't cheat on him. Not once. I don't know why he'd even think that.'

The detective sat forward in her seat. 'Would you like to take a break? This is obviously very distressing and maybe—'

'No! I'm not going anywhere until you listen to me. Andy did not commit suicide.'

'You seem very sure.'

'What else do I have to say to convince you?' She took a deep, shuddering breath. 'Andy was murdered! Got that? It wasn't suicide. He would never, ever leave his kids.'

Chapter 38

Sorrell

WEDNESDAY

As her students file out of her pottery studio, cheerily calling, 'See you next week!' and 'Looking forward to decorating my piece!', Sorrell forces a cheery smile and raises her hand in goodbye. 'Baby Love', by the Supremes, plays on the radio as she wraps each of the student's works in plastic sheeting and transfers them onto the shelf. Then she bags up the fresh clay, throws the students' scrap clay into a tub to be reclaimed later, wipes down the table and washes the various knives, tools and boards in the sink. Only when everything is as it should be does she drop into a chair and let herself cry.

Harper and Henry knew something was wrong the moment their eyes met hers at school pick-up yesterday.

'You look weird,' Henry said, his brows pinched together in confusion.

'Mummy, have you been crying?' Harper took her hand then wrapped herself around her arm.

'I'm fine, guys, honestly. I think I've got the start of cold.'

Neither child looked convinced but at that exact moment, Scout, squirming angrily in his buggy, started to cry. She made it back to the house without any more questions but the moment she let the two older children into the house, a new interrogation began.

'Mum! When's Dad coming home?'

'He wasn't here this morning!'

'I miss him!'

'Can we call him?'

She told them more lies, that he was too busy on his course to take a phone call, but he'd return home very soon. The truth was, she hadn't heard from him since she'd kicked him out the day before and she didn't want to. She was still trying to process what she'd been through in Andy's flat on the high street, just a couple of hours before.

As Victoria was helped into a squad car by a police officer, Sorrell had stumbled onto the high street with Jude and followed her to her Fiat Uno, too dazed to speak. Once inside they sat in silence for several minutes until Jude slumped over the steering wheel and said, 'Jesus fucking Christ.'

When she finally started the engine, they spoke sporadically, a phrase here, a comment there until words would fail them and they'd drift back into their own shocked, silent worlds. For Sorrell it was as if time had stopped, but seconds ticked into minutes on the clock on the dashboard and beyond the window, life went on as the rest of the world shopped, chatted and laughed.

'I can't believe that really happened,' Sorrell said eventually.

'I know,' came the reply from beside her. 'It just doesn't feel real.'

It was the same strange, disconnected phrasing Jude had used when Sorrell had tried to get her to let go of the DNA test instructions, like she was trapped in the past.

'Had you . . .' Sorrell ventured. 'Had you experienced something like that before?'

In the pause that followed, she wished she hadn't said anything, then Jude sighed softly.

'Yes. My dad.'

'Oh God, Jude. I'm so sorry.'

They lapsed into silence again, then Jude opened up, the words spilling from her like an unlocked dam as she told Sorrell about her father, how he'd been hounded to his death.

The further they travelled from Andy's flat the more easily they talked. They shared their mutual shock and horror about what they'd witnessed, the desperate hope that Andy might be resuscitated and Victoria's silent, still reaction to the news of his death. When Jude pulled up on a back road near the school, they swapped numbers and hugged tightly before they got out of the car.

Sorrell's plan had been to look for Jude on the school run this morning, but she'd barely stepped foot through the gates before she was swarmed by Shahina, Sara, Dawn, Caz and Audrey. The comments and questions came thick and fast.

'How's Victoria? She won't answer her phone.'

'Is it true Andy was in the bath in his clothes?'

'Do you think it was suicide or murder? God, those poor kids.'

'How was V when you found her? I'm just so shocked by what happened.'

She had to battle through them, crying, 'I'm sorry I can't talk about it,' to get Harper and Henry to the door before the last bell. The other mothers were waiting for her at the gates when she returned, huddled together like woodlice, and they pinioned her, Dawn and Audrey each grabbing an arm, galloping along beside her as she tried to make her way down the street. She felt so smothered by their attention, it was all she could do not to break into a run. As it was, her phone saved her. It was only a student, no doubt ringing to say they'd be late or they'd have to miss class, but she'd clamped it to her ear as though it was an emergency, shouting, 'I really have to take this,' and hurried away at a trot.

Now, she swipes at her eyes, and she sits back in her chair and she tries to sort through her feelings and decide what to do. Her plan had been to tell Andy the truth about Robyn and the blackmail but now she's back to square one – she's the only person in Lowbridge, other than Finnley, who knows that Robyn is alive. There's a part of her that's tempted to confide in Jude – to repay her openness and trust with similar – but that wouldn't be fair to Will. He has to be the first person she tells, then she'll go to the police.

Decision made, Sorrell gets up from the chair and lugs the tub containing the dried clay for reclaiming onto the table. It's her least favourite job but she's too wired to do anything else. As she fetches the bucket of slip her brain tunes in to the radio. The local newsreader is speaking.

'. . . And, finally, Arnold Patterson, seventy-four, has pleaded guilty to failing to stop after an accident and causing death by dangerous driving, after police unearthed dashcam footage of the accident by a passing motorist. Hit-and-run victim Sherri Toser, forty-seven, died in Mallhampton General yesterday. Sentencing will take place tomorrow.'

Sorrell stares at the radio as the news sinks in.

Of course Finnley wasn't responsible. He'd never actually admitted to doing it and her worry had revolved around the shape of the dent in the car. The *evidence* Robyn claimed to have was a lie. The voice note wasn't proof he'd knocked down a woman, but Sorrell had been so stunned by the mention of Robyn's name that the logical side of her brain shut down. What had appeared to be blackmail was actually a scam to extort money out of her.

She glances up at the clock on the wall. One hour until she takes Will Ledger to one side at school pick-up and tells him everything. It's going to be the slowest hour of her life.

Chapter 39

Jude

WEDNESDAY

Jude is labelling the drawers in Betsy's room when the doorbell rings. She hasn't done a scrap of work all day and the house is unusually clean and tidy, something Betsy remarked on when she returned home from school. Jude has spent hours scrubbing, sorting and polishing. Anything to avoid sitting still and thinking. Hiding her emotions by being the 'funny one' is all well and good when she's around other people but when she's alone . . . the laughter dries up. Not that there was any laughter when she drove Sorrell from Andy's to St Helena's yesterday and she told her everything, about the rape allegations, her dad's suicide and finding his body in the barn. Jude can only pray that it doesn't go round the school mums like a case of chlamydia and that Sorrell's as trustworthy as she seems.

'Betsy!' she shouts now, the television blaring downstairs. 'Can you get that?'

When there's no reply and the doorbell sounds again, she stomps down the stairs herself. She reaches for the door handle, braced to tell any religious sorts or canvassing politicians to go away, and throws open the door.

'Will?' She stares in surprise at the handsome man with cropped hair, shiny shoes and an old man's suit standing on her doorstep. He doesn't return her smile. 'What are you doing here?'

Will's sombre expression doesn't change. Obviously, he hasn't come round to apologise for snapping at her the other night.

Unsettled, Jude focuses on his daughter instead. 'Hi, Mills! What a lovely surprise.'

'We've got a playdate.' Milly stares up at her accusingly. 'You were supposed to pick me up from school. They had to ring Dad because I was the last one in the playground.'

'I was supposed to . . .' Jude's gaze flicks back to Will. 'Oh shit, I'm so sorry. I completely for—'

'Mum, don't swear! It's embarrassing.' Betsy has appeared beside her and couldn't look less impressed.

'You didn't tell me!' Jude says to her. 'Why didn't you remind me that Milly was coming home with us?'

'I tried, but you were on your phone. You said I'd got the days muddled up.'

'If now's not a good time.' The flint in Will's gaze intensifies. 'Then we can just—'

'No, it's just . . . oh God, you don't know do you? About what happened yesterday?' She shoos Milly inside. 'You go on in. Betsy, don't mess up your room.'

Her daughter doesn't deign to reply. Instead, she grabs her best friend by the hand and two pairs of feet pound their way up the stairs. Jude's stomach flip-flops as she looks back at Will. She's never seen him this frosty but she's starting to understand why the other school mums normally give him a swerve. When his guard's up, as it is right now, he's completely unapproachable.

'I'm sorry,' she says. 'For . . . for making out that I've got any idea what Milly's going through. It wasn't my place. I just . . .' She shrugs. 'I just didn't want you telling her off on my behalf. But, like I said, it wasn't my place. If Emma told me how to parent Betsy, I'd probably set fire to her curtains.'

Will's mouth stretches into a slow smile. 'Set fire to her curtains? Seriously. Couldn't you just be normal and throw something at her?'

'Too much risk. I might miss. A lighter never lets you down.'

She's being childish but she doesn't care. What matters is that the light has come back on in Will's eyes and he's no longer treating her like the enemy. He shakes his head, mock-judging her but the smile hasn't left his face.

'I'm sorry too, for snapping at you. It just . . .' he sighs '. . . I hate using this word because it makes me feel like a grandad trying to get down with the kids, but it triggered me. Robyn was forever criticising my parenting and . . . and I know she loved Milly but she's my daughter. I was there when she was born. Robyn didn't meet her until she was school age. No one knows her better than me.'

'I get it, honestly.' Jude touches a hand to his arm, feeling the strength of his bicep under her palm. The memory of their kiss in his hallway comes rushing back and she feels her cheeks warm. 'Do you want to come in?'

'You haven't told me what the news is yet? Something happened yesterday?' As he slides his hands into his pockets, Milly's pink rucksack slips off his shoulder and hangs in the crook of his elbow. He looks like Professor Indiana Jones meets Daddy Daycare with a dash of Tom Hardy. It shouldn't work but Jude finds it endearing, and sexy as hell.

'Yeah, right, sorry,' she says. 'Yesterday . . . I . . . well, we . . . we found him in the bath, in all his clothes, unconscious and we tried to save his life but . . .' She tails off, her throat tightening. This isn't how things work with Will. She makes stupid jokes to get him to laugh and open up; she doesn't share her own dark and upsetting shit. But she did with Sorrell in the car yesterday and she saw warmth and sympathy, not judgement or indifference, in her passenger's eyes.

Will's eyes widen in alarm. 'Who are you talking about?'

Jude blinks. 'Andy. Andy Routledge. Victoria Routledge's ex.'

Will draws away from her as though stung.

'It was awful,' Jude continues, too wrapped up in the horror of what happened to spot that a shutter's come down over Will's eyes. 'Really, really upsetting. I don't know if it was a deliberate suicide attempt or an accidental drowning but it was one of the . . . it was one of the most awful moments of my life and . . .' She tails off, feeling exposed, as though she just shed a layer of her skin.

Will stares at her, unblinking. 'I'll be back to collect Milly in a couple of hours.'

Then, without saying another word, he turns away from her and walks back down the path.

Chapter 40

ROBYN'S DIARY

Me again! Still not miserable you'll be pleased to hear! What am I talking about? You're a piece of paper in a book who can't hear anything! Sorry, that's STUPID. I'm a bit drunk. If I can read any of this back tomorrow I'll be very surprised.

Went out with 'the girls' again tonight. Yes, I am finally part of the inner sanctum! I'm part of the mamas WhatsApp group and I get invited to all the nights out. Still don't feel like I a hundred per cent fit in but they've accepted me and that's better than hanging round the school gates with the other rejected mums. Look, yes they're shallow and judgemental sometimes but they can be really funny and entertaining. And I take back everything I said about Victoria – she's absoluteley brilliant. So funny. And she's totally got her shit together. Nice house, fit husband, good figure, two lovely kids, clients that adore her, everyone knows who she is! It would be amazing to be like her. Someone that other people want to be around. I don't know if it's charisma or what but when you're chatting to her – just you and her – you feel like everything you say is amazing. She's so interested in other people's lives.

Anywayyyy . . . I have SO MUCH GOSSIP to report! Honestly, get a bit of Pinot Noir down those women's necks and they'll spill everything! Well, most of them. There are a couple that have a got a bit more self-control – will say no to another glass of wine and get themselves a water instead, will excuse themselves to the loo if the conversation gets a bit raunchy.

So . . . just in case this diary is ever stolen or read by someone who shouldn't read I'm going to give the women pseudonyms. I'm going for animals because I'm too drunk to think of anything clever. Okay, here we go . . .

1. – *Fox admitted that she's started dragging her kids to church on Sundays so she can get them into the local Catholic secondary school (Outstanding Ofsted but you can only go if your priest writes a letter about what a good Catholic you are)*
2. – *Badger gets so bored of sex with her husband that she suggested they put porn on when they go to bed, just so she's got something to watch!*
3. – *Also Badger, when she met her husband she told him she'd only slept with seven men when the total is more like thirty! Also, she went to a sex party in London when she was in her twenties and basically took part in an orgy. He doesn't know about that either.*
4. – *Flamingo admitted that her first child wasn't the 'oops I had a stomach upset when I was on the pill and I'm pregnant' mistake that she made it out to be. She really wanted a baby so she stopped taking her pill.*

IT'S ALWAYS THE HUSBAND

5. – *Owl has a secret savings account that her husband doesn't know about.*
6. – *Tiger, Blowfish, Cheetah and Chihuahua I've got nothing on. They're the ones that keep an eye on how much they drink.*

ANYWAY. It's a good job I'm not a complete arsehole because, with tea like this, a blackmailer could make a lot of money. A lot of money INDEED.

Chapter 41

Jude

WEDNESDAY

Jude rereads Robyn's diary, then she takes her phone out of her pocket and takes a photo of the page. With everything that happened yesterday, reading Robyn's diary had been the last thing on her mind but, after Will's strange reaction to Andy's death just now, she went straight up to her room, closed the door to the girls' bickering, and dug it out from the bottom of the wardrobe where she'd hidden it.

While the page she's just read hasn't thrown any light on Will and Robyn's relationship it says a lot about Robyn. Who writes down all their friends' secrets in a diary, gives them animal pseudonyms, then ends the entry with a thinly veiled threat? And who are Badger, Fox, Flamingo, Owl, Tiger, Blowfish, Cheetah and Chihuahua? The school mums certainly had enough to say about Robyn at Victoria's 'drinks and nibbles' evening to make her think that the six birds and animals could be Victoria, Sorrell, Shahina, Audrey, Dawn, Sara and Caz. But that's seven women and there are eight animals. Who is she missing? Robyn hinted at blackmail at the end of the entry. Did she actually go through with her threat and one of her victims killed her? Otherwise, it looks a lot like her murderer could be Will. As convinced as Jude's been of his innocence, only a fool would ignore the evidence that's starting to mount up.

First Robyn vanished and now Andy, one of the cops who investigated her disappearance, is dead. Are the two things connected? In a town as small as Lowbridge it would be a hell of a coincidence if they weren't, particularly when Robyn confessed in her diary that she had a crush on Victoria's husband.

Might Will have read the diary and put two and two together about Robyn continually going out? He hasn't hidden his dislike for Andy Routledge, openly cheering whoever punched him in the face. Did he discover an affair the night Robyn was last seen when he argued with her? Did he lose his temper and snap? But why murder Andy now? Was he close to revealing the truth?

With Andy and Robyn dead they can't answer any of her questions and, if Will really is a murderer, he's hardly going to hold up his hands and confess. But what she *can* do is follow up her blackmail theory and that means matching the 'animal' confessions to the other school mums. When she's got a list of potential suspects she can do some more digging, try and work out which one of them could have been Robyn's target, assuming she blackmailed them at all.

The only trouble is, she doesn't know any of the women well enough to take a guess at who lied about how many people they slept with, watches porn because she's bored in bed, or has a secret savings account. Maybe there are more clues later? She turns the page then jolts as the bed bounces beneath her.

'Betsy!' She flips the diary shut and slides it onto the floor. 'What have I told you about knocking before you come into my bedroom?'

'Sorryyyy.' Her daughter couldn't look less apologetic. 'You said you were going to make pizza with me and Milly. Or have you forgotten that as well?'

'No,' Jude lies. 'Of course I haven't. We might have to pop to the corner shop to get a few things but . . . um . . . nope, haven't forgotten at all.'

'You're the *best*.' Betsy throws her arms around her neck and Jude feels her mum points climb from rock bottom. 'Can we get ham, and olives and pineapple? Milly wants anchovies but they're gross.'

'No they're not,' a little voice says from the doorway. 'Robyn thinks they're tasty. And so do I.'

Two hours later, after a forty-minute round trip to Tesco to buy pizza ingredients, the girls are playing in Betsy's bedroom and Jude finally has a minute to herself.

Keen to get back to Robyn's diary, she trudges up the stairs to her bedroom, pushes open the door and stares at her bed. There's a smooth sea of blue cotton where a book should be nestling. She could have sworn she slapped the diary shut when Betsy came in then tucked it out of sight behind her.

No, that's not right. She closed it when Betsy came in and then she nudged it onto the floor. She rounds the bed, relieved, then stops short again. There's a couple of make-up brushes and an errant sock on the carpet, but no diary. Did one of the girls kick it under the bed while they were playing? She drops to her knees to check but, other than a shameful amount of dust, there's nothing there. She gets back up and looks behind and then on her bedside table. No diary. She checks under the pillow and the duvet. No, nothing there either. Where the hell has it gone? She painstakingly searches her bedroom, peering into the gap between the chest of drawers and the wall and the clean clothes piled up on her chair, then gets back on her knees, turns on her phone's torch, and takes another look under the bed in case she missed it the first time. But it's not there. The diary has completely disappeared.

She wanders into Betsy's room and has a good look around. Maybe one of the girls found it while they were playing hide-and-seek and, intrigued, took it to share with their playmate. But there's no sign of it anywhere. It's not on the landing, in the bathroom, or discarded in the hallway downstairs.

Jude pokes her head around the living room door where the two girls are sitting side by side on the sofa, watching a programme about a dance academy. They're suspiciously quiet, like butter wouldn't melt.

'Have either of you . . .' Jude begins, then tails off as their heads turn sharply in her direction, like two Chucky dolls brought to life. Her gaze swivels to the pink rucksack at Milly's feet. Might she have taken the diary? Is that why she's keeping her bag so close?

'Hey, Milly.' Jude keeps her tone light and playful. 'Could I have a look at your reading record please? I need some ideas for books for Betsy.'

The bag's snatched away before she can touch it. Milly's gripping it like it's a life buoy and Jude's a great white shark.

'Mum!' Betsy wails. 'You're so embarr—'

The doorbell sounds, cutting her off and, defeated, Jude scurries away.

'Hi!' She greets Will with a faltering smile. Shit. If Milly's taken the diary, she's never going to get it back now. 'Milly,' she calls into the hallway, 'your dad's here to collect you!'

She looks back at Will, who's giving her strong 'I really don't want to be here' vibes. 'Is everything okay?'

He nods curtly, his gaze flicking away to the hallway. 'Yeah fine, you?'

The atmosphere is so toe-curlingly awkward that Jude's tempted to head back upstairs and leave him to stew in his icy-cold aloofness, but she stands her ground instead. Emma's right – Will isn't a red flag, he's a nuclear bloody siren – and she's tired of tiptoeing around him. That's definitely not who she is. Sod Betsy and Milly's friendship, her daughter's going to have to learn how to make some new friends.

'Why were you so weird earlier, when I told you that Andy had died?'

He stares at her, wide-eyed, then blinks rapidly and clears his throat. 'I was weird?'

'Yeah, you just walked off.'

The confusion on Will's face vanishes and rage sparks in his eyes. 'What did you expect me to say when the man is – was – a fucking arsehole? He hounded me for months and treated me like a murderer. No, no that's not true. He *called* me a murderer. He sat across from me in an airless fucking room and he *told me* that I'd lost my temper with Robyn, murdered her and buried her body. He turned my house upside down. His team fucking ransacked Milly's room. I was suspended from my job while I was under investigation and pretty much ostracised by everyone I knew. And people still suspect me! They still believe that I killed her. You heard Victoria at the school gates. Have you got any idea how many people at work still refuse to be alone with me? What it's like to walk into the staffroom and have almost everyone else walk out? Do you have any idea what it's like to stand in front of a room full of students and see fear and suspicion in their eyes? Have you got any idea at all?'

Jude, who's taken several steps back into the hallway, buffeted by the force of his anger, doesn't answer. Her heart's pounding and she feels light-headed and breathless like she was caught up in an emotional tornado then spat out without warning. Will didn't raise his voice once when he spoke, but she feels as though he screamed in her face. When she presses her lips together she swears she can taste his rage on her skin. How can he be that angry and also guilty? She can't make sense of how she feels.

Emma has always accused her of seeing the world in black and white and maybe her sister's right. People aren't good or evil. They're not right or wrong. They're messy, contradictory and unpredictable. God knows she's the same.

'Got everything?' Will asks, and it isn't until Jude feels Milly and her backpack brush past her that she realises that he isn't still talking to her. All she can do is stare into the distance as Will, Milly and – quite possibly – Robyn's diary, move down the path, and disappear.

Chapter 42

Victoria

WEDNESDAY

Sophia and Noah have been crying on and off for hours and Victoria is broken. She thought she'd prepared herself to break the news to the children – as prepared as she could be, given she felt like a shell herself. But, when she crouched on the floor in front of the sofa, gripping each child's hand in hers, she couldn't speak for crying. Her tears and choked sobs – for Andy, for her children, for herself – terrified them. She could see it in their wide, fearful eyes. Afterwards – after she wrestled the words from her throat, and absorbed their emotions, soaking up their grief like a sponge – she held them both in her arms as her heart shattered and splintered. All she'd ever wanted to do was protect them but there was nothing she could do to extricate their pain. There was no salve for this hurt. No quick fix, no phone call, no visit to school.

IT'S ALWAYS THE HUSBAND

Even as she pulled her children against her body, guilt nipped at her grief. The DNA test instructions, laid out on Andy's coffee table were haunting her. She hadn't killed him, but he'd died believing that Noah wasn't his son.

Her lies began in high school. Bullying had made her primary years miserable. She was a shy, unconfident child and when she was excluded from games at playtime, taunted because she was skinny, had wide-set eyes and a large forehead, her fragile self-esteem was destroyed. She withdrew into herself and stopped raising her hand to answer the teacher's questions lest she draw more ire from the rest of the class. She sat by herself during break time, perched on the edge of the sandpit, drawing circles in the sand repeatedly. The only time she flourished was during the annual school sports day. Light and agile, she sped along the bumpy school field during the running races, easily beating her nearest competitor. During 'house' races against the year above, the competition was greater because the children were taller and stronger, but her natural athleticism meant she still won every race. The teachers begged her to take part in team sports and represent the school, but she refused to, only acceding to cross-country because that was one sport she could do on her own.

When Year 6 ended, she cried every day during the summer holidays, not through relief that school had ended, but because the prospect of high school was terrifying. If primary school was a locked cellar she couldn't escape, then high school would be a prison, the inmates hardened, and battle-scarred. Her frantic mother took her to a therapist, a kindly-faced woman in her fifties with expressive hands, frizzy hair and broken veins on her cheeks. Maggie was warm and kind and patient and, session after session, she tried valiantly to repair Victoria's shattered self-esteem through a combination of talk, role-play and visualisation. The visualisation exercises were what Victoria enjoyed the most.

When Maggie told her to imagine a child at primary school who was popular, confident, and happy, she thought about a girl called AJ who seemed to drift through each day on a cloud of laughter and hugs, surrounded by children who clung on to every word she said, fascinated by florid tales of her home life, her weekends and her holidays. Nothing AJ said was boring or weird. Maggie had her mentally step out of her own body and into AJ's. She made her imagine what AJ saw, how she felt. Victoria always left those sessions smiling, feeling bigger, stronger, loved and adored. 'You need to find your tribe,' Maggie told her during their last session. 'You'll bond with people you have something in common with and, as you've told me that you're good at sport, I think you should join at least one sports team at high school. Everyone feels nervous meeting new people but if you step into your best, most radiant self then no one will know that you're feeling nervous too. Your energy and your confidence will attract people to you.'

'I should be more AJ,' Victoria had said, sitting up straighter as she mentally stepped inside the girl she'd so admired.

Maggie's brow had creased with concern, 'No my dear, you should be more you.'

But Victoria let the words wash over her. Why would she want to be herself when who she really was was quiet, weird and scared?

On her first day at high school she walked into her first class with her chin up and her shoulders back. When Elodie, the girl sitting beside her at their shared desk, asked her what she'd done in the holidays she pushed down the truth – about the tears and the therapy – and instead told her a fabricated tale about a safari in Kenya when a lion had jumped up at their jeep. Her new friend's eyes grew wide with awe and wonder and when Victoria wrapped up her story, Elodie said, 'Wow. Your life is so exciting. I just went camping in Devon for a week,' something powerful blossomed deep inside of Victoria. Captivating Elodie the way she had made her feel good. So good that, for the next five years of high school, she did it repeatedly. Now, she barely registers the lies that she tells.

Her thoughts return to Andy and the DNA test instructions, and the weight of guilt in her chest lightens, as a realisation takes hold and anger claims its place. Someone in her friendship group has betrayed her.

She snatches up her phone, hammers out an angry accusatory message.

One of you shared what I said the other night about Noah's paternity when it was obvious I WAS FUCKING JOKING. Because of you Andy died thinking that Noah wasn't his and I WILL find out who you are.

It's an empty threat because she hasn't got the first idea how to track down the culprit, but she has to do something to rid herself of the irritating, uncomfortable sensation in her body, as though hundreds of ants are crawling beneath her skin. No one is who she thinks they are – not Theresa, the 'mamas', or Jude and Sorrell. They tried to help her save Andy but she's got no idea why they turned up to see him or even that he knew who they were. She doesn't know what's going on in Lowbridge. Her sense of security was only ever an illusion. The foundations of her world are shaking but there's no one to cling to because she doesn't know anyone at all.

It's killing her, sitting around, doing nothing, waiting for the police to investigate Andy's death. There's no way it can be anything other than murder and whoever killed him is still out there, planning God knows what. She'd assumed Andy's killer was a criminal – the murder had been staged to look like a suicide and it seemed like a professional job. He'd played a role in the sentencing of hundreds of crooks during his years in the police force. Had one of them left prison and decided to take their revenge?

Or is Andy's killer closer to home? Someone who knows the family? A friend of her and the kids? The thought sparks fireworks in her belly and she rushes to the front door then pulls on the handle to check that it's locked. When she raises her head, sensing she's being watched and sees two figures standing outside, beyond the glass panels of the door, her breath catches in her throat, before fresh tears fill her eyes.

'Mum! Dad!' She throws the front door open, sees the heartache on her mother's face and the concern in her father's eyes and collapses into their arms.

Chapter 43

Sorrell

WEDNESDAY

Will Ledger opens his front door, his eyes clouding with confusion as he looks from Sorrell to Harper and Henry, then at Scout, rubbing his eyes and grizzling in her arms because it's almost his bedtime.

'Oh, hello, Sorrell!' he says with surprise, then glances at his watch.

'I know it's late' – Sorrell shifts Scout onto her hip – 'and I'm sorry to turn up unexpectedly but it's really important.'

When Will didn't appear at school pick-up, her heart had sunk. There was no way she could endure a night alone at home, knowing what she knew about Robyn. She *had* to tell Will Ledger, even if that meant staking out his house. She'd returned home with the children, fed them, then loaded them back into the car and drove round to Will's. All the lights were off and there was no car in the driveway. She drove home, waited an hour, then did the same thing, with the same result. When she'd loaded the children into the car for the *third* time, all three kids were so frustrated and miserable she swore there wouldn't be a fourth time.

'Sorry, Will,' she says now. 'I wouldn't have brought the kids but I . . . I really had no choice.'

He must hear the note of desperation in her voice because he opens the door wide and says, 'Don't worry, come in!'

Sorrell ushers the two older children in first, then steps into Will's hallway and closes the door behind her.

'Shoes!' she says to the children as they turn on the spot, taking in their surroundings. They've never been inside this house before, but she's visited, just once, briefly, when Robyn still lived there. She'd volunteered to pick up book donations for the school fayre and, with Robyn out somewhere, Will had sorted out a pile that Milly had outgrown.

'Milly!' Will bellows up the stairs. 'We've got visitors!'

Thirty seconds or so later, his daughter's head appears over the top of the balcony. When she spots Harper and Henry standing in her hallway, she raises her eyebrows in surprise. The children don't hang out in the same friendship groups at school and, although they obviously know each other, Sorrell's pretty sure they've never played together before.

'Can they hang out in your room for half an hour?' Will asks. 'Take turns on the Switch or something? Remember that they're guests. If it's a two-player game you should offer to sit out.'

An objection forms on Milly's lips, but she doesn't voice it. Instead, she shrugs and beckons the twins up the stairs.

After the bedroom door clicks shut Will inclines his head towards the living room. 'Do you want a tea? Coffee?' He gives her an appraising look. 'Something stronger?'

'Better not. I drove over. I'm sorry about this. I won't keep you long.' She plops Scout onto the floor, upends the small bag of toys and teething rings she brought with her, then sits down on the sofa.

Will takes a seat in the armchair, runs a hand over his cropped hair and smiles at her awkwardly. Other than nods of hello at the school gates, and the book donation visit, they've barely spoken. She's surprised he even remembers her name. 'So, what's up? You okay? What's this important thing that can't wait?'

The warmth in his voice, and the fact she can't remember the last time someone asked her how she was, makes tears well in her eyes but she blinks them away. She didn't load the kids into the car and drive all the way over for a pity party.

'Okay, this is . . . it's complicated but I'll try to keep it short.' Sorrell takes a steadying breath then tells him about Finnley's hit-and-run and the blackmail that followed.

'I told them I was going to block their number unless they provided evidence that proved Will was responsible for the hit-and-run and they . . . they sent me this . . .'

She takes her phone out of her handbag, hits play on the voice note then looks intently at Will, monitoring his reaction.

He gasps at the mention of Robyn's name, his body stiffening. 'No, no that's not possible.'

'They've been having an affair.'

Will grips the sides of his head, his fingers entwined in his hair. The skin is pulled so tight across the back of his fists that Sorrell can see every vein and sinew in his broad, weighty hands.

It's the reaction of a man who was utterly convinced that his partner was dead, but is that anger she can see, shining beyond the dazed expression in his eyes? Or fear?

If Finnley was telling the truth about Robyn disappearing

because she was scared of Will then Sorrell's just handed him an axe. Last month, last year, she would never have dreamed of putting another woman in danger, but Robyn's no innocent.

'Play it again,' Will says and Sorrell does as he asks.

As the voicemail ends he runs a hand over the stubble on his jawline, his gaze fixed on a spot on the carpet on the other side of the room. 'I don't believe it. Regardless of how she feels about me there's no way she'd leave it this long without trying to contact Milly.'

'I'm sorry but it is true. She's alive. Finnley told me everything, before I kicked him out. He's probably with her now.'

'Ring him.' Will turns sharply to look at her, the soft cloud of his incomprehension replaced by a hard-edged decisiveness. Wasn't this what she wanted? For him to act, take control?

'Ring Finn?' she repeats, delaying.

'Yeah. Ask to talk to Robyn. Put the call on speakerphone.'

Sorrell glances down at Scout who's slamming a plastic piano toy with the flat of his hand whilst making discordant noises of his own. Two days have passed since she ordered Finnley out of the house. Yesterday he sent a text asking after the children. Her reply was a simple *Get fucked*. He'd been planning to leave them for Robyn – how dare he pretend that he cared.

Emboldened by the energy flowing out of the man sitting across from her, Sorrell touches her thumb to her phone. The call's answered almost immediately but there's a pause before Finnley says, 'Hello?'

The sound of his voice – a reliable, predictable soundtrack to almost twenty years of marriage – lands a blow to her belly that winds her. She forces herself to reply.

'Where are you?'

Another pause then: 'In a hotel.'

'Where?'

'Can I speak to the children?' Her teeth clench in irritation but Will makes a circling gesture with his hand, telling her to keep the conversation moving.

'They're sleeping.' Almost on cue Scout smashes his hand against the piano again and Sorrell hears a soft gasp on the line.

'Sorrell, please.'

'Is Robyn with you?' She glances at Will, who nods.

This time there's no answer for so long that she checks the call hasn't disconnected but the timer's still ticking down the seconds. Finnley's just taking his sweet time.

'Finnley,' she bites at his name. 'Is she with you?'

'Not yet.'

Will's expressions shifts – somewhere between frustration and 'I told you so'.

'Have you heard from her?'

Another pause and then: 'Yes.'

'What's the plan now then, Finnley?'

'Sorrell, please let me talk to the children. I can hear Scout babbling. Can you put the phone next to him so I can talk to him?'

'No I fucking cannot!' The words explode out of her with such viciousness that Scout looks up at her, fear moistening his eyes. She softens her expression for her baby and in a sing-song voice says, 'It's okay, Scout. It's okay, baby,' but her son still looks on the verge of tears.

Will, no doubt anticipating a full meltdown, slips off the sofa and onto the floor. He lifts up a colourful, chiming ball and rolls it on the carpet. Distracted, Scout's chin stops wobbling and he crawls to claim the ball for himself.

'Has Robyn told you that she's been blackmailing me?' Sorrell makes her voice as flat and emotionless as she can.

'What?' There's genuine surprise in Finnley's reply. 'No. She would never—'

'Want me to send you the texts?'

'Why would she do that that when I've already given her—' He catches himself and breaks off.

'When you've given her *what*, Finnley?'

No reply.

'When you've given her WHAT?'

She can hear him breathing, a rapid nasal breath, that lasts for several second before the phone goes silent. He's cut her off. Her first instinct is to call him back; her second is to check her banking app.

It's been a while since she checked the balance but, with interest rates being what they are there should be nearly twenty thousand pounds in their joint account. She breathes shallowly as the screen refreshes and—

It's gone.

Zero pounds and zero pence.

She jabs at the transactions link, her eyes widening with horror as she watches her life savings vanish in two-thousand-pound increments. Withdrawn to an account in the name of Finnley S Edwards. He's cleared their savings account of every last penny. That was money for their children's futures, and he's taken it all for Robyn and himself.

When she looks up from the screen Will's staring at her intently. 'What's happened?'

'My savings, they're gone. They've cleared me out.'

'Shit.'

'I can't even call the police because it was a joint savings account.'

Will continues to gaze at her, his eyes roaming her face

and she senses there's something he wants to say but he's wary of saying it.

'What is it?' she asks.

'I'm really sorry about what's happened but . . .' He tails off.

'But what?'

'None of this proves that Robyn's alive.'

She stares at him, frustration building in her chest. She's just poured out her heart to him, she's played him the voice note, she's even rung her husband on speakerphone and he still doesn't believe that—

'Has he seen her?' Will asks. 'Robyn. Since she disappeared? Face to face?'

'I . . . I don't know. How would I—'

'Ring him back. Ask him.' There's that authoritative tone again, only this time it grates on her so much that she can't hold back.

'No. How about you answer my questions now. What makes you so sure that Robyn's dead? Unless you killed her.'

She sees the effect of her words immediately. He looks like someone who's just been punched in the face.

'I think it's time for you all to go home now,' he says, his voice flat and emotionless. 'I'll get Harper and Henry from upstairs.'

Chapter 44

Jude

THURSDAY

The diary has gone. Last night Jude spent hours frantically searching, not just her own bedroom, but the entire house. She questioned Betsy – 'Did you see a book on the floor by my bed? Or see Milly pick it up?' Betsy stared at her blankly, repeatedly shaking her head. It was obvious that she had no idea what Jude was talking about. When Milly had hidden the diary, she'd done it without her best friend seeing a thing. As tempted as Jude is to fess up to Will, she's wary of his reaction. The fact he was triggered when she told him not to reprimand Milly has made her reticent about mentioning Robyn at all. The only lead she's got that might shed some light on Robyn's disappearance is a photograph of the page where Robyn gave the other school mums animal pseudonyms and revealed their secrets.

'Sorrell!' She spots the other mother crosses the road after the morning school drop off and hurries after her. 'Wait up!'

There's a wary expression on Sorrell's face as she turns to see who called her name, but it melts away as Jude draws closer.

'Are you okay?' Sorrell asks.

'Yeah, fine. Have you got a minute? I'll get us some coffees in the park.'

Sorrell nods agreeably but as Jude makes small talk during the short walk to the park, she can tell that Sorrell isn't really listening. She looks distracted, as though there's something playing on her mind.

'You sure you've got time for a chat?'

'Yes, course. I just . . . sorry, I didn't get much sleep last night.'

'I know that feeling.' Jude's pretty sure she's not the only one that sees Andy's lifeless face when she closes her eyes.

Once in the park she buys two coffees from the stall then gestures towards a bench. The sun's out and the sky's blue, but there's enough of a nip in the air that she's glad she's wearing a coat. Jude takes a sip of her coffee then slides her phone out of her pocket. What she's about to do feels risky. There's a chance that Sorrell could go to the other school mums and tell them she stole Robyn's diary, but she has to trust someone. She saw enough at Victoria's drinks evening to recognise a fellow outsider. And besides, Sorrell knows all about her dad's suicide and, from the lack of sympathetic glances at the school gates, Jude's pretty sure she hasn't mentioned a thing.

'Okay so . . .' She flashes Sorrell a smile. 'Don't judge and don't ask questions about how I've seen this. Actually, sod it, I stole it from under Will's bed, but for the right reasons. Not that that would stand up in court.' She laughs nervously as she tilts her phone towards Sorrell. 'That's . . . um . . . that's a page of Robyn's diary and—'

'Robyn's?'

'Yes, and I've read it, well, most of it. The thing is, everyone seems convinced that Will killed Robyn and I think this page might prove that he didn't. Look, she's detailing all the secrets that the other school mums shared and she gives them animal pseudonyms then, at the end, she mentions blackmail. My theory is that maybe she went through with the threat – she actually blackmailed one of them and they . . .' she shrugs awkwardly, suddenly aware of how insane she might sound '. . . they killed her, to stop their secret getting out. If I can work out who the animals are I might find my suspect and . . .' She tails off, perturbed by the change of expression on Sorrell's face.

'What is it? What's the matter?'

Sorrell takes her phone out of her handbag. 'There's something you should listen to. The voice you'll hear is Finnley, my husband. The message is less than a week old.'

Intrigued, Jude leans closer.

Her jaw drops as the message ends. All this time she's been right. Will *didn't* kill Robyn. She's been alive the whole time, and Finnley Edwards knew.

'Did you know too?' she asks. 'That she was still alive?'

Sorrell laughs bitterly and runs a hand down the length of her braid. It's a self-soothing gesture Jude saw her do in the car after they left Andy's flat. 'She was having an affair with him, *is* having an affair with him. I only found out two days ago.'

'Oh shit. I'm so sorry. That's awful.' As she touches a sympathetic hand to Sorrell's shoulder she sees tears well in her eyes. 'Does Will know?' Jude asks her. 'That Robyn's still alive?'

'Yeah. I told him yesterday. He couldn't have looked more shocked, then he asked me to ring Finnley so we could speak to her and then . . .' She shrugs miserably. 'I'm not sure what went wrong but when Finnley said Robyn wasn't with him Will started acting like I was an idiot for believing that she was alive so I . . . I asked him how he could be so sure she was dead, unless he'd murdered her, and he kicked me out of the house.'

Jude stares at her, trying to process what she's saying. Knowing what she knows about Will she's not surprised he kicked Sorrell out for calling him a murderer but why react so intensely if Robyn was still alive? Surely there was no greater vindication. He was weird with me yesterday too, when I told him about Andy.'

'Exactly the same!' Sorrell says as Jude finishes telling her what happened. 'He went really cold and he asked me to leave and then—'

'Wait!' She holds out her phone. 'Sorry to interrupt you, but Will just texted me and asked for your number.'

'You're kidding.' Sorrell's eyes are wide and worried.

'The bastard didn't bother apologising for getting angry yesterday. Just, *have you got Sorrell's number?* Want me to ignore him?'

'No. Give it to him. I want to hear what he has to say.'

Jude replies with Sorrell's number then they both fall silent, staring at their phones expectantly. Sorrell jolts as her mobile starts to ring.

'It's him!'

'Answer it!'

She's not sure why but a tight knot forms in her stomach as she listens to Sorrell's one-sided conversation with Will Ledger. She should feel relieved, knowing that Robyn's alive and he's off the hook but something's not sitting right and she's not sure what.

'Well?' she asks Sorrell as she tucks her phone back in her handbag. 'What did he want?'

Sorrell runs a hand down the length of her braid and stares off into the distance, her eyebrows low over clouded, worried eyes. 'He wanted to apologise for what happened yesterday.'

'Good. That it?'

'No.' She turns to look at Jude. 'He wants me to help him search the local hotels for Finnley this evening. He wants to confront him, and Robyn, face to face.'

Chapter 45

Sorrell

THURSDAY

There's a strange, strained atmosphere in Sorrell's living room. Jude is on the sofa, clutching a cushion, laughing a little too loudly whenever Sorrell says something even vaguely amusing, whilst Will's perching on the edge of the armchair, barely speaking, his hands pressed between his knees. He acknowledged Jude's presence, when Sorrell showed him into the living room: a curt nod of the head and tight-lipped hello. And Jude, who'd moved to stand up when she saw him, hovered as he greeted her coolly, then promptly sat back down. Normally Sorrell would find the awkwardness of their interaction unbearable but, on this occasion, she finds it reassuring. Will knows that Jude is there to babysit the children and Jude knows that Will and Sorrell are going to try and find Finnley but they obviously haven't talked to each other about what's happening, and

Will obviously hasn't apologised yet. Sorrell's heard the rumours that they're sleeping together but hasn't asked Jude about it. She's got enough going on without getting involved in that.

Standing on the street outside her house, where Will's car is parked, Sorrell pauses as he gestures to her to get in. His plan to confront Finnley and Robyn involves searching for her Ford Fiesta in hotel car parks (Finnley's been using it since his own car was damaged), then report a car park collision – with the Fiesta's licence plate – to the receptionist and wait for Robyn and Finnley to come down from their room. The idea had appealed to Sorrell earlier, but now she's having doubts. What if only Finnley comes down? What if Will wants to beat the shit out him? As much as she loathes her husband she couldn't just stand by and watch him get beaten up. Not unless she was doing it herself. The truth is she barely knows Will Ledger and what he's capable of. There were rumours when Robyn was still in Lowbridge that he had quite the temper. Given what he's been through over the last eighteen months she's worried that, if he starts hitting Finnley, he won't be able to stop.

Will, who's already in the driver's seat, rolls down the window. 'What is it? What's wrong? You look as nervous as I feel about my mother coming to stay this weekend.'

Sorrell pulls her cardigan tighter around her body. Now the sun's set there's a nip in the air. 'Are you sure you just want to talk to Robyn and Finnley?'

'As opposed to what? Beating the shit out of them?' He must clock the horror on her face because he quickly adds, 'I was joking, Sorrell. I'm not a violent man. If I'm honest, I'm doing this more for you than myself.'

'What do you mean?'

He sighs heavily then opens the car door and gets out. At six foot four he towers over her five-foot-five frame. 'Listen.' He shoves his hands deep into his pockets. 'I'm not saying I don't believe you about Finnley and Robyn having an affair. God knows I suspected as much. Not about Finnley per se, but I was pretty sure she was sleeping with *someone*.' There's a resigned acceptance to his words, as though he's too exhausted to get angry. 'What I don't believe, or what I'm having trouble accepting, is that Robyn is the person he's been messaging. I mean it might be, yes, it's possible, but, unless she turns up at reception with him, or he can prove that he's seen her in person then . . . no, I don't believe it. And not because I killed her or—'

'I'm so sorry,' Sorrell says quickly. 'For saying that yesterday. I didn't . . . I was just—'

'I get it. It's fine.'

'Finnley's been sending money to Robyn. Surely he wouldn't do that unless he'd actually—'

'He wouldn't be the first man to be catfished.'

She stares at him in alarm. The thought hadn't even crossed her mind.

'Maybe I'm wrong. Maybe I'm completely barking up the wrong tree, but that's why we need to do this. We'll find out the truth one way or another.'

'I can't see it.' Sorrell looks desperately at Will. 'I can't see my car.'

For the last hour they've driven from one side of Lowbridge to the other, pulling into hotel car parks, getting out and checking each car. 'This is the fifth hotel we've visited and there's no sign of it.'

'He definitely said he was staying in a hotel?' Will asks, for the third time that evening.

'You were there when I called him. You heard him.' Sorrell fights the urge to snap back but it's not Will she's irritated with, it's her husband. 'He's obviously not in Lowbridge.'

Will blows out his cheeks in frustration. He may not have said as much but she knows he was pinning a lot on finding Finnley.

'We could go wider,' Will says. 'Check out the hotels in Wyrethorpe and Mallhampton or just drive round the streets. There's a chance he's still local, because of the kids.'

He runs a hand over his hair as he scans the car park again, in case Finn's car might have miraculously appeared. 'This was a shit idea, I'm sorry. I got carried away, trying to prove a point to you. Maybe you should try ringing him again? Lure him out another way.'

'The diary! There might be clues.' The words are out of her mouth before she can stop them.

Will's eyes narrow. 'What diary?'

Sorrell blinks uncertainly, her stomach churning. Shit. Why did she have to go and open her mouth?

'It's nothing . . .' She stares desperately around the dark interior of the car, racking her brain for an explanation that isn't completely idiotic. 'H . . . Harper. She lost her diary and er . . . I was going to help her look for it. She'll be upset that she didn't get to write in it before bed.'

With her eyes lowered to her hands, clasped in her lap, she can't see Will's reaction, but she can feel it. His silence is cold and weighty, like a wet towel draped over her shoulders.

'That's not true, is it, Sorrell?'

The sharp edge to his question makes her feel childlike and she wishes to God she hadn't said anything.

'Sorrell?' Will says again.

If she tells him the truth, he'll know Jude found and read

the diary. He'll get angry, confront her and she really doesn't want to be responsible for that.

'Has this got something to do with the diary I found in Milly's bag the other day?' His tone is steady, emotionless, giving away nothing.

'I've got no idea,' Sorrell replies truthfully. Hopeful that the interrogation is over she lets out a small sigh.

'The diary that wasn't in her bag until she visited Jude's house.'

Sorrell says nothing. She can't. She's trying very hard not to cry. Will isn't openly intimidating her and she's not scared of him per se, but she can't help but feel like she's opened the lid of a dark box and she doesn't know what lies inside.

Will starts the engine then yanks at his seatbelt. 'I think we need to go and have a word with Jude. Don't you?'

Chapter 46

Jude

THURSDAY

'Any luck?' Jude asks as Sorrell and Will traipse back into the living room. The atmosphere instantly becomes more strained. Whatever happened when they were out looking for Finnley and Robyn, it obviously wasn't good.

'No sign of him.' Sorrell perches on the edge of the sofa beside her but doesn't meet her gaze. 'He's obviously not in Lowbridge . . .' As she continues to talk rapidly, her body language as tight and tense as her voice, Jude becomes aware of Will staring at her from across the room, the oddest expression on his face.

'Sorry, Sorrell,' she says, 'I don't mean to interrupt, but Will, why are you looking at me like that?' Before he can reply she glances back at Sorrell and the pieces fall into place. 'Oh fuck no. You told him about the diary, didn't you? Sorrell, you—'

'I didn't. I swear.' There's panic on Sorrell's face now. 'I just said the word "diary" and then he put two and two—'

'Jude,' Will interrupts her. 'Did you take a diary from my house?'

'Yes, but only to try and prove your innocence.' The accusation in his eyes puts her on the defensive and she sits up taller. 'Half of Lowbridge thought you were a murderer and—'

'Only half?'

The upwards twitch of one of his eyebrows makes her pause, but only for a split second because she's in full flow and she's not going to let him interrupt her again. 'I think she blackmailed someone and that's why she was killed and that, if we can just identify whose secrets she knew then—'

Sorrell speaks so softly that Jude continues talking for another couple of seconds until her brain registers what was just said. 'What was that?'

'Robyn.' Sorrell's eyes are pale and haunted. 'She's been blackmailing me.'

Jude listens, heart pounding, as Sorrell tells her the details then she asks for her phone. 'So I can read Robyn's messages,' she clarifies and Sorrell hands over her phone. She bends over the screen occasionally shaking her head, brow furrowed as she scrolls through the texts.

'We need to go to the police,' she says when she finally looks up.

'And say what?' Will asks.

'That Robyn's alive and she's been blackmailing Sorrell.'

A resigned smile lifts the edges of Will's mouth but it doesn't match the expression in his eyes and Jude feels a twinge of irritation. Robyn's alive and he's off the hook for her murder. Would a little bit of joy go amiss? She'd be punching the ceiling if it was her.

'What's that sceptical look for?'

When he doesn't immediately respond she looks at Sorrell who shrugs desolately.

'He thinks the person who's been blackmailing me might be a catfish.'

'What? No! No way. Look at this.' Jude holds her and Sorrell's phones out towards Will. 'Here's the proof. Look at the spelling of "absolutely" in this diary entry. She adds an "e" after the second "l". She does the same in one of her messages to Sorrell. Same person. See!'

'That may be true but it's not Robyn.'

'Of course it is! The spelling of absolutely is the same in the—'

'It's not her diary.'

Jude's brain fills with white noise as she stares at him. *Of course* the diary is Robyn's; it was in a box with the rest of her things. Why would he lie about it being her diary? Was he the one who ripped out the last two pages? Was there something incriminating in it that he doesn't want her to read?

'Why would you say that?' she asks.

'Because it's not her handwriting.'

'I don't believe you.'

'The police do. They searched my house remember? They took everything that might be evidence – clothes, laptops, phones, that diary – then they gave them all back, eventually. I know Robyn's handwriting, Jude, and whoever wrote that diary, it wasn't her.'

'But . . . but who . . . why? Why would she have someone else's diary? Whose is it?'

'I don't know.' Will sits forward in his seat and cups his jaw with his hand, his eyes on hers. 'I didn't even know it existed until the police searched the house. I've read it, obviously, and I've got no idea who it belongs to. I don't know if Robyn found it and was planning on returning it to its owner, or if she stole it for a joke or if there was something more malicious behind it but . . .' he shakes his head and the warmth in his eyes cools '. . . there's a conversation to be had about *you* stealing it and keeping that from me, but I think maybe we should leave that particular chat for another time.'

Not in front of Sorrell, is what he's trying to say. Jude shifts uncomfortably in her seat. That's not a conversation she's in a hurry to have.

'So, who's been blackmailing me?' Sorrell clutches her arm. 'And who's Finnley been messaging and giving money to? He's trying to meet up with her – with Robyn – but she doesn't even seem to exist. He's stopped answering my calls. What the hell do I do?'

'Call him again. Tell him you'll go to the police if he doesn't reply. I'm not saying he's in any danger, but . . .' Jude lets the sentence drift. Andy's dead. Robyn's almost certainly dead too.

Her gaze slides across the room to Will Ledger, sitting back in his seat, his hands interlinked behind his head, elbows angled towards the ceiling, eyes closed. After everything that's transpired that evening she's stressed, Sorrell's panic-stricken and Will's acting like he hasn't got a care in the world.

Chapter 47

Sorrell

THURSDAY

Sorrell pours herself and Jude a second glass of red wine and takes a long, desperate glug, trying not to focus on the phone on her coffee table – taunting her. One week ago, she would have viewed her phone as a source of work, distraction or irritation. Right now, it's as terrifying as a bomb.

'You've got this,' Jude says beside her. 'If he doesn't answer, you call the police. If he does, you tell him what you know.'

They're calming words but Jude's as anxious as she is. Sorrell saw the way she jolted when Will Ledger said he needed to get back to pay the babysitter, and the way her eyes trailed after him as he left the living room and disappeared into the hall.

'Right, fine, okay.' Desperate to get it over and done

with Sorrell puts down her wine glass and snatches up the phone. There's a part of her that really doesn't want to talk to her lying, cheating husband. He's dug this hole, let him lie in it and rot. But he's also her children's father and if something happened to him, she'd never be able to forgive herself. If Will is right, and the person pretending to be Robyn is a catfish, who knows what they might do to avoid their real identity being uncovered. Wherever Finnley is, whatever he's doing, his silence is worrying. She needs to warn him how much danger he might be in, if it's not already too late.

She jabs at the call icon on the screen and listens to the dialling tone, her heart racing. After several seconds the call goes through to voicemail.

'No joy?' Jude asks and she shakes her head.

'I'll text him.'

Finnley, I know you're screening my calls. Pick up the next time I call you or I'm going to go to the police to report you as missing.

Jude, who's peering over her shoulder, says, 'Should you mention he's potentially in danger?'

Sorrell nods and adds, *You could be in danger,* then she presses send.

A couple of seconds later a reply appears.

I'm fine. Don't involve the police in domestic matters. This has nothing to do with them.

What's domestic about being blackmailed? she replies. She glances at Jude who shakes her head.

'Don't let him know you're pissed off or he'll stop replying. Call him. You need to tell him what you know.'

Sorrell sighs loudly but she deletes the text, unsent.

I have something important to tell you, she taps out instead. *I'm going to call you. Pick up the phone.*

When she calls his number for a second time – on speakerphone so Jude can hear it – she's so certain that he'll ignore it again that, when the call does connect, she gasps into the phone.

'Finnley?'

'Yes.' She can hear the exasperation behind the word.

'You're being catfished. Whoever you've been messaging and sending money to, it isn't Robyn.' The urge to give him hell for clearing out her savings account is almost more than she can bear but she knows he'll put the phone down on her if she does. She'll tell him exactly what she thinks of him when she's sure that he's safe.

There's a pause then: 'You're wrong.'

'I'm not. I've got proof that it's not Robyn.'

His barked laugh in reply makes her blood run cold. 'What is this? What are you playing at?'

Anger swells in her chest and tightens her throat. Playing? Playing! A heavy hand on her knee snaps her back into herself. Jude's looking at her with concern.

'Finnley,' she squeezes out his name then reaches for her wine glass and takes a big gulp. 'Whoever has been blackmailing me and sending me your voicemails is not Robyn Lewis. We all thought it was because—'

'Who's we?'

'We need to go to the police about this, Finnley. Tell me where you are.'

'Who's we, Sorrell?'

'Me, and Jude and Will Ledger. What does it mat—'

'You told *him* about Robyn? When he's the reason she ran away? The reason she's too scared to come back to Lowbridge and—'

'IT'S . . . NOT . . . ROBYN. It's someone pretending to be her. LISTEN TO ME! Jude found a diary in Will's house and we thought it was Robyn's because she makes the same typo that my blackmailer does. But Will says the diary isn't in her handwriting. You haven't been texting Robyn. It's a catfish, pretending to be her.'

There's an intake of breath on the other line but, instead of responding, Finnley falls silent. So silent that Sorrell's about to ask if he's still there when he says, 'Will's lying.'

She slumps forward, cups her forehead with her hands and sighs despairingly. How can such a clever man be so stupid? Has love really blinded him so much that he can't see what's right in front of his face?

'Finnley—'

'Will Ledger's lying, Sorrell. Do you know how I know?'

'I'm sure you'll tell me.'

'Because I saw Robyn this morning. And she's very much alive.'

Her lips part but the line goes dead, before she can reply.

'Fuck,' Jude breathes as Sorrell places the phone on the coffee table and reaches for her wine. She's aware of the movements her body makes – the outstretched arm, the pincer movement of her fingers, the tang of the wine on her throat – but it's as though she's watching herself from the ceiling.

'Do you believe him?' Jude's clutching her wine glass like it's a rope and she's free-falling. 'Or do you believe Will?'

Sorrell shakes her head numbly. There are thoughts in her brain, but they're as fragmented as broken glass.

'Still want to go to the police?' Jude asks.

Something sparks inside Sorrell – rage, injustice, a fury that she's been pushing down for days. 'No,' she says firmly.

'I'm going to find out the truth and confront Robyn, or whoever's responsible for trying to destroy my family, face to face.' She gives Jude a long look. 'I think it's time to bring Victoria in on this, don't you?'

Chapter 48

Victoria

FRIDAY

Victoria grabs the wine bottle from the table and pours a hefty measure into her glass. It's early afternoon and she never drinks in the daytime, or if she's looking after the children, but screw it. Noah and Sophia, who haven't returned to school since she broke the news about their father's death, are out for the day with her parents and it's going to take more than two glasses to get drunk.

Wine glass empty she reaches for the bottle again then jolts as the doorbell sounds. She jumps up and heads for the front door. She throws it open, expecting to see her children and parents on the doorstep. Instead, two women smile tentatively at her before one of them thrusts a huge bouquet of roses and lilies at her chest.

'These are for you,' Jude says, while Sorrell, beside her, her long hair unplaited, steps nervously from foot to foot.

'That's very kind. Thank you.' Victoria buries her nose in the blooms, hiding the unexpected rush of emotion she feels. Of all the people she thought would turn up on her doorstep to check on her, she never would have picked these two.

'I've been thinking about you,' Jude says earnestly, the brightness of her blue jumper clashing with her sombre expression.

'We both have,' Sorrell adds.

'Thank you, for everything you both did.'

As an awkward silence settles, Victoria looks from one woman to the other, trying to read the tension in their faces. There's something they want to say but they're not sure how to say it. She hopes to God it's not more platitudes, or questions, about Andy. She's heard enough from the other school mums to last her two lifetimes. If she hears the words 'sorry' or 'condolences' again she'll scream.

'Do you . . .' she ventures. 'Do you want to come in?'

'If now's not a good time,' Sorrell says, 'we totally understand.'

'You're grieving,' Jude adds.

Sorrell meets Jude's eyes and shakes her head sharply. 'It's too early. I'm sorry, Victoria, we really shouldn't have come. I don't know what we were thinking.'

'Yeah,' Jude says. 'Yeah, you're right.'

As they turn to go, Victoria calls after them. 'Too early for what?'

Sorrell shrugs off the question and raises a hand in goodbye but Jude turns back. 'It's not important. It's about Robyn.'

Robyn? Victoria jolts in surprise. Of all the words to come out of Jude's mouth that definitely wasn't one she was expecting.

'You can't just drop that name and leave.' She opens the door wider. 'Please, come in.'

'Have you heard anything from the police?' Jude asks as they congregate on Victoria's plush grey velvet sofa. 'About Andy?'

At the mention of her husband's name Victoria's heart cramps in her chest. It's been less than seventy-two hours since she, and these two women, hauled her husband's body from the bathtub. She can't close her eyes without seeing Andy's pale, slack-jawed face. It's like a memory from a horror film or a nightmare – visceral, horrific – but at the same time, it doesn't feel real.

'No.' She shakes her head. 'I mean, yes. The family liaison officer checks in daily but I don't really get told anything. Just, you know, active investigation, lines of enquiry, all that stuff. It's frustrating and I hate the fact that I don't know exactly what's going on . . .' She tails off. 'Anyway, can we . . . can we talk about something else? God knows I need the distraction. What's happened with Robyn? Has Will Ledger finally admitted killing her? Has her body been found?'

She listens, eyes widening, as Jude and Sorrell tell her everything – from the reason they both visited Andy in the first place, the blackmail, the diary and their confusion about whether Robyn is alive or dead. How could all that happen in Lowbridge without her knowing? Has she been fast asleep for the last eighteen months?

'You know Theresa was being blackmailed too,' she tells Sorrell, 'About her kleptomania. Or at least she claimed to be, and she had the audacity to point the finger at me.'

When Sorrell and Jude exchange a look she adds, 'It wasn't me, obviously.

'No, no. That wasn't why we did that,' Jude says, reaching into her handbag for her phone. 'It was because we forgot about her, Theresa I mean. We've been trying to work out who the women are that are referred to in the diary and the numbers aren't adding up – but it makes sense now, with Theresa.'

'We're trying to work out who's been blackmailing me,' Sorrell adds. 'Now we know it's not Robyn.'

'You believe Will, that the diary's not hers?' Victoria raises an eyebrow.

'Absolutely. Why would he lie? I'm almost certain that one of the other school mums has been blackmailing me and catfishing Finnley. Possibly blackmailing Theresa too.'

'This is the photo I took of the diary entry.' Jude hands Victoria her phone. 'If you can remember whose secrets these are then we can eliminate those women. Sorrell thinks she's the one with the secret savings account. Finnley found out about it; that's why she had to give him access.'

'Okay.' Victoria zooms in on the image, her eyes flitting over the words. 'That's Caz.' She jabs a fingernail at the first secret. 'She's the one who started going to church to get her kids into St Augustine's.'

Beside her, Jude scribbles in a notebook *Fox = Caz*.

'That was me.' Victoria slides her nail down to Badger. 'Truthfully, which married woman of ten, fifteen years wouldn't rather watch telly than have sex?'

She looks at Sorrell, who shrugs.

'Me again.' She points at the revelation about the sex party. 'Long time ago, pre-Andy. What can I say? I've lived. Flamingo's Sara. She secretly stopped taking her pill. No judgement from me.'

'So . . .' Jude, who's been frantically scribbling, puts her pen down. 'That means that Tiger, Blowfish, Cheetah and

IT'S ALWAYS THE HUSBAND

Chihuahua must be Shahina, Theresa, Audrey and Dawn. No wait, that doesn't work.'

'Because you're forgetting about Robyn,' Victoria says. 'She could be one of the mums who didn't share a secret, assuming Will was telling the truth of course. Oh wait, hang on. I've just thought of something. Dawn can't be the one who wrote the diary because she wasn't on the night out when I was talking about the sex party and watching telly in bed.'

'So not Dawn.' Jude hastily scrubs her name out from the list.

'So either Shahina, Audrey or Theresa,' Sorrell says, 'wrote the diary, blackmailed me and is pretending to be Robyn.'

'Yeah. Shit.' Victoria runs her hands through her hair. She can't quite believe that one of her friends would do this. 'How sure are you that the diary writer actually went through with their blackmail threat? It might have been a joke.'

'Pretty sure,' Sorrell says. 'They make the same typo in the texts to me and the diary entry. They can't spell the word *absolutely*.'

Victoria looks back at the screen. 'Okay, that's pretty damning.'

'I don't suppose you recognise the handwriting?' Jude asks. 'I know everyone just texts each other these days but—'

'Birthday cards!' Victoria jumps up. 'It was my birthday a couple of months ago and Noah made me take them out of the recycling. He said it was mean to throw them away. I meant to chuck them when he wasn't looking and . . . I'm pretty sure I forgot.' She darts out of the living room and into the kitchen where she frantically opens and closes drawers.

'Got them!' She returns, victorious, to the living room, a wad of thin cardboard in her hand. They pore over the diary entry again, comparing each card against the untidy scribble on the page.

As they compare the last card the bubbling, excited sensation in Victoria's chest fizzes out. 'It's not any of them. How is that even possible?' Jude and Sorrell both look as deflated and disappointed as she feels. 'Are there any more entries?' She scrolls to the next photo on Jude's phone. 'Any other clues?'

Jude shakes her head. 'I haven't got any more photos but whoever wrote it mentioned feeling left out and excluded at the school gates. That could be anyone. Oh, they also had a crush on Andy.'

Victoria's eyes widen in alarm. One of her friends had a crush on her husband? And there's that feeling again that she doesn't know *anyone* as well as she thought. 'What did they say?'

'Not much. A crush, they were putting make-up on for the school run. That's about it.'

Victoria feels sick. 'Was it an affair?' She's pretty certain Andy cheated on her but she assumed it was with his colleagues, not one of her friends.

'I don't know. I don't think so. I mean, he's not mentioned again but she does call another, unnamed school dad a lady-killer. Sorrell thinks that's probably Finnley, given what we now know about him and Robyn although—' She breaks off again. 'Sorrell, are you all right? What are you staring at?'

Victoria turns to see what she's talking about and, sure enough, Sorrell's staring across the room, a peculiar expression on her face.

'Can I . . .' Sorrell gestures across the room. 'Can I just look at something?'

IT'S ALWAYS THE HUSBAND

'Yeahhh,' Victoria says slowly.

She glances across at Jude as Sorrell gets up and walks across the living room, but Jude shakes her head. Neither of them has a clue what's going on.

Sorrell points up at the living room clock then turns to look at Victoria. 'Is that connected to the Wi-Fi or something?'

'No, why would you connect a—'

'There's a light, at the bottom. It's been intermittently blinking, subtly. It's done it twice since we sat down.'

Victoria stands up and joins her. 'It takes batteries and . . . hang on.' She pauses beneath the clock and looks up at it. She must glance at it several times a day but she hasn't looked at it properly since she bought it last year. 'That's not my clock. I mean, it looks a lot like it, but mine had a thin silver band around it and that one's all white.' She lifts it off the wall and turns it over in her hands. It looks like a regular clock. Why on earth would it blink?

'Can I see that?' Sorrell asks.

Victoria hands it to her as Jude joins them.

'The blinking was here.' Sorrell touches number 10. She peers at it, then angles the clock from side to side.

'What are you looking for?'

'I'm not sure. Does that . . . in the middle of the number one . . . does that bit look slightly domed to you?'

'Yes. It's not flat like the rest of the numbers. What does it mean? Why would it blink?'

Sorrell turns the clock over and removes the batteries. 'My brother's a software salesman and he does a lot of travelling for work, stays in a lot of hotels and Airbnbs. He's paranoid about being spied on. He sent me an article about it, warning me to be careful when I go away with the kids. It's really scary how subtly these things can be hidden.'

Victoria shivers. If Sorrell's right, then someone's been spying on her. As if her life isn't fucked up enough.

'Here, look.' Sorrell runs her fingernail under a small piece of black plastic in the centre of the battery compartment and a small door flips open. 'Here's the SIM.' She jabs at the clock again and a SIM card pops out from the back, like it does from a mobile when you stick a pin into the side. 'Maybe it's full and that's why it was blinking?'

'Who has access to your house?' Jude asks.

'Me, my cleaner, my parents, Andy and . . .' Victoria turns to stare at the front door, her mind whirring. 'Absolutely everyone I've ever invited round for drinks.'

Jude and Sorrell stare at her. They're thinking what she's thinking – that whoever blackmailed Theresa and Sorrell has been keeping an eye on her too.

'We need to find out what the hell is on this SIM card,' she tells them. 'Anyone know how?'

An hour later, after a call to Sorrell's brother and a quick trip into town to buy a SIM card reader, the three women pore over Victoria's laptop as she opens the folder. Her heart rate quickens as she double clicks on the AVI file and Windows Media Player launches. Whatever's been recorded it's related to Andy's death she's certain, and a more sensible woman would have taken the clock and the SIM straight to the police. And then what? More torturous waiting as they investigate. Well fuck that. Whatever she's about to see she'd rather know now.

For a split second there's nothing on screen apart from

a reddish orange blur and she feels a stab of disappointment, but then the image sharpens, and a hand comes into view, moving away from the camera. Then there's a body, and a face, staring straight up into the camera.

'Andy!' She looks from Jude's dropped jaw to Sorrell, her hand clutching her mouth. Andy replaced her clock with covert CCTV? Why? It doesn't make sense.

'Look!' Sorrell jabs at the screen then hurries across the room to the TV and ducks behind it.

Victoria looks back at the video, where Andy's doing exactly the same thing.

'Look at this!' Sorrell rushes back, brandishing the sort of air freshener you'd find in a pub toilet. 'I'm guessing you don't normally keep one tucked at the back of your TV stand?'

'Seriously?' Victoria says, which makes Jude laugh. 'I wouldn't let that monstrosity in my bin, never mind my house.'

'It's another camera. You can see the camera there, in that little hole.' Sorrell prises the front off, revealing a black box with a port in the side. Her eyes shining with excitement.

'There's more.' Jude gestures at the screen as Andy moves across the room and plucks what looks like a phone adapter plug out of a socket and turns it over in her hands. 'It looks like he put devices everywhere. They're probably all over your house.'

The hollowing sensation Victoria feels is so sudden, so violent that she presses a hand to her chest. It's as though the air has been stolen from her lungs and she can't breathe. Her home was her safety, her sanctity, the nest she made for her children.

'Why?' she gasps. 'Why?' She looks into Sorrell and Jude's eyes but all she sees is her own confusion, horror and incomprehension reflected straight back at her. Once upon a time her life was almost boring in its predictability, but now even the ground beneath her feet doesn't feel real.

Chapter 49

Jude

SATURDAY

Jude is worried about Victoria. Once the shock at discovering that Andy had bugged her house had worn off, an unbridled rage took its place. She stalked through the ground floor of her house, alternately ripping photos, pictures and smoke detectors from the walls or screaming, 'You fucking bastard! What were you doing? Why were you spying on me? Why?' Jude and Sorrell followed her, initially begging her not to destroy her house before they too joined in the search. Between the three of them they discovered four more devices – in the hallway, landing and kitchen. Despite a thorough search of the bedrooms, no more devices were found.

When Victoria eventually collapsed, emotionally exhausted, on the sofa her brain refused to be stilled. When she wasn't trying to work out 'why the fuck Andy would want to spy on me' she was ranting about Theresa, Robyn, Will, Andy's murder, the diary, blackmail and the fact she was certain they were all interconnected and that 'not one bastard in Lowbridge is who they pretend to be'.

Only a knock on the front door, heralding the return of her parents and children, finally silenced her although she didn't answer it until she'd hissed to them both, 'Tomorrow. We need to talk more about this tomorrow. I'll text you. Tell you where to meet.'

To Jude's surprise, that place ended up being a chip shop on Lowbridge high street, which is where they're all sitting now.

'There's a massive flaw in your plan.' She dips a chip into ketchup, keeping an eye on Betsy who's on a separate table with Henry, Harper, Sophia and Noah. It's pouring with rain outside, Victoria's original plan to meet in the park abandoned within minutes of them all parking up. 'We haven't got the charity shop stuff.'

'Doesn't matter.' Victoria lifts the batter from her fish with a wooden fork and jabs at the white flesh beneath. 'We can pretend.'

Before they met up Victoria rang every charity shop in the Devonshire town where Tony and Theresa live, asking if they could remember a donation that included a gold Eames bird, a penguin ornament from Tiffany's and a blue glass bowl. Her plan was to drive down and retrieve the items only, none of the volunteers she spoke to could remember the items apart from one, who had a vague memory of a gold bird but said that it had probably sold.

Sorrell, who's doing her best to stop Scout from smearing her jumper with chip grease and ketchup, shakes her head. 'What's the point of doing this if Theresa is on holiday?'

'She'll be back by now. It was Monday when Tony said he was taking her to Cornwall for a few days.'

'But how are you going to text her when she's blocked you?'

'I won't text her. Jude will.'

'And you really think she'll drive all the way up from Devon to get the diary?' Jude says, 'Assuming it's even hers.'

'It can't be her.' Sorrell wipes Scout's fingers on a napkin. 'She was blackmailed too, remember.'

'You're assuming she was telling the truth.' Victoria's still sporting the same determined expression she's had since the conversation began. She's fixated with the idea that they can flush the diary writer, and Robyn's potential murderer, out of suburbia and into their trap. 'We can't discount anyone. You two should think yourselves lucky that I even trust you.'

She's smiling now, and so is Jude. She's not sure if she judged Victoria too harshly when she first met her, whether Victoria's mellowed, or she's fallen under her spell, but she finally understands why she's so popular. She's bossy, sure, an attention seeker, and preternaturally self-confident, but she's funny and, underneath her Barbie-like exterior, there's an actual beating heart.

'You know this could be a massive waste of time,' Jude says, reaching for her can of Diet Coke. 'We might be *way* off the mark narrowing it down to Audrey, Theresa and Shahina.'

Victoria shrugs nonchalantly. 'Maybe, but if we don't lure them out that's three less suspects.'

'Fewer.'

Victoria shoots her a *what the fuck?*

'What?'

'Don't be an asshole like Andy.'

Jude's cheeks grow warmer. It's not the first time in her life she's been called a grammar pedant. 'Sorry. Part of the job. Anyway—'

'If there were more of us . . .' Victoria crosses her arms over her chest, her fish abandoned. 'I'd suggest we keep an eye on Will's house too.'

'He didn't write the diary and blackmail Sorrell!'

'He might not have written the diary, but he's involved in this somehow.'

'How?'

Victoria gives her a cool, measured look. 'You really need me to spell it out for you?'

Jude feels a prickle of irritation at the other woman's patronising tone. 'Please do. I'm stupid like that.'

'I think he murdered Ali, and he probably killed Andy too.'

'But not Robyn?' Sorrell asks.

'Oh, I'm pretty sure he killed her. But if he didn't, then they're in on this blackmail plot together. I don't trust a single word that comes out of his mouth.'

A dozen comebacks bubble in Jude's brain then pop just as quickly. A couple of weeks ago she would have leapt to Will's defence and had a raging argument with Victoria. Now . . . well . . . she's not as keen to be his shield, especially when she's got a lot of questions herself.

'Guys, please.' Sorrell places her hands on both their shoulders. 'Let's not do this again. If we go ahead with the plan tonight, to flush out whoever wrote the diary, then we'll know for sure who's lying – Will or Finnley – and whether Robyn's my blackmailer or not. Whoever it is, hopefully I get to punch them in the face.' She takes a breath. 'So, childcare allowing, are you two in or not?'

'Obviously,' Victoria says, 'It was my plan after all.'

After a pause, Jude gives a grunt of agreement.

'Good.' Sorrell shifts Scout onto her shoulder when he starts to grizzle and gently rubs his back.

Jude looks down at the notes she's tapped into her phone. 'So at 8 p.m. I text the mamas WhatsApp group and say that Theresa, in a fit of guilt, sent all the stolen stuff to Victoria who has passed it on to me to give to everyone at school on Monday. Then I'll add a photo of the diary and say that we don't know who it belongs to but Theresa obviously stole it. I'll say that it hasn't been read, just a peek in the inside cover to see if there was a name, and I'll put it in the clear recycling box outside my house if the owner wants to collect it.'

'Then you'll text Theresa anonymously,' Victoria adds, 'Include the photo of the diary and say, "I believe this is yours," and include your address.'

'And while all this is going on,' Sorrell continues, 'I'll be watching Audrey's house, Jude will be watching Shahina's and Victoria will be watching Jude's to catch Theresa or anyone who might have slipped through the net.'

Jude raises her hand. 'I still think it makes more sense for me to watch my own house.'

Victoria shakes her head sharply. 'Not when Shahina knows my car really well.'

'So we swap cars?'

'How about you just stick to the plan?' And there it is again, the 'do not fuck with me' steel in Victoria's eyes. An objection forms on Jude's lips but she lets it go. Given everything Victoria's been through is she really *that* bothered about staking out her own house? No, she's not.

'Mummm!!!!' Harper whinges from the next table. 'Henry's taken my lemonade and he won't give it back!'

'On that note . . .' Sorrell slowly gets up from the table.

'Meeting over. If no one goes to Jude's to claim the diary then we go to the police tomorrow and tell them everything.

'Not going to happen.' Victoria gets up too. 'I think a lot of questions are going to be answered tonight.'

'Talking of the diary,' Sorrell says, 'I really want to read it. See if I can spot any clues that you might have missed. Do you think you could get it back from Will Ledger?'

Jude doesn't immediately reply. She's remembering the last time she saw him, in Sorrell's living room after they'd returned from looking for Finnley. While she was freaking out about the fact that Robyn hadn't written the diary, he had his hands clasped behind his head, acting like he didn't have a care in the world. He hasn't texted her since, and she hasn't texted him either. She's not sure if 'relationship' is the right word for what they've been doing but, whatever it was, it's definitely been paused.

'I think . . . you might have to ask him,' she says slowly. She glances at Victoria, expecting a question or a sarcastic comment but, for once, Victoria's mouth remains closed.

Chapter 50

Victoria, Jude and Sorrell

SATURDAY

Jude looks at her watch – 7.57 p.m. – and her pulse quickens. She's parked up down the street from Shahina's house and there's only three minutes to go until she hits send on the message that could reveal the identity of Sorrell's blackmailer. It took forever, going back and forth between the three of them, until they were all decided on the wording but it's in the WhatsApp group now, ready to send, along with a photo of the diary.

Hi all! (Victoria had insisted on *Hi guys!* but Jude had objected, saying she'd rather chew off her own fingers than start a message like a sixteen-year-old YouTuber).

Hi all! Just to let you know that, when I visited Victoria earlier today to take her flowers, she gave me a box that Theresa's husband Tony had sent her, containing several items that had been stolen (her bird, Caz's ornament, Audrey's bowl. Not gift card, sorry Shahina), and she will return them to everyone next week. This diary was also in the box. Does it belong to anyone? We've respected the diary owner's privacy and only checked inside the cover for a name (there isn't one). Victoria wasn't sure what to do with it so, because she's not in a great head space right now, I said I'd try and return it to its owner. I'm off out tonight but if you're desperate to get it back I've put it in the clear recycling box in my front garden (it's clean, with a lid on!) If no one claims it I'll bring it in when I get home later. My address is 15 Beechwood Drive. Take care. X

She composed a different text to Theresa:

Hi Theresa, we didn't really get know each other before you left but I'm Jude, Betsy's mum. Sara gave me your number. I'm trying to track down the owner of this diary. If you happen to be visiting Lowbridge this weekend I'm leaving it in a clear plastic recycling box outside my house so the owner can claim it – 15 Beechwood Drive. If it's yours let me know and I'll bring it into the house instead. Jude. x

Her gut instinct is that it's highly unlikely that Theresa will jump in a car and drive to Lowbridge from Devon, even if it is her diary, but Victoria insisted that the message was sent. Jude checks the time again – 8.00 p.m. – and hits send.

Parked up near Audrey's house in the thickest coat she owns and a beanie, Sorrell dims the screen on her phone. When

Jude sent the group text, it lit up like the local garden centre's Christmas display, and the last thing she wants is for someone to spot her, sitting alone in Finn's car with a massive dent in the front. It's not the dent she's worried about – she stopped believing that Finnley hit anything other than an animal a while ago – but she really doesn't want Audrey to rumble her. So much rests on tonight's plan going well.

She waits, nervously, for the 'mamas' to respond to Jude's text but a minute passes, then two, then five and still no one's commented. Surely they're not all having such amazing Saturday nights that they're too busy to check their phones.

Her phone bleeps with a message. It's from Jude, posted into the group chat that's just for the three of them:

Caz just privately messaged me. Asked that I bring her Tiffany penguin to her house tonight! The cheek. Have I got Uber stamped on my forehead or what? I haven't replied what with me being in the 'pub' and all.

Sorrell types back, *Good decision. Save the argument for another day.*

Victoria replies too. *Ignore her. Ignore all of them. Anyone see anything suspicious yet? I borrowed my dad's car so mine won't be recognised. REALLY hard convincing him not to open the bonnet of my car to look for the 'fault' I said I was having! I'm parked just down the street from Jude's.*

Sorrell's gaze drifts from her phone's screen to the enormous mansion-sized house at the end of the very exclusive street. She was so impressed by the sheer size of the place the first time Audrey invited her round for a drink. With its six bedrooms and elegant, expensive interior design it was the kind of home she could only dream of. Now she finds it as cold and uninviting as its owner. About as communicative too.

Restless now, she opens the glove compartment and takes

out the diary. Earlier, when she'd texted Will, asking to read it, she'd expected him to say no outright, or make an excuse. Instead, he texted back almost immediately. *I can drop it round now if you're home.*

She turns the first page and, using the dim light from her phone, she begins to read.

Parked up in her dad's white Range Rover, across the street from Will's house, Victoria looks from the tall, elegant Victorian terraced home to the glowing screen of her daughter's mobile phone. She wrangled it from Sophia earlier, telling her that it needed a system upgrade and she'd return it later. The discussion went as well as she'd imagined it would, but the promise of horse-riding lessons eventually calmed Sophia down, and now Victoria's in possession of a burner phone of her own.

But now she's worried about the wording of the text that she's drafted:

I know where Robyn is. Transfer £100,000 via Paypal to noonespuppet@outlook.com or the police will receive a tip-off.

In 'theory' she should be parked up outside Jude's house. What's she's actually doing is setting a trap for Lowbridge's Poundland Tom Hardy, the man who's dickmatised Jude. Jude looked so appalled when Victoria cast suspicion in Will's direction there was no way she could tell her what she was actually planning. She hasn't told Sorrell either because she's as convinced as Jude that Will's been telling the truth. He might have pulled the wool over their eyes but Victoria's never been a fan of lanolin; it smells sour and it makes her skin itch.

IT'S ALWAYS THE HUSBAND

The way she sees it there are only three possible outcomes when she sends the text to Will: either he ignores it, he leads her to where Robyn's hiding, or he goes to check that her body's still wherever he buried it. If he goes for either of the last two options she'll follow him and if he just ignores her message then she'll . . . scream.

She rereads the text again. She needs to add something heavier, darker, that he definitely won't be able to ignore.

Pursing her lips together, she adds an extra line at the end of the text message. In the improbable event that Will's innocent (and she's ninety-nine per cent sure that he's not) he's unlikely to tell the police about an anonymous threatening message. Not when he openly distrusts them. He made that perfectly clear to Andy, over the years.

Andy.

A pang of regret pierces her heart. She's still desperately angry with him but she can't shake the thought that she could have saved his life if she'd got to his flat sooner. That's one 'what if' that keeps her awake at night.

She runs a hand through her hair and looks back at the curtained windows of 19 Hollyhock Terrace. What if she's right? What if Will killed Robyn and Andy? That makes him very dangerous indeed. If anything happened to her, her children would be orphaned. By doing this is she making a terrible, terrible mistake? She shoves the thought away. Nothing's going to happen to her. All she's going to do is follow Will. She's not going to confront him. He won't even know that she's there.

As she continues to watch the house a male silhouette drifts past one of the windows and the spark of rage she feels is so intense, so scorching, that she jabs at her mobile's screen.

The text has been sent.

* * *

There's movement in Shahina's house. Jude's seen Kwame, her husband, wandering around in the kitchen and living room, blinds and curtains open, oblivious to the fact that she's watching every move he makes. There's also been movement in an upstairs bedroom, a silhouette behind closed curtains, that can only be Shahina. Is she waiting for her husband to settle, so she can secretly slip out of the house?

An hour has passed since Jude sent the text and photo, and Audrey's going nowhere, according to Sorrell. No sign of anything untoward happening back in Jude's garden either. Victoria texted to say that no one had even walked past.

Maybe they've got it completely wrong, and it isn't Audrey, Shahina or Theresa. Maybe there was someone else at the parties and nights out that Victoria's forgotten about? Maybe one of the 'mamas' shared everyone's secrets with another school mum? Maybe they're following the wrong scent?

Jude's phone vibrates on the passenger seat. Will again. It's the third time he's tried to call her in as many minutes. He's obviously stressing about something but she doesn't trust herself to answer in case he asks what she's doing. She's always been a terrible liar. Emma says her voice goes up half an octave, and she's awful at keeping a straight face. If Will suspects what they're up to he'll either try and get involved, or he'll ruin everything and call the police. Either way, whatever he wants to talk about, he's going to have to wait.

A pang of guilt hits her – what if something's happened to Milly? She pushes the thought away. After their row about her criticising Will's parenting she's pretty sure she's the last person he'd call.

She taps the 'decline' button. Will Ledger can wait.

Sorrell yawns and rolls back her shoulders. She's been watching Audrey's house for an hour and a half and the most exciting thing that's happened is an upstairs light going on. She finished reading the diary ages ago and, despite her optimism that she might find something that Jude missed, she's still as clueless as her. The only real lead in the whole thing, other than the blackmail list, was the confession about fancying Andy, but she hasn't got the first clue who that might be.

She moves her seat as far back as it will go, bends and straightens her legs to try and get the blood moving again. Regular Pilates classes stretch out her back and shoulders when she's been throwing and decorating pots for hours on end, but none of those moves are going to help her now.

Her thoughts switch to her children, left at home with a babysitter they've never met before, and she feels a strong pang of guilt. There was a time when she and the other 'mamas' would exchange babysitting tokens and take turns to sit with each other's kids. Falling out with Audrey changed all that. Suddenly everyone had 'other plans' when she wanted to use one of her tokens and many of her texts were left unread.

The memory sparks an urgency within her. She's sick of being left in the dark. 'Jude, Vic, I'm sorry,' she whispers as she opens the car door. 'But there's something I've got to do.'

The shapely silhouette behind the living room curtains makes Victoria sit up straighter. Will's got a woman in his house. It's not Jude, so who is it? Either he's got more friends than she gives him credit for, relatives she doesn't know about or he's seeing someone other than Jude. She takes a photo of the silhouette to show to Jude later, then presses a hand over her mouth as the automatic flash goes off, filling the car with a blinding white light. She slithers down in her seat, the phone pressed against her heaving chest, her breathing as shallow and rapid as it was when she gave birth.

'Fuck! Fuck! Fuck!' She screws her eyes tightly shut, teeth clenched, braced for a knock on the driver side window. She's too scared to open her eyes again in case it's Will Ledger's face she sees, leering in at her from outside the car. After what feels like an age she calms her breathing and risks a peep at the driver side window but there's nothing outside but houses, a streetlight, and gloom.

She cranes her head towards the roof and rubs a hand over the back of her neck. She's going to give herself a heart attack if she stays here much longer. She should just go, drive to Jude's as planned.

Sensing movement and light she twists to look back at Will's house. The front door is open and he's standing in the doorway with a woman who can only be his mother. They've got the same shaped nose and jawline. They have a short conversation then Will's mother steps back into the house and closes the door. Will steps out onto the street and heads towards his car. It flashes as he unlocks it but, instead of opening the door, he heads for the boot and rummages inside. He turns something over in his hands, as though appraising its weight and size, then carefully puts it back, closes the boot and opens the driver side door.

As he starts the engine and pulls away Victoria makes a split-second decision: follow him or go to Jude's house? It's an easy decision to make when Will's driving off with a shovel locked in the boot of his car.

Jude's phone has finally fallen silent but the urge to return Will's call is nagging at her, more out of boredom than anything else. Victoria and Sorrell's updates have all but dried up and she's wasted two hours of her life parked up in the middle of Lowbridge. Shahina's not even at the top of her list of suspects. The urge to just drive back home is strong.

'Ooh!' She sits forward in her seat as Shahina's front door opens and she steps into the front garden, triggering the security light. A couple of seconds later Kwame joins her on the patio, both of them dressed to the nines. Surely, he's not going to drive her to pick up the diary, looking the way that they do?

As they get into their car, Jude sinks down in her seat. With the light off in her car, it's pretty unlikely that they'll spot her but she's not taking any chances. She waits for their car to pull off, then starts the engine, her heart pounding in the base of her throat.

She waits until they drive to the bottom of the street and turn left, then follows them. It's nearly ten o'clock and the roads are near empty, but she gives way at the T junction to allow another car to slip between her car and Shahina's. Less chance of being noticed that way. Her excitement builds as they head east, towards her house. Maybe the fancy outfits are all part of a ruse, so if they're spotted driving through Lowbridge they can claim they were heading somewhere else? But why wouldn't Shahina just go on her own? Why drag Kwame along too?

Jude's mobile, on the passenger seat, flashes with a new message as Shahina's car takes a left rather than the right that she'd been anticipating. Maybe they're not going to her house after all. Perhaps they're going to warn someone that the diary's been discovered? But why not just call?

When the buffer car turns right, Jude glances at her phone then indicates left. She's hoping for an update from Victoria or Sorrell but it's her sister's name on the screen.

Betsy finally asleep, the first part of the message reads.

With her eyes on the screen, rather than the road, it takes her a second to notice that the red brake lights on Shahina's Mercedes are beaming and she does an emergency stop, bringing her own car to a shuddering halt. Seemingly oblivious to the fact that the car behind them has stalled, the Mercedes continues on down the street for another ten or fifteen metres, then the right indicator flashes. Jude looks from the parking spot that Shahina pulls into, to the house three doors away, festooned with lights and balloons. The outfits aren't part of an elaborate ruse, they're going to a party!

Sighing, she messages Sorrell and Victoria with an update then adds, *I don't know about you two, but I think we should call it a night. Heading home now unless either of you have updates?*

She waits a minute or so for a reply then, when the double ticks don't appear and the car behind her beeps its horn impatiently, she starts up the engine. Home it is, then.

Barely breathing, Victoria follows Will at a distance, keeping to the shadows as he strides down the street, holding the shovel in his hands like a weapon. She'd expected to follow him to the woods at the north of the town, or the countryside out near Mallhampton. What she didn't expect, was to follow him all the way to Jude's house.

As Will walks down the path to the front door, Victoria hovers by the gate, shielded from view by the bushes. Either Will's turned up at Jude's house to attack her with the shovel or, in the world's biggest coincidence, Robyn's buried in the garden. The house is rented, she knows that much, but she hasn't got the first clue who it belongs to. *Surely* Will isn't Jude's landlord. She would have told her if he was.

She risks a peek around the hedge and discovers that Will

has disappeared. He can only have gone around the side of the house to the back garden. What the hell's he planning on doing there?

Every muscle in her body tensed and primed for running, Victoria silently makes her way through the garden, wishing she hadn't left her phone in the car. Even muted, it might have flashed with a message and given her away but now she's left without any way of calling the police.

At the sound of laboured breathing she panics – Will's coming back and there's nowhere to hide. Frantic now, she squeezes herself into the small space between a large black bin and a wall. She listens, her hand clamped over her mouth as heavy footsteps crunch on gravel. She really, really doesn't want to die.

Chapter 51

Jude

SATURDAY

Jude slows the car as she passes Victoria's dad's white Range Rover, parked towards the bottom of her street. She blinks, confused as she peers inside. It's empty. Where the hell has Victoria gone?

Her breath catches as she realises the significance – Victoria must have caught someone looking in the recycling box and confronted them. That's why she didn't reply to her last text.

She parks up hurriedly, worried that there might some kind of altercation in her front garden, and runs across the road. The only light is the soft glow of the TV screens and lamps of her neighbours. Apart from the wail of an ambulance in the distance the street is completely quiet. That's not unusual in itself but she'd expected to hear the raised voices of two women. She desperately hopes that Victoria's all right.

IT'S ALWAYS THE HUSBAND

Muscle memory makes her reach for the catch on her gate, but it's already open. She steps tentatively into the garden, scanning the ground, fearing the worst. Victoria might be strong but God knows how much of a psychopath Theresa is. She's clearly unhinged to lie about being blackmailed when she was actually blackmailing Sorrell, but how would she have known about Finnley's hit-and-run? That's what she's struggling to work out.

A shadow flickers in her peripheral vision, making her start, but when she looks towards the side of the house, there's nothing – and no one there. She swears softly then glances at her phone, checking for two ticks or a message from Victoria but she still hasn't replied.

Where are you? she types then drifts towards the left of the garden, where the bins are kept. If Theresa's been there she'll have rifled through the clear plastic tub.

Sure enough, the lid is lying on its side and some of the brown packing paper Jude had filled it with is strewn on the ground. She glances over her shoulder, twisting sharply, expecting to find someone creeping towards her but the garden's still empty, no one's there. Maybe she should go back to the car and call Sorrell about Victoria. They need to find her. If anything's happened to her, she'll—

The large bush outside Jude's living room window rustles, then a beam of light reflects off the glass.

'Victoria?' she whispers. 'Is that you?'

She's almost knocked off her feet as someone barrels into her. She raises her arms defensively but, before she's completely regained her balance, she's shoved again, away from the bins and in the direction of the gate.

'Run!' Victoria screams at her. 'Run!'

The fear in the other woman's voice makes Jude's stomach lurch and her muscles tighten and she takes off, sprinting out of the garden and onto the street when a male voice barks,

'Jude! Jude stop!'

She stops running so abruptly that Victoria crashes into her.

'What are you doing?' Wide-eyed and sweating, Victoria shoves at her, trying to get her to continue down the street. 'Jude, you have to run!'

'Why?' She takes a step back towards her garden but Victoria grabs her, terror in her eyes.

'He's dangerous. Please Jude, just run!'

'Jude?' Will steps out onto the street, clutching what looks like a large stick, his fists clenched his arms raised. As his gaze flits from her to Victoria, who's cowering in fear, he lowers it and she sees the sharp metal square of the spade.

'What the actual fuck?' She feels like she's caught in a nightmare.

Will wipes the back of one hand over his brow and sighs. 'You're okay. Thank God.'

'Why wouldn't I be?' She looks back at Victoria questioningly. Did something happen that she doesn't know about? 'What the hell's going on?'

'I received a blackmail text, that threatened to hurt those I'm close to if I told the police.' Will steps closer, reaching into his pocket for his mobile. 'That's why I was ringing you, to make sure you were safe. When you didn't answer I told Mum to lock all the doors and windows and not to let Milly out of her sight until I came back. Now I know you're okay, I'm calling the police.'

'Wait!' Victoria shouts at the same time Jude says, 'What kind of threatening text?'

'Don't ring the police.' Victoria steps around her, holding her palm out to Will.

'Why not?' A frown creases his brow, but he doesn't lower his phone.

'I . . . I . . . I did something stupid.'

'What? Exactly?' Will's eyes narrow.

'I sent you that message. I . . . I don't know what I was thinking.'

Jude stares at her. 'You're the blackmailer?'

'No! Not that one. I messaged Will. I had to find out what he knew. I thought he would lead me to Robyn, or her body. I saw him put that spade in the boot of his car.'

'I bought it for the school allotment!' Will bellows, brandishing the spade. 'Or have you forgotten that the PTA strong-armed me into helping? If you'd care to check my boot, you'll also find a fork, a trowel, some pots, some seeds, and sixty litres of compost!'

'You weren't tending the allotment when you were creeping around Jude's house and garden like you were going to take someone's head off!'

'Because I thought she was in danger, and I don't own a baseball bat!'

'Stop it, both of you!' Jude holds up her hands then stares, accusingly at Victoria. 'Seriously? You sent Will a threatening text – while he was at home with his mother and daughter? What the hell were you thinking?'

'I didn't. I wasn't—'

'Someone came here, Victoria! They went through the recycling bin, looking for the diary but, because you weren't here, we still have no bloody idea who it was. This whole thing has been a massive, massive waste of time.'

'What whole thing?' Will asks as Victoria says, 'Jude, I'm sorry.'

Too frustrated to speak she can only clutch her head and groan.

'Give me one reason why I shouldn't call the police,' Will barks at Victoria.

'Because I used my daughter's phone to text you. Because I'm grieving for my ex-husband. Because my whole life is a shit show.'

'Tell me you think I'm an innocent man and I'll consider it.'

There's a pause then, in a voice so quiet it's barely audible Victoria repeats the phrase. There's no sincerity in it, no apology. Jude can tell she doesn't mean a word of it and if anyone's going to stop Will from calling the police it will have to be her.

'Victoria.' She straightens up and looks at her. 'I think it's time you went home.'

'What's been going on then?' Will asks as he joins Jude in the hallway. 'Why did you need her to watch the house? What was all that about a recycling bin and the diary? I thought Sorrell had it.'

'It's a long story.' Jude rubs at her arms. 'I'm going to have to put another jumper on. Do you mind checking that the boiler in the kitchen's working? It's bloody freezing in here.'

Leaving Will in the hallway, Jude climbs the stairs to her bedroom. It's the kind of cold that either means the boiler's broken or Betsy's left a window open. She pops into her daughter's room and pulls back the curtains to find the windows shut. Broken boiler then, great.

Sighing to herself – another thing to talk to the landlord about – she continues on to her bedroom, opens the door and freezes in the doorway. Every drawer is either open or has been upended on the floor. Her double bed, which has a storage compartment beneath, is hinged upwards, the wardrobe door's open and the suitcases that were stacked on top of it are lying open on the floor.

'Jude, there's something I need—' Will, who's just appeared beside her inhales sharply. 'Holy shit you've been burgled.'

Jude stares at the bomb site that used to be her bedroom, as she struggles to make sense of what she's seeing.

'I came up to tell you that the glass in your kitchen door has been smashed,' Will says grimly. 'That must be how they got in.'

'They were looking for the diary,' Jude mumbles, her shock making way for anger. 'Fucking Victoria! Why the hell didn't she go through with the plan?'

Chapter 52

Victoria and Sorrell

SATURDAY

As Victoria drives home, she mentally kicks herself. Not only did the trap she set for Will fail spectacularly, but she missed the diary writer/blackmailer turning up at Jude's house.

She was right about them rushing things. They had one opportunity to try and catch the blackmailer and they've completely screwed it up.

It's been five minutes since Sorrell returned to her car after having an argument with Audrey and she's going through the messages on her phone.

There's a voice note from Jude saying, 'Shahina and Kwame have gone to a party. Victoria says there's nothing going on at my house. We should probably just call it a night.'

IT'S ALWAYS THE HUSBAND

The second voice note is also from Jude. 'Someone checked the tub for the diary then broke into my house. I'm fine. I'm with Will, waiting for the police. Victoria didn't see anything. She's just gone home.' Sorrell's heart judders. Thank God Jude wasn't at home with Betsy when someone broke in, but how awful to have her house ransacked. Worried by what happened she calls her babysitter, then slumps back in her seat as the young woman answers. The house is fine, the children are asleep, everything is okay.

She allows herself the first deep breath of the night. When she'd spontaneously decided to stop watching Audrey's house and confront her instead, the conversation about their failed friendship went as terribly as she'd expected it to. Audrey had answered the door in a pale pink silk robe and matching pyjamas and stared at her like she was something the cat had dragged in from the street.

'What are you doing here, Sorrell? Do you know what time it is?'

'I'm sorry, I know but I need to talk to you about what went wrong with our—'

Audrey moved to close the door. 'I'm busy.'

Sorrell jammed her foot between the door and the frame. 'Audrey, please. Just talk to me.'

'Take your foot away.'

'Not until you talk to me.'

Audrey attempted to slam the door then, but Sorrell pushed against it before it hit her foot. Years of lugging bags of clay, and heavy boxes of pottery around have made her stronger than she looks.

'For God's sake, Audrey. What did I do that was so awful that you ghosted me?'

'What makes you think that you were the problem?'

'I'm sorry?'

'Maybe you should have a conversation with your husband, instead of me.'

'Finnley?' A shiver passed through her. What else doesn't she know about her husband? 'What did he do?'

Audrey's sigh is pure exasperation. 'Remember the evening we were all supposed to go for dinner, but Sully couldn't make it, because he was ill?'

Sorrell did remember; a new restaurant on the outskirts of town was offering a ten-course tasting menu and the two couples, who'd forged a genuine, if unlikely friendship, had been enthusing about it for weeks. When Sully had gone down with a heavy cold the day before their reservation, he'd insisted that Audrey go without him. It had felt strange, sitting at a table for three, instead of four, and while Sorrell had initially missed Sully's jovial presence, the glass of wine served with each course soon made her loosen up and, by the end of the evening, her sides hurt from laughing. Finn, who'd driven and stayed sober, dropped her at the house to pay the babysitter and then drove Audrey home.

'Well,' Audrey said curtly. 'Finnley parked up outside my house, locked me in the car, and propositioned me.'

Sorrell stared at her, horrified.

'He told me he'd always found me beautiful. That he thought about me all the time. He said my husband was too old for me and he'd make a better lover. That we were meant for each other, that he'd leave you. I only had to say yes.'

'I . . . I . . . don't believe you.' Even as the words left her mouth she could taste the lie on her lips. A month earlier she would have accused Audrey of getting the wrong end of the stick, but not anymore. Of course Finnley made a pass at her. Of course he did.

'Now you know, goodnight.' Audrey pressed her weight into the door, but Sorrell didn't budge.

IT'S ALWAYS THE HUSBAND

'Why didn't you tell me?'

'And be blamed for the end of your marriage? That wasn't my place. If anyone should tell you it was him.'

'You were my closest friend!'

'And you were one of my many friends.'

Stung, Sorrell blinked back angry tears. She wouldn't give Audrey the satisfaction of seeing her cry. 'Did you tell Sully? About what Finnley said?'

'Of course not. Why complicate things because your husband can't keep his dick in his pants?'

'You should have told me!'

'And what? Have you blame me? Tell the other mums I tried to steal your husband? I'm not stupid, Sorrell, it's always the woman who is blamed. And if you think Finnley didn't try it on with someone else after I turned him down then you're more of a fool than you look.' That time, when Audrey pushed at the door, Sorrell didn't bother to push back. She remained on the doorstep for a couple of seconds, shaking with anger, then made her way back to her car. If she'd had a heart left to break, then it would have shattered into shards.

Now, she takes another deep breath and cups her hands over her face. Eyes closed, she breathes in the warmed air through her nose, taking it deep, deep into her lungs. She holds it, then exhales slowly. She breathes in again, slowly, but the air's expelled in a rush. Reliving the conversation with Audrey, she's just realised something.

The diary owner's identity has been under their nose all along.

Audrey calls her husband Sully – short for his surname Sullivan – because she struggles to pronounce his first name: Hugh. Excited now, Sorrell opens Facebook and scrolls through her friend list, gasping as a surname jumps out at her.

The W that the diary writer refers to isn't Will Ledger. It can't be if it doesn't belong to Robyn. Why did none of them notice that before?

Victoria enters the keycode to the front door, slips off her shoes, removes Sophia's phone from her bag, then chucks her knock-off Louis Vuitton onto the sofa and heads straight for the fridge. Her fingers wrap the cool neck of a bottle of Sauvignon Blanc, but only for a second. She'll have a drink after she's checked on the kids. As she walks quietly up the stairs she hears the sound of her father snoring, drifting from the spare bedroom on the first floor.

Phone clutched to her ear; Sorrell prays that Sara is awake. She doesn't know her that well and she's not even sure if she'll answer, but she's the only mum she's aware of who doesn't bother to upgrade her phone every twelve to eighteen months.

Sorrell's pretty sure she knows the identity of her blackmailer but there's something she has to check to be sure.

'Hello?' She can hear the surprise in Sara's voice as the call connects. 'Sorrell? Is everything okay?'

'Yeah, fine, um . . . sorry to ring you so late. This is going to sound weird but, how far back do your WhatsApp messages go? There's something I need you to check . . .'

Having looked in on Noah – tossing and turning but seemingly asleep, clutching his teddy – Victoria carefully opens the door to Sophia's room and peers inside. Both children have been sleeping with night lights on since Andy's death and she can see her daughter's relaxed profile above the line of her duvet, her blonde hair splayed out on the pillow. As she crouches

IT'S ALWAYS THE HUSBAND

down to return Sophia's phone to its charger, she hears a faint ringing. It must be her phone, still in her bag downstairs. She'll have to answer it. There's no way she'll be able to sleep if she doesn't find out who it is.

She leaves Sophia's bedroom and pauses on the landing, listening for the sound of the phone but it's stopped ringing.

She stiffens as a new sound reaches her ears. It's the sound of someone opening and closing drawers, and it's coming from her room. Moving quietly, she crosses the landing, listening intently, trying to work out what the hell it could be. The only person she hasn't heard or checked on is her mother. What could she possibly want from her bedroom in the middle of the night?

She stands beside the door to her bedroom, still listening. Whoever's inside hasn't closed it properly and there's a centimetre gap. She can't see who's in there but from the flashes of light on the wall, they're using a torch. That discounts her mum.

She slams open the door and flicks on the light. 'What the fuck are you doing?'

A woman, bent over the top drawer of her dressing table, rummaging through it, turns and looks at her but she's not shocked or frightened. There's an eerie calmness to her expression, as though she was interrupted part way through a meditation or a yoga class.

Dawn crosses her arms over her chest. In black running leggings and a tight long-sleeved T-shirt – stripped of her normal school-run uniform of oversized jeans and baggy sweatshirt – there's definition in her biceps, shoulders and quads. She was one of the heavier, more unfit school mums when they met in Reception, but she's transformed her body. Now she looks incredibly toned, and strong.

'Where is it?' Dawn asks.

Victoria walks into the room and closes the door behind her. Dawn doesn't so much as flinch. She's acting like it's perfectly normal for her to be rooting around in Victoria's bedroom in the middle of the night.

'Is it in your handbag? Your car? I've looked pretty much everywhere else.'

Victoria's gaze flits around the bedroom. Compared to the hell site that was Jude's house, Dawn's been neater here, more orderly in her search of the room. Other than a sock hanging out of the chest of drawers, and a plant – in a plant pot she bought from Sorrell at a local craft fayre – lying on its side near the doorway, everything else is in place.

'Where's what?' she asks steadily.

'My diary. Jude lied about having it. You know, you're making a mistake hanging out with her and Sorrell.' There's a flash of hurt in her eyes. 'They're using you; you know. You need to be careful who you're friends with, Victoria – not everyone's as loyal as me.'

Victoria pastes on a smile as something inside her tightens. Was that an implied threat? Over the past few weeks she's learned that no one is who she thinks they are. So what, exactly, is Dawn?

'You can't just let yourself into my house.'

The look Dawn gives her is pure, *Why not?* 'I wanted my diary back.'

'My children are asleep, as are my parents! Can you hear how mad you sound?'

'Don't call me that.' A nerve twitches below her eye. 'I was just doing what you'd do in the same situation: trying to protect my family.'

'From what?'

Dawn's eyes narrow. 'Don't lie and pretend you haven't read it.'

'I haven't.'

'Liar!'

'I swear to God.' Victoria holds her hands palms out. She's telling the truth for once, or at least partially. Something shifts in Dawn's expression. It looks a lot like relief.

'Good. Where is it?'

'I haven't got it.'

'So where is it?'

'Why did you blackmail Sorrell and Theresa?'

Dawn blinks rapidly then shakes her head, a small smile incongruous with the innocent widening of her eyes. 'I don't know what you're talking about.'

'You've been pretending to be Robyn. You've been messaging Finnley, asking for money.'

The other woman's body stiffens and her expression shifts from guileless to defensive. 'Has Sorrell been feeding you lies?'

'Spell the word "absolutely".'

'Don't fucking patronise me.' Her calm demeanour shatters and there's anger in her eyes. 'I'm not stupid, despite what some of the group might think. You're better than that, Victoria.'

Victoria doesn't reply. She's trying to work out what it was that Dawn just swiped from her dressing table and is hiding behind her back.

'The others don't deserve what they've got,' Dawn continues. 'They don't appreciate it. They take it for granted, showing off about their fancy holidays and private tutors and their massive houses. That's not you. It's not you at all. I'll be honest, I didn't take to you initially but when I got to know you, I saw a different side. Yeah, you're funny and witty and all that but, unlike the other women, you say it like it is. You won't stab someone in the back, you'll stab them in their front.' She laughs. 'And you've got it all, well, maybe not so much now with what's happened recently but you're inspiring – with your lovely house and your business and your figure and all that. I was never going to take anything from you, Victoria. If anything, I wanted to be like you.'

Dawn takes another step towards her and her eyes darken. 'I trusted that you hadn't read my diary but now I'm starting to wonder if that's true. What were you planning on doing with it, Victoria? Sharing it with the others like Robyn said she'd do?'

At the mention of Robyn's name Victoria tenses and she takes a small step backwards, towards the door.

'What happened to her?' She can feel her heartbeat in her throat.

'I don't know.'

The words *I think you do* play on the tip of Victoria's tongue but she doesn't say them. If she backs Dawn into a corner her hackles will go up, and she still doesn't know what's in the hand that's tucked up behind her back. She has to be cleverer, make Dawn think she's on her side.

'You know I didn't like her, don't you? That I had my suspicions that she slept with Andy.'

'You'd have been right and—' Dawn breaks off, suspicion clouding her eyes. She's trying to work out if Victoria read the diary entry where she admitted her crush.

'There were some days,' Victoria says quickly, 'when I'd happily have given Robyn a slap.' Dawn's smirk tells her that she's on safer ground. They're two friends, having a gossip, bonded by their mutual dislike of one of the other mums. 'I wasn't even that bothered that she didn't turn up to my drinks party,' Victoria continues. 'I was more excited about you coming along. I just thought it was rude, that she'd cancel without telling me.'

IT'S ALWAYS THE HUSBAND

'Oh, she was planning on coming all right.' Dawn's body language has altered. She's more relaxed, leaning into the conversation. Out of all the women in Victoria's friendship circle Dawn was always the one to hang on to her every word. Andy used to joke that she hero-worshipped her, which Victoria always said was ridiculous, but now she's not so sure.

'Was she?' she asks, playing along.

'Oh yeah. I saw her standing on the side of the road, a couple of streets down from her house, when I was heading out. She was drunk, had had a raging row with Will, and was trying to call an Uber to yours but her phone had died. I pulled over, wound down the window, and offered her a lift. She repaid me by being an absolute bitch.'

'What happened?' Victoria holds her gaze.

Dawn's mouth stretches into a wide, self-satisfied smile as though she's enjoying being the sole keeper of a secret. 'Wouldn't you like to know.'

'Yes, I would! So what happened? Did you boot her out' – she fakes a laugh – 'and leave her stranded on the other side of Lowbridge?'

'Oh no, she made it all the way to your party.' Dawn tilts her head to one side, her smile tightening. 'Well, nearly. I parked up on the verge by your field – I know you'd rather we all park there than in your driveway. Anyway, we got out and we were walking through the field to your garden when she casually mentioned that she'd caught Theresa trying to steal my diary.'

'What?'

'Seriously. It was when I was hosting drinks at my place. Robyn went to use the upstairs bathroom and saw Theresa opening the drawers in my bedroom. She walked in and caught her red-handed, trying to put my diary in her bag.

Theresa left in a rush – do you remember? She came into the living room and said she wasn't feeling well, that she had to go?'

She does remember; it was an unusually hurried exit.

'Instead of putting it back,' Dawn continues, her cheeks flushed, a droplet of sweat escaping from her hairline, 'or telling me what happened, Robyn took it home with her. Can you believe it? *Two* thieves in our friendship group.'

'Wow,' Victoria says softly. She's got a horrible feeling she knows where this story is heading but she doesn't want Dawn to stop talking.

'Anyway, we were part way across your field, when Robyn said that she'd brought the diary with her and she was going to read bits out, give everyone a laugh. Can you believe that? I couldn't let her humiliate me like that, not in front of you.'

Victoria fumbles for the door handle as Dawn takes another step closer. There's less than a foot between them now and she's pretty sure she can talk Dawn out of doing anything stupid but she's not going to take any chances.

'I didn't know that she was bullshitting, and it wasn't in her bag. She could have just told me that. I wouldn't have tried to grab the bag if I knew she was lying but did she admit that? No, she fucking didn't. She got up in my face instead, pulling on the bag strap, shoving me, calling me a fat bitch and a loser, saying I was a laughing stock. I shoved her, anyone would have. It wasn't my fault she hit her head on the cesspit lid. I just wanted her to shut up and give me my diary back and—' The door handle creaks as Victoria turns it. 'What are you doing?'

'I'm just—'

'I trusted you, Victoria. Why would you try and leave?' Dawn's arm swings from behind her back and she lunges

IT'S ALWAYS THE HUSBAND

towards her, something shiny and metallic in her hand. Victoria raises her arms defensively but it's not a knife in Dawn's hand, it's hairspray and, in an instant, she's blind and choking, a chemical mist filling her airways and burning her eyes. She fights to breathe, to open her eyes but, before she can do either, she's shoved to the floor and then Dawn's on top of her, her hands around her throat.

'I'm sorry.' Dawn's voice is a whisper. 'I'm really sorry. I thought you understood me but you don't, do you? I saw the fear in your eyes.'

Victoria swipes at her blindly, writhing and bucking, trying to escape, but Dawn's too heavy, too strong and she can feel herself getting weaker as the grip on her throat tightens. She's going to die. Dawn killed Robyn and now she's going to kill her too.

Frantically, she feels around either side of her, fingers spidering over the carpet, searching for something, anything, she can use as a weapon against her. In between Dawn's laboured breaths she hears someone call out 'Noah' but she's not sure if it's real or in her own head. She can't die, she can't. She can't leave her children. She won't. She sweeps her arms wildly across the carpet and her fingers graze something cold and ceramic, but when she plucks at it, it rolls away. It's too far to reach now and darkness is closing in. She's going to black out.

'Dawn, stop that!' a female voice rings out from behind her.

'Audrey?' Dawn says, and the pressure on Victoria's throat eases. Through stinging eyes she sees the small, slight shape of her son, standing in the doorway, clutching the teddy Andy gave him.

'Get a refill.' The sound's coming from the teddy in Audrey's voice. 'Please! I can't stand that disgusting noise.'

'Run!' Victoria tries to shout but the only sound that escapes her mouth is a raw, raspy groan.

'Mummy!' Noah shouts as footsteps fill the air and he's whisked away from the doorway as Sorrell barrels into the room. Skin flushed, nostrils flared, she grabs Dawn's hair and yanks her backwards, away from Victoria, and onto the floor.

She hears a sound like a bowling ball being repeatedly dropped on the carpet and Sorrell screaming, 'You fucking bitch, I'll kill you.'

'Sorrell, stop!' Now Jude's in the bedroom too. 'Sorrell, stop it. Let her go. The police are coming. No one else needs to die.'

Chapter 53

Jude

SATURDAY, SEVEN DAYS LATER

As garden parties go, the gathering around Sorrell's firepit couldn't be more different than the last time Jude sat around drinking with the other school mums. Jude, Sorrell and Victoria are the only ones present for a start, bundled up in coats and blankets, sipping wine and staring into the flames. The mood is sombre as they discuss the fact that Victoria's own garden, and the field beyond is festooned in police 'scene of crime' tape, with a white tent erected over the disused septic tank where Robyn's body was found.

Whilst Dawn hadn't openly confessed to Victoria that she had killed Robyn, what she had said – recorded on a fake phone charger that they'd missed when they'd searched the bedroom for hidden cameras – was more than enough for the police to arrest her and begin a fingertip search of the field. Dawn had been charged with murder – Victoria's family liaison officer had told her – attempted murder, and two counts of blackmail.

Victoria pulls the blanket tighter around her shoulders then takes a sip of her wine. She was discharged from hospital after twenty-four hours, but the physical evidence of the attack is still visible: bruising and scratches to her neck as well as redness around her eyes. The mental scars . . . well, Jude can only guess at how deeply they run.

'Dawn knew about the septic tank even before she killed Robyn,' Victoria says. 'I'd warned the mamas about the field the first time I had them over. I told them that if they parked in the lane, to keep to the edge where Andy mows it because the rest's full of nettles and there are bits of old farm material embedded in the soil, as well as the disused septic tank. It's why we never let the children down there.'

'How are the children?' Sorrell asks. She looks exhausted. There are dark circles beneath her eyes and her face looks pinched and pallid, even in the light from the fire.

Instinctively Victoria glances towards the house. Through the double glass door to Sorrell's living room she can see her son and daughter, curled up under duvets on blow-up mattresses on the floor. With her bedroom a crime scene, as well as her garden, she temporarily moved into an Airbnb in the centre of Lowbridge with her parents and children. She takes Sophia and Noah everywhere she goes, unwilling, and unable, to let them out of her sight.

'They're both still grieving their father. Sophia's started wetting the bed again. She's become scared of the dark and she's barely eating. Noah's regressed several years. He clings to me like he did when he was a toddler and he has nightmares about what he saw in my bedroom and the sound of the police, stampeding up the stairs. Thank God

IT'S ALWAYS THE HUSBAND

Jude snatched him up and out of the way before he saw any more.'

Jude nods, her chest tightening at the memory – poor little Noah, clutching his teddy as she'd hurried him away from the bedroom, crying because the lady was hurting his mummy and there was a black box in the back of his favourite toy, and it was saying really weird things. The police revealed to Victoria that Andy had placed the recording device in his son's teddy, and cameras and listening devices in her house. No one was entirely sure why he'd done it but they were pretty sure it was to do with their impending divorce.

'We're going to therapy,' Victoria adds. 'Separately, and as a family. What happened has made me reassess my life and my priorities. Fuck the house and money and all the rest of that shit – all that matters is the people I love. You two saved me. You and Noah. I was about to black out when he turned up at my door, playing the recording of Audrey's voice. He'd discovered the device in his teddy and had come to tell me.'

'Thank God we turned up when we did,' Sorrell says. 'Will would have been there too if Jude hadn't asked him to stay at hers, in case the police showed up.'

Victoria looks at Jude, regret filling her eyes. 'I fucked up, accusing him of killing Robyn. When you see him next can you tell him how genuinely sorry I am?'

Jude shivers despite the warmth of the fire and blanket. Twenty years ago, when her dad was hounded to his death for a crime he didn't commit, she was desperate for those responsible to apologise. When she moved to Lowbridge and met Will she thought that clearing his name would make her feel better, that it would help heal the wounds of the past; but Victoria's apology has done none of those things.

Instead of feeling liberated or vindicated she feels very, very sad. Will might be able to rebuild his life now but that can never happen for her dad, as much as she'd love to rewind time.

After the police turned up at Victoria's and Dawn was arrested, an ambulance was called for Victoria whilst everyone else was separated to be questioned. On the sofa, after she'd given a lengthy statement to a detective, Jude had asked him whether he, or another police officer would break the news to Will about Robyn? When the detective told her that he'd be informed about the development in the investigation she asked if she was free to go. She didn't want a stranger to tell him the news. If anyone was going to break his heart and reveal what Dawn claimed had happened to Robyn, then it really had to be her.

Twenty minutes later she arrived home to find that the police burglary team still hadn't turned up, and Will had patched up her kitchen door with wood and nails that he'd found in her shed.

The next hour of Jude's life was one of the most upsetting she'd ever experienced. Will was too stunned to react initially but as the minutes ticked by, and the news sank in that Dawn had probably murdered Robyn, he crumpled into himself. She held him as he cried.

'How is he?' Sorrell asks now. 'How's Will?'

Jude looks deep into the fire. 'Not great. Believing that Robyn was dead was one thing, finding out the truth was another. There was love there, despite their issues, and a lot of questions that will never be answered. And obviously, he's had to break the news to Milly.'

Sorrell's eyes fill with tears as she looks from Jude to Victoria. Jude can tell that she's thinking about her children.

'Have you heard from Finnley?' she asks.

IT'S ALWAYS THE HUSBAND

Sorrell shakes her head. 'Not since I messaged him after Dawn was arrested. Oh, but I finally heard back from Amit, the friend he was pretending to meet at the Bat and Badger – he said he hadn't seen Finnley for years.'

'Helpful,' Jude says tightly.

'Henry and Harper . . .' Victoria ventures. 'Are they—'

'Asking questions, yes. They want to know when he'll get home from his course. I'll have to tell them the truth very soon.'

'Yeah.' Jude says as Victoria sighs heavily, then all three women fall into a wistful silence, the kind of companionable silence you only get when you know the people you're with really well.

Typically, Jude's the one to break it. 'Can we just talk about the way Sorrell smashed Dawn's head into the carpet like a WWF wrestler?'

Sorrell and Victoria both laugh.

'I'm not saying it was satisfying,' Sorrell says, 'but . . .' A smile plays on her lips.

Victoria takes another sip of her wine then sets it on a side table and reaches her hands towards the fire. She wasn't joking when she said that the experience had changed her. Jude can't pinpoint what it is about her that's different but it's there. She can feel it, like the hard edges have been rubbed off.

'What's really bugging me' – she looks from Jude to Sorrell – 'is that I didn't realise that the W in the diary was the Woodster when Dawn calls Simon that all the time!'

Jude shrugs. 'I didn't even know that her last name was Wood. She's *Dawn – Eva's mum* in my phone. Like Sorrell is *Sorrell – Henry and Harper's mum* and Victoria is *Victoria – total bitch.*'

It raises a smile from Victoria, which is what Jude had hoped.

'It wouldn't have occurred to me if Audrey hadn't called Hugh "Sully" when I confronted her.' Sorrell gets up and refills all their wine glasses. 'I had to check Facebook to see which of the mamas had a W surname. I didn't think it could be Dawn because Victoria said she wasn't on the night out when she'd shared her secrets but then it occurred to me that maybe something had been written about them in the WhatsApp group. It wasn't on my phone because I'd upgraded so I rang Sara to check and . . .' she shrugs '. . . I was right.'

'Well,' Victoria says. 'You're definitely sharper than me.'

'You're the one who realised why the birthday cards didn't match the handwriting in the diary,' Jude says, trying to cheer her up. 'You worked out that Dawn broke her wrist around the time of your birthday, and her husband must have written your card.'

'I realised that *yesterday*, Jude.'

Sorrell takes a sip of her wine. 'What I don't understand, is why she only blackmailed me and Theresa when she had so many secrets to choose from?'

Jude shrugs. 'Those secrets were openly shared. Yours weren't.'

'I guess so. And if Finnley ran out of money to give her, then the hit-and-run call gave her the perfect opportunity to extort more money from me.'

'What do you think she was going to do with it?'

'I don't think it was about that,' Victoria says. 'I think it was about feeling important, like she was in charge. I think she believed Robyn when she told her that everyone was laughing at her behind her back. Maybe it had something to do with that.'

'That would make sense, with her pretending to be Robyn,' Jude says. 'Dawn tried telling me that everyone had an issue with Robyn but maybe she was envious of her too, in a weird way. Why not play-act at being Robyn to see how it felt to have that kind of power over people? Robyn created a stir in Lowbridge; she certainly couldn't be ignored.'

Sorrell runs a hand over her hair, as though searching for the end of her plait, then presses her hands between her knees. 'The only thing worse than being talked about is not being talked about.'

'Exactly!'

'Changing the subject back to me,' Victoria says, and they all laugh. 'Why would Theresa accuse *me* of blackmailing her when there were so many school mums it could be?'

Jude flashes her a grin. 'Can I refer you to the *Victoria – total bitch* entry in my phone. I'm joking,' she says quickly, reaching for Victoria's hand. 'You know that, don't you?'

'Maybe . . .' Victoria narrows her eyes suspiciously, but her smile gives her away. 'Talking of phones, mine hasn't stopped bleeping with texts from the other mamas, desperate to find out the goss about Dawn. Apparently, there's a rumour going round the playground that she was the one who killed Andy.'

The three women exchange a look. As usual, the whisper network has got things wrong. Dawn didn't kill Andy, but they know who did and, very soon, they're going to flush the real murderer out.

Chapter 54

Sorrell

SUNDAY

Sorrell's always hated hospitals. Even after Harper and Henry were delivered, by elective caesarean, she was too stressed out by her surroundings to embrace new motherhood. Everything from the crisp white sheets to the swish of green curtains, the scent of disinfectant, the clipboards, the squeak of shoes on lino and the sound of other people made her feel anxious and out of control. She wanted to be at home with her babies, surrounded by her blankets, her furniture, familiar smells. But today she's got no choice but to sit on an uncomfortable chair in the foyer of Mallhampton General, one short corridor away from A&E. It's the only way in, and the only way out for the general public. She queued to speak to the receptionist to check.

More scared than she's ever been, she opens her WhatsApp messages. There's one from Jude: *I hope everything goes okay.* And one from Victoria: **Thinking of you.** There's also an email message from Finnley: **I'll be there as soon as I can.**

It's a reply to the message Sorrell sent him four hours ago, along with a photo of Scout lying on crisp white sheets, his eyes wide and startled and an oxygen mask, with a tube running from it, covering his nose and mouth. A terrifying image even without the text she'd written below it. *At Mallhampton General. Scout went into respiratory distress earlier today. The doctors suspect congenital heart disease and are running tests. Get here as soon as you can.*

Now she taps the toes of her shoes on the horrible squeaky lino. It's been four hours since she sent the email to Finn and two since he replied. Is he even going to show up to be there for his son? She left him a long voicemail, the day after Dawn was arrested, telling him that Dawn was his blackmailer, that she'd murdered Robyn and disposed of her body in a disused septic tank in Victoria's field. It was over, she told him, the children missed him and could he please come home. When he didn't reply she sent the same message via WhatsApp message. Two ticks appeared, he'd read it, but he didn't reply. Twenty-four hours later he messaged her:

I can't come home.

That was five days ago. The message about Scout is the first thing he's sent her since.

A man hurries into the foyer, but it's not Finnley. In the last four hours she's watched hundreds of people stream through the doors of the hospital – staff, contractors, worried parents with small children, terrified women and pale-faced men, a teenage boy propped up between two of his mates limping, several people bleeding profusely, hands wrapped in tea towels, one man with a bed sheet wrapped around his head. At least five of the men who've hurried into the hospital looked so like Finnley that she stood up sharply, attracting attention, only to sit back down heavily again.

'Come on, come on,' she mutters, looking back down at her phone. She taps out a message to Jude, asking how Harper and Henry are doing at her house with Betsy, then glances up, her senses tingling, and spots her husband, already halfway down the corridor that leads to A&E.

'Finn!' she shouts, heart pounding. 'Finnley! I'm over here!'

As he hurries towards her she clocks the beginning of a beard on his top lip and jawline, the baseball cap pulled low over his eyes and his hideous nylon tracksuit. Out of the corner of her eye she spots two men across the room, getting up from their seats.

'Where's Scout?' Finnley looks gaunt with worry. 'Why are you out here? Has something happened? Oh my God, Sorrell, please tell me he's not—'

'Why couldn't you come home?' She looks him in the eye, feels herself grow stronger and more powerful. She's been fantasising about this moment for days. 'You know Robyn's dead, don't you?'

His skin pales and sweat beads at his temples as his gaze darts from her to the corridor behind her. He looks like he's fighting the urge to run.

'You lied about seeing her in person. Didn't you? Why would you do that, Finnley?'

'Where's Scout?' He reaches for her arm but she steps away before he can make contact. 'I need to see my son.'

'Why did you lie about seeing Robyn? Why, Finnley?'

'Because you wouldn't shut up!' He sprays the words at her, his brow furrowed, eyes glassy, blood flushing his throat and his cheeks. 'You kept on and on, saying she wasn't real.'

'I was right though, wasn't I, Finnley?' A calm has descended over Sorrell. The nerves she's been feeling for days, suddenly gone. 'The real Robyn dumped you and slept with Andy. The person you were messaging after she disappeared was Dawn. Dawn was the one who begged for your help, it was Dawn you professed your love to and made plans for the future with. It was Dawn you gave money to, *my* twenty thousand pounds.' The two men from across the room are standing behind Finnley now but he hasn't noticed them. He's staring at Sorrell, rage and disbelief filling his eyes. 'Robyn never loved you, Finnley. It was all in your head. None of it was real and when Andy tried to tell you that you—'

'What the fuck is this? Scout's not ill, is he? You lured me here, you fucking stupid—'

'Finnley Edwards.' The taller of the two men takes his arm. 'I'm arresting you for the murder of DS Andrew Routledge. You do not have to—'

Finn tries to make a run for it but the detectives are too quick for him. They bundle him to the floor and twist his arms behind his back. Handcuffs click shut over his wrists as he writhes and wriggles. 'You do not have to say anything. But it may harm your defence if you do not mention when questioned something which you later rely on in court. Anything you do say may be given in evidence.'

A little after 8 p.m., five days earlier, two plain-clothes detectives turned up at Sorrell's door, asking for Finnley.

'We need to talk to your husband,' the female detective told her, perched on the armchair in Sorrell's living room as her children slept upstairs. 'Do you know where he is?'

Sorrell shook her head. 'He left me for Robyn Lewis. I know she's dead,' she added as the two officers shared a look, 'but he's in denial. I don't know where he is. I haven't heard from him since last Sunday when he sent me a text saying he couldn't come home.'

She noticed the female detective's left eyebrow twitch upwards as she said the phrase 'he couldn't come home'.

'What's this about?' she asked. 'Why do you need to speak to him? What's happened?'

The male detective, a weary-looking man in his late forties, with a receding hairline and a green wool jumper that looked like it had seen better days, rolled back his shoulders. 'We've got some questions for him, concerning the death of DI Andrew Routledge.'

Sorrell said nothing as his words sank in.

'Andy? You think *Finnley* killed Andy?'

Her initial reaction was shock, denial and anger, in quick succession, but as she combed through her memory, resignation and acceptance settled in. Finnley had been off work 'sick' for a month, but he'd jumped at the chance to do a sedated extraction. It was for Andy Routledge. What was it that Finn had said, 'we can't let our police force be in pain'? He'd returned home later than expected and she'd sensed the tension in his body even as he'd pretended to be normal, and when she'd kicked him out after the conversation about Robyn he couldn't move fast enough. It was almost like it was a relief to leave.

He couldn't come home, not because he was in denial about Robyn's murder. It was another death he was running from.

'He won't come home voluntarily,' she told the two officers, 'but I've got an idea how we could trick him out of hiding. He might have been happy to abandon me and the children but he'd act if he thought one of them was seriously ill . . .'

* * *

IT'S ALWAYS THE HUSBAND

The hardest part of Sorrell's plan was breaking the news about Finnley to Victoria. Whilst the police hadn't openly admitted that he was a suspect, it was pretty obvious from their desire to track him down. Not that they'd shared their suspicions with Victoria. When Sorrell told her everything – nursing cups of tea on Victoria's patio – she could see the shock in her eyes.

'I couldn't plan this with Jude and the police, and not tell you.' She took Victoria's trembling hands in her own. 'We've been through a lot, the three of us, and we've built up so much trust that I couldn't keep this from you. And if you hate me forever, I get it. How can you be friends with someone whose husband killed the father of your children? The man you once loved.'

When heavy tears filled Victoria's eyes, Sorrell braced herself for the worst. Their friendship was over, of course it was. She'd been fooling herself if she'd expected anything else. 'Hate you?' Tears streamed down Victoria's cheeks as she shook her head sharply. 'How could I hate you? None of this is your fault.'

Jude's contribution to the plan was introducing Sorrell to her sister Emma. Knowing that Finnley was medically trained, Sorrell had thoroughly researched oxygen masks for babies, poring over photograph after photograph on Google. She'd even managed to source one on Amazon. The issue was what to feed into it to make Scout look like he was in 'respiratory distress'. Emma came to the rescue, providing the tube from her son Blaine's nebuliser. Then all Sorrell had to do was put white sheets and a thin white pillow on a bed, put Scout in his pyjamas, fit the mask and take a photo. She compared it to the photos she'd found online and, to her eyes, it looked damned near perfect. But what she thought didn't matter. The whole plan rested on Finnley believing that his son was really in hospital. The night before she sent the text message, Sorrell didn't sleep at all.

Now, still shaking and breathing shallowly, Sorrell watches as the two detectives, flanking Finnley, lead him out of the hospital.

'She loved me!' Finnley twists round to take one last look at her, tears streaming down his cheeks. 'Robyn loved me! She did!'

'No she didn't,' Sorrell whispers. 'But I once did.'

Chapter 55

Jude

FRIDAY

Jude joins Sorrell and Victoria in a small huddle near the gates of St Helena's, as they wait for their children to leave school. Sara, Caz, Shahina and Audrey flash tight smiles across the playground but none of them ventures closer. After Dawn and Finnley's arrests, Victoria decided to extricate herself from the 'mamas' and it's as though she's erected an invisible force field around herself. Only Jude and Sorrell can pass through it.

It's a protective bubble that they're all grateful for, particularly Sorrell.

After Finnley's arrest, he told the police everything, and Victoria's family liaison officer paid her a visit. She told her that, when Andy was consciously sedated for his extraction, Finnley had sent the nurse out of the room on an errand, then pumped him for information about Robyn, knowing that Midazolam is almost like a truth serum for some patients. He'd heard some shocking confessions over the years. The drug had worked as he'd hoped, and Andy had admitted that he'd slept with Robyn and she'd talked to him about Finnley. The conversation ended abruptly when the nurse walked back into the room.

Desperate to know what Robyn had said, Finnley visited Andy at home later, having looked up his address. He spiked his drink with the crushed tablet form of the drug and set about questioning him; only this time Andy wasn't as cooperative. He laughed at Finnley, called him a loser that Robyn couldn't wait to be rid of, and made a joke about his sexual performance that could only have come from her.

When he showed Finnley the door, Finnley flew into a rage and punched Andy in the back of the head, knocking him out. Scared he'd end up in jail for assaulting a police officer, he'd dragged Andy into the bath, drowned him and staged a suicide, hoping the DNA test instructions on the table would prove just cause. Then he'd returned home to Sorrell acting like nothing had happened, only to be confronted about his affair.

None of them know why Finnley lied about meeting up with Robyn. Victoria thinks it was to save face under Sorrell's questioning. Sorrell thinks it was because he couldn't accept that his love was a lie, and Jude can't work out what he was thinking at all. What they all agree on is the fact that he became so obsessed with a woman he'd had a brief affair with that he was willing to believe that she'd cast him as her saviour and hero, even though she'd unceremoniously dumped him to sleep with another dad and then 'disappeared'. Finnley's fantasy world has destroyed two families, leaving five children without a father and they all, all three of them, hope that he rots in jail.

IT'S ALWAYS THE HUSBAND

It's three days since Robyn's funeral, and a week since Jude and Will chatted briefly at the school gates. It was Milly's first day back at school after Will had broken the news about Robyn and he was nervy and impatient, keen to get away before the other parents descended. Jude had exchanged a few texts with him since he'd sobbed in her arms, but it was the first time she'd seen him in person. He looked drawn and exhausted, his hair in need of cutting. She'd asked how he was doing, about Milly, the funeral, but his answers were short and perfunctory. It was like he'd completely withdrawn into himself.

'I think it's best that you don't come to Robyn's funeral. For Milly,' he'd said suddenly.

'Of course, absolutely. No problem.' She'd touched him on the arm to let him know that she understood. The request wasn't exactly a shock.

'I don't want you to feel hurt, after everything you've done, after . . .' He'd tailed off, his eyes meeting hers, but he didn't have to finish his sentence. She knew exactly what he meant. *After the way we felt about each other, after the sex, our daughters' friendship and the ghost of Robyn's disappearance following us everywhere we went.*

'Wrong place, wrong time.' Her hand had slid down his arm to his hand and she'd given it a firm squeeze. 'I get it. I've been thinking the same myself.'

He'd looked at her oddly then, like he couldn't follow what she was saying, and Jude had realised her mistake. He was apologising for not inviting her to the funeral, while she was trying to end their relationship.

It was something she'd thought about a lot over the last few weeks. She'd become so wrapped up in the excitement of their physical and emotional connection, so impassioned by the similarity between his situation and her dad's, that the red flags in their relationship had completely passed her by. She'd done the same with her ex, only realising too late that his unpredictability and his outbursts weren't fiery and exciting, they were destabilising and unnerving not just for her, but for Betsy too. She could spend the rest of her life making excuses for Will's mood swings. She could justify stepping on eggshells, but what kind of role model would that be for her daughter? Being alone was not the same as being lonely and with Emma, Sorrell and Victoria forming a tight, protective triangle around her, there was certainly no danger of that.

Three single women. It was a great name for a Beyoncé rip-off band, but the timing wasn't great to crack that joke to Will. Instead she'd said, 'I hope there's no hard feelings. I don't want to make life any more difficult for you than it already is.'

She'd seen a flash of disappointment in his eyes before he'd forced a smile. 'God no, definitely not.'

Now, she spots Betsy walking hand in hand out of an open school door with a little girl called Morgan, while Milly has Eloise, Sophia and Jasmine crowding around her, hanging on to every word she says.

She and Will weren't the only ones to move on. In the playground the children are forming and dissolving alliances, making friends, breaking friends, gossiping and whispering. Little tiny people, battling to be understood and heard, to form connections, a microcosm of the parents themselves.

Chapter 56

DAWN'S DIARY

Welcome to hell, aka my prison diary. Ha ha! Me again! My parents finally came good with my canteen so I've got pens and paper, as well as a shitload of ramen, crisps, sweets and chocolate. It says a lot about this place that it feels like Christmas Day. The other thing I really wanted, but couldn't get, was an eye mask to help me sleep. It never gets properly dark in this place.

I got some post earlier – in a brown envelope with my name and prison number typed on the front. I assumed it was from my solicitor but the prison staff aren't allowed to open those so it can't be. I'm hoping it's from the Woodster. He hasn't replied to a single letter I've sent. When Mom came to visit with the kids she said it's because he's struggling to come to terms with what I did. Maybe if he came to see me he'd understand. I just want the chance to explain.

Robyn and I just had a bit of a scrap when I was trying to get her bag off her so I could take back my diary – just pushing and shoving, that sort of thing, until the bitch started calling me names. I didn't plan for her to fall backwards and hit her head on the metal lid of the septic tank. I thought about going to get help but when I checked her pulse I panicked.

It wasn't like anyone in Lowbridge would miss her. She rubbed everyone up the wrong way, starting arguments, swanning around like she was Milly's real mother and sucking up to Victoria when she was secretly sleeping with her husband! She screwed Sorrell's husband too, although that privileged bitch absoluteley got what she deserved. Who shows off about a secret bank account apart from a total wanker?

You wouldn't catch Victoria doing that. She's a grafter, like me. She didn't have Mummy and Daddy give her a wodge of cash to buy her house; she bought a run-down shit heap and did it up and she worked hard to build up her PT business. After Andy left her she was pretty much a single mum.

So no, I don't feel guilty about taking money off Theresa and Sorrell – Theresa's a thief and Sorrell's a show-off, and that husband of hers is a dick. If he was prepared to leave his family for Robyn, then why shouldn't he pay? All I had to do was buy a burner phone and message him. He totally bought the fact that she wouldn't want to use her normal phone and risk being traced (which was just as well as her actual phone was in the sceptic tank with her). I pretended to be her, which wasn't hard given the amount of gag-worthy flirting I'd witnessed while she was alive. He totally bought it. Men and their egos, eh?

I mean, who hits an animal in the middle of the night and doesn't stop to put it out of its misery? You could say I did the same for Robyn. Ha ha.

Anyway, it wouldn't have occurred to me to try and blackmail Sorrell if Finnley hadn't left me a voicemail about the hit-and-run and I hadn't been scrolling through Facebook a few hours later and seen the local police update about that woman who ended up in Mallhampton General.

I knew Finnley hadn't hit her because he was miles away at the time, but Sorrell didn't know that. If she'd trusted Finnley she would have just ignored my message. She didn't though – she tried to catch me out, the absolute bitch. She wasn't cleverer than me though was she? I was one step ahead of her the whole time. Her and Robyn.

I was the only one in Lowbridge who knew she was sleeping with Finnley and Andy. I wrote in my diary about how I caught her out. Me and the Woodster were having an anniversary meal out in Wyrethorpe and when I went to the loo I saw them together – Robyn and Finnley – holding hands in a table in the corner. They were too busy staring into each other's eyes to notice me (back then I didn't have blue hair). I kept an eye on them after that, saw the lingering looks they gave each other across the playground, watched them texting on their phones, grinning. It was obvious that it was an affair. I knew immediately when they'd split up because Finnley turned up to pick-up looking like thunder, and Robyn wouldn't look him in the eye.

A couple of weeks later I noticed her making a beeline for Andy and she couldn't have made it more obvious that she was into him – flicking her hair, wearing low-cut tops, simpering and smiling. It made me sick. The day I saw them subtly touching hands I knew I had to tell Victoria, but not straight away. I had to find a way to make Robyn pay before I did anything else. And pay literally. If she was well off enough to afford a Gucci handbag then she could chuck a few quid my way.

I had it all planned out in my diary, how I'd blackmail her, and then bloody Theresa came round to my house and Robyn ended up with my diary! Not that I knew she had it until that night in Victoria's field. She told me that she was going to take the diary to the police and then she was going to expose me to the whole of Lowbridge. She laughed at me for writing down everyone's secrets. Asked what kind of weirdo I was to do something like that. Said I couldn't have much of a life of my own to be so fascinated with everyone else.

Turns out she was lying about going to the police. My solicitor was given photocopied pages of my diary by the prosecution and the pages about Robyn's affairs weren't there. She must have ripped them out. Didn't want anyone else to find out she was cheating with Finnley and Andy. She deserved everything that happened to her. I was right about her being a bitch.

Anyway, now I've got that off my chest I'm going to open the letter from the Woodster. I hope he doesn't try and guilt-trip me about the children. I was a mess after I saw them at visitation. I might have to ask Mom and Dad not to bring them again. You can't survive here if you fixate on what you're missing out on, it's like jabbing your brain with pins. I'd rather pretend the kids don't even exist.

I've always been good at turning off my emotions but I'm not going to get into the reasons. Don't want to give anyone ammo if they read this. My padmate's okay – she knows I'm the boss of this cell – but I don't trust the others. Bloody druggies and thieves everywhere but if I could survive the school run then prison should be a walk in the park.

Right, going to read the letter now. Back in a bit.

What the actual hell?! It wasn't a letter from the Woodster at all. It was a single piece of printer paper, typed, and all that was written on it was: You beat me to it.

That was it! No signature, no date, nothing else, not even my name! The letter has a Lowbridge Mail Centre postmark but that's my only clue.

Who'd send me something like that, and what does 'You beat me to it' even mean? What are they talking about? Beat them to what? Prison? Blackmail? Killing Robyn? I've put the letter straight in the bin. There are too many weirdos in this world.

Chapter 57

There's a brisk wind blowing in the Devonshire market town that Lillian calls her home. Hands pushed deep into the pockets of her favourite winter coat, she strides down the high street, slowing down as she reaches the door to the Oxfam shop where she works.

'Oh for goodness' sake.' There are black bags piled up beside it, torn open, clothes spilling out. She put a note in the window, several weeks ago, telling people to please *not* leave bags of clothes and donations outside when they're closed and to hold on to them until they're open instead. But have they listened? No. Because everyone thinks that notices like that don't apply to them.

She ties up the bags as best as she can then hauls them into the shop. As she carries them into the back room she nods at Phoebe, a local English Literature undergraduate and volunteer, sorting through a huge pile of books on the floor.

Why Phoebe didn't think to bring the bags in herself she doesn't know, but she doesn't chastise her; she needs all the volunteers she can get. Instead, she says, 'I'm so glad you're sorting through the books – we're running out of space back here.'

IT'S ALWAYS THE HUSBAND

Day to day, there isn't time to check each donation against eBay to see if they've been given anything valuable, and God knows none of them are antique experts, but they try and do their best.

A fashion fan since she was a teenager, Lillian's the shop's resident clothes 'expert' and she'll keep back anything from Biba and Burberry to vintage Tommy Hilfiger and Levi's to research online and price it up later. She also has a keen eye for vintage dresses from the Twenties to the Eighties and can't bear for anything valuable to be sold for a few pence.

Her only full-time volunteer, Karen, does the same with the vinyl. She's got an almost encyclopaedic knowledge about rare records and if Lillian hears an excited squeal from the back room she knows that Karen's found gold.

Their newest recruit, Phoebe, does the same with books but, as she's only in the shop twice a week her shelves take the longest to empty. As for the ornaments, plates and dishes they get given in huge quantities, all the staff are pretty clueless when it comes to glass and pottery and she hates to think how many valuables have slipped through the net.

'Found anything good?' she asks Phoebe as she turns on the kettle.

'Just this one.' She holds up a copy of Margaret Atwood's *The Handmaid's Tale*. 'It's a first edition and . . .' she breathes '. . . it's signed too. I thought it might be a reprint when I was rushing to look through all the bags a few months ago but I put it to one side just in case.'

'I remember,' Lillian says. 'It was in that box of stuff with a gold bird and some other stuff that sold really quickly. You were really excited. Have you researched the value online?' She doesn't mind admitting that she's clueless about the value of books.

Phoebe nods excitedly. 'It's worth around two thousand pounds.'

Lillian's jaw drops open. 'I'm going to have to tell head office about this one, get it listed on the website.' She takes the book from Phoebe and flicks through it, eliciting a horrified gasp.

'Lillian be careful! There might be some loose—'

Lillian's stomach turns as a page drifts from the book to the carpet. She crouches to retrieve it as Phoebe gently takes the book from her hands. 'I'm so, so sorry. I really hope I haven't devalued it. I'd never forgive myself if . . . oh. It's not a page – it's fine.'

She unfolds the piece of paper that evidently wasn't part of the book. There's something written on it but, without her glasses she can't tell what it says. As Phoebe leans closer to take a look, Lillian lifts her reading glasses from the chain around her neck and perches them on the end of her nose.

'*If you're reading this,*' she begins tentatively. Written in fountain pen ink the letters are smudged and faint, as though water was spilled on them or, she thinks darkly, maybe tears. '*If you're reading this,*' she repeats, '*and this book isn't in my house, my possession, or been passed on to my daughter then it's been stolen or something has happened to me.* I would never willingly part with this book.*'

Phoebe laughs softly. 'I'm the same about my favourite books. You'd have to put them in my coffin with me.'

'Wait,' Lillian says, 'there's more, an asterisk and tiny writing at the bottom. *Last week I got into a raging argument with my husband and he said I should watch what I say because he could easily kill me and make it look like an accident – that no one would ever know. Afterwards he said he was joking but he scares me and I don't know who to tell.*'

IT'S ALWAYS THE HUSBAND

A shiver passes through her and she shoves the letter at Phoebe, not wanting to hold it a moment longer. For several seconds, neither of them say anything then Phoebe screws the piece of paper into a ball and tosses it into the bin in the corner.

'It's someone's idea of a joke.' She puts a reassuring hand on Lillian's shoulder. 'It's like it's part of Offred's diary or something. It was probably a GCSE homework assignment or something and they forgot all about it. Although who'd let their child even touch a signed edition I don't know. Some people have more money than sense.'

Lillian nods, feeling a lot less worried. If she'd been alone, and not in the company of a book nerd like Phoebe, she'd have taken that letter to the police.

'Tea?' she asks as the kettle begins to boil and she opens the tea caddy. The signature at the bottom of the letter said *Ali*. She wonders who that is.

Acknowledgements

Huge thanks to my editor Helen Huthwaite for her patience, belief in this book and seeing the wood for the trees. To Maddie Wilson, Emily Hall and Jessica Whitehead for all your hard work. Becky Hunter and Laura Sherlock, you're both publicity queens. Thank you. Thanks also to Toby James for the stunning cover, the sales team, digital team, production team, and everyone involved in bringing this book to life. I am also indebted to Clare Corbett who has been narrating my audiobooks since *The Missing* and unfailingly brings them to life.

To my amazing agent Madeleine Milburn and the whole team, thank you for all you do to keep me motivated, organised and optimistic. I am very lucky.

To my parents, Reg and Jenny Taylor, thank you for supporting me during all the ups and downs of my sixteen-year career as an author, and for being my biggest cheerleaders (I love that you go up to random strangers on cruise ships who are reading my books, and tell them that the author is your daughter). Thank you to my brother

Dave Taylor who is the only person I know that's interested in discussing sales figures and statistics with me. To my sister Bec Taylor, who buys armfuls of my books to give to her friends and relentlessly promotes my new releases on social media (my brother does that too but none of his friends read books!).

Thank you to Sami Eaton for putting up with Dave and being such a brilliant mum and stepmum. Thank you Louise Foley for looking after Bec and for being my champagne partner. Ana Hall and Angela Hall, my Dancing Queens, I couldn't have asked for better sisters-in-law. James Loach, superstar DJ, thanks for putting up with us all. And lots of love to Steve and Guin Hall, and my nieces and nephews Frazer, Sophie, Oliver, Rose and Mia.

To Seth and Chris, thank you for putting up with the fact that I'm always disappearing off to events, or into my own head, for loving me, supporting me and for making me laugh every day. You two have my heart.

To Nat Beare, Claire Bagnall and Tez Travarthen, I love our Cornish get-togethers. Cath, Vic, Sarah and Gill, I love our swims, even if I don't love the early mornings! Big love to Helen Kara, Leigh Forbes, Jenny Beattie, and to my uni mates Kat Little, Joe Wood, Steve MacMurray, Rob Newnham, Mel Chilman, Ian Holley, Simon Smith and Adrian Goodrich.

To Wendy Calder, thank you for all the wonderful pottery lessons over the years. Hopefully I didn't get too many things wrong when I wrote about Sorrell's career as a ceramicist, I relied on my memory . . .

Kat, Sarah and Jenny – you're probably surprised to see your names in the dedication but you three kept me sane and entertained on the school run. As a shy introvert (I know, I hide it well), I really appreciated the school gate chats.

Claire Douglas, you definitely won the word race this time, and you're ahead again, damn you! Thanks for always being there to let me vent.

To the retailers, booksellers and librarians who stock my books, thank you so much. To the bookstagrammers who spread the word about my books, I'm so grateful. And to you, the reader, I wouldn't have a career without you. Thank you so much for reading my books.

If you'd like to be informed when my next book is out, and want to be one of the first people to get a sneak peek at the title and cover, do sign up to my newsletter. I also recommend books by other authors, run bookish giveaways and you'll even receive a free ebook for joining.

cltaylorauthor.com/newsletter

Keep your friends close and your enemies closer . . .

> The only way to stop a stalker is to become one yourself
>
> 'Twist after brilliant twist'
> CLAIRE DOUGLAS
>
> 'Clever, tense and satisfying'
> ANDREA MARA
>
> 'I absolutely loved it'
> LISA JEWELL
>
> **EVERY MOVE YOU MAKE**
>
> C.L. TAYLOR
>
> FROM THE SUNDAY TIMES BESTSELLING AUTHOR OF
> THE GUILTY COUPLE

The chilling and terrifyingly real thriller that will keep you up all night – and looking over your shoulder for days to come . . .

What would you do if your husband framed you for murder?

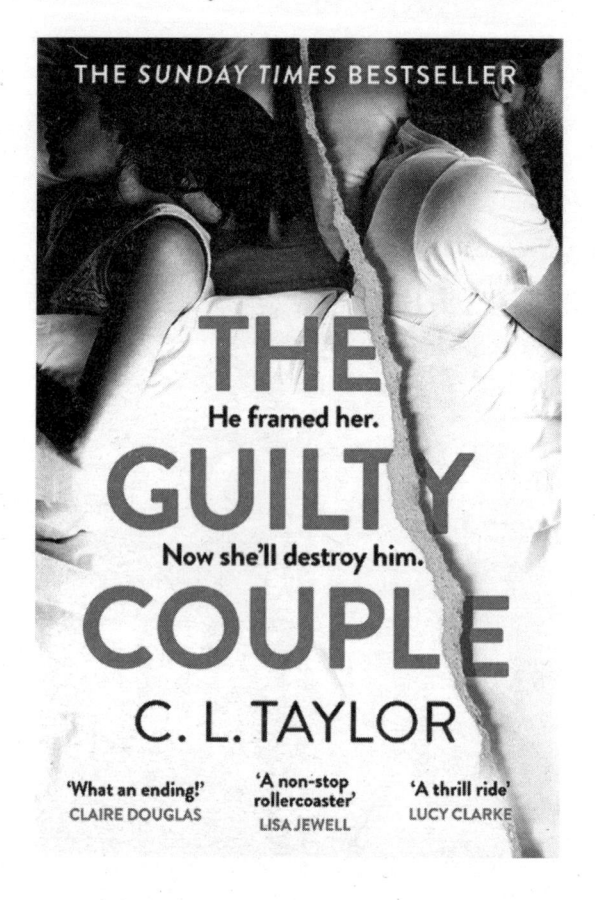

THE SUNDAY TIMES BESTSELLER

He framed her.
Now she'll destroy him.

THE GUILTY COUPLE
C. L. TAYLOR

'What an ending!'
CLAIRE DOUGLAS

'A non-stop rollercoaster'
LISA JEWELL

'A thrill ride'
LUCY CLARKE

The smash-hit Richard & Judy Book Club pick from the million-copy crime thriller bestseller.

You come to Soul Shrink to be healed. You don't expect to die.

FROM THE *SUNDAY TIMES* BESTSELLING AUTHOR OF
SLEEP

'The absolute queen of the page-turner'
Elizabeth Haynes

HER
One retreat.
LAST
Three victims.
HOLIDAY
No escape.

C.L.TAYLOR

The addictive and suspenseful psychological thriller.

Three strangers. Two secrets. One terrifying evening.

Strangers

C.L. TAYLOR

A gripping novel that will keep you guessing until the end.

Seven guests. Seven secrets. One killer.

The addictive Richard & Judy Book Club pick from the psychological thriller bestseller.

Sometimes your first love won't let you go...

The sensational thriller from the *Sunday Times* bestseller.

What do you do when no one believes you . . . ?

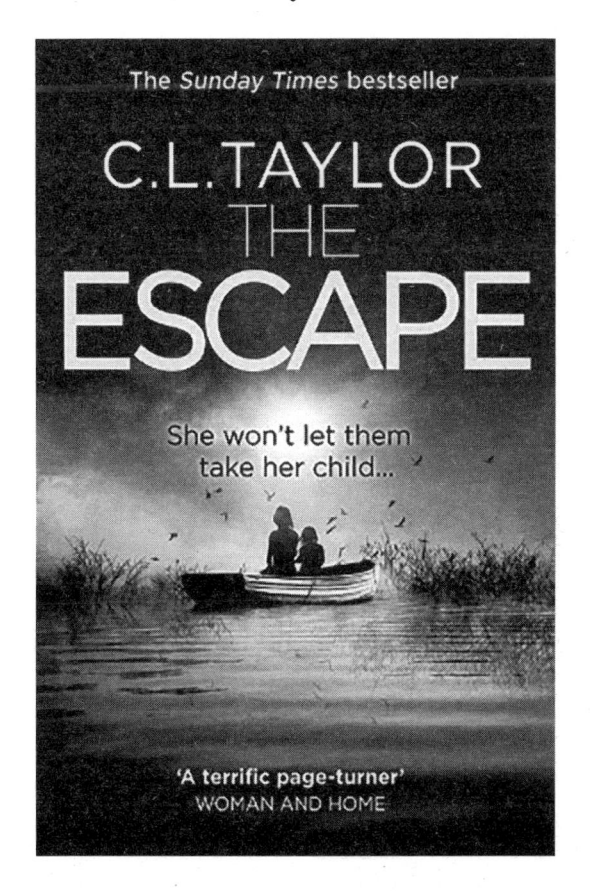

The nail-biting, twisty thriller from the
Sunday Times bestseller.

You love your family. They make you feel safe. You trust them. Or do you . . .?

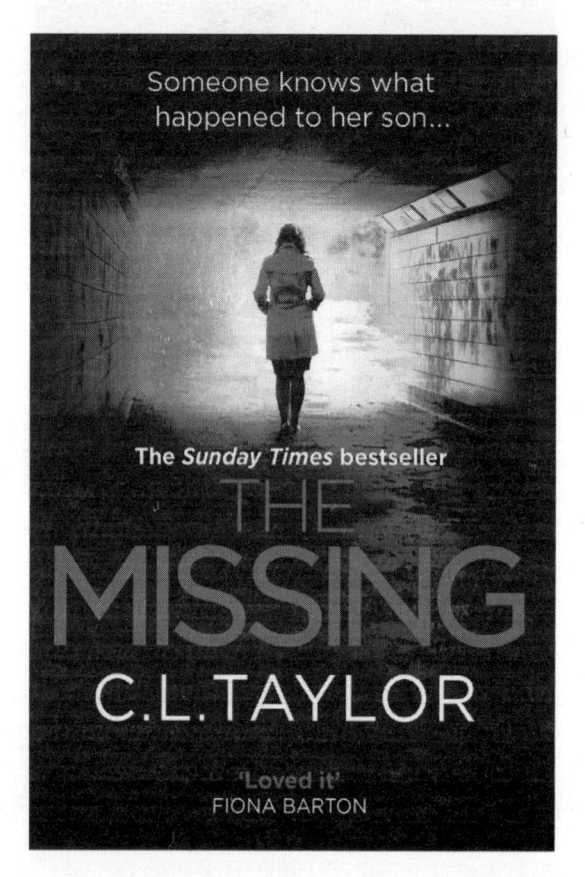

Someone knows what happened to her son...

The *Sunday Times* bestseller

THE MISSING

C.L. TAYLOR

'Loved it'
FIONA BARTON

The unputdownable psychological thriller that will leave you on the edge of your seat.

She trusted her friends with her life . . .

She trusted her friends with her life...
THE LIE

'Haunting and heart-stoppingly creepy'
SUNDAY EXPRESS

C.L. TAYLOR
The *Sunday Times* bestseller

A haunting, compelling psychological thriller
that will have you hooked.

Keeping this secret was killing her . . .

A riveting psychological thriller from the
Sunday Times bestseller.